CHAPTER ONE

San Francisco, California
Thursday – March 25

G rief was a monster.
It had taken up residence inside Jack the night he lost his family. Every day for four years, his squatter took pleasure in eviscerating him until he no longer recognized himself and every inch of his body cried out in anguish.

His leather jacket creaked as he reached for the bottle of Jameson he'd taken from Nick's office the day of his funeral. Jack's hand shook as he poured a measure into the two cut crystal tumblers then set them aside.

Not yet.

As was tradition, he'd wait until he was ready before downing his.

He'd switched off his phone's ringer earlier, but it started vibrating on the table in front of him, telling him there was an incoming call. He pushed it away. He didn't want to talk to anyone, and certainly didn't want anyone talking him out of what he was here to do.

Tears coursed down his cheeks like liquid fire. He squeezed his eyes shut, trying to block the burning pressure behind them. His pounding heart forced blood into his head until it felt like his skull would explode. The firm whoosh in his ears drowned out any ambient sounds. He raked his fingers through his hair, then pressed his palms against his head to force away the pain. It didn't help.

He pulled the leather jacket tightly around him, hugging his

1

arms around his middle, and rocked back and forth, trying to suppress his sobbing.

This was Jack Slaughter, losing his shit.

Not yet, he kept chanting to himself.

Jack hadn't been back to the house since the day he'd found the dead man slouched behind the dining table—where he currently sat—chunks of his brain, skull, and hair stuck to the wall in the splatter. The forensic team had removed as much of it as they could, but the blood stain still fanned out across the plasterwork where the man had held his head before pulling the trigger. Memory forced the man's distorted face into the splatter void. Jack looked away with disgust.

The man had broken in to commit suicide, but there was still no answer as to why he'd done it or chosen Jack's house to do it in. Just the note he'd left behind simply saying *I'm sorry*.

Jack wasn't upset about the man's suicide. Once someone decided to take their own life, there was no talking them out of it. He was pissed eight ways from Sunday because, in his last moments, the guy could have explained a few things before calling it a day. *I'm sorry* wasn't a confession or the typical last note suiciders left behind.

What had the asshole's note meant? Was he sorry for breaking the door glass when he accessed the house, and that was why he'd carefully stacked it on the table and left it beside his vague note? Was he sorry for choosing this house to kill himself because it looked abandoned? Or was he sorry because he was the one responsible for destroying Jack's family and could no longer live with himself?

So many questions Jack would never have answers to, and without them, he felt his monster pulling him so deep into his anguish, there was only one way out.

For all Jack knew, the guy was probably the only link to what had happened to Leah, and the only one who could have told him why his daughter had to die—she'd only been two, for fuck's sake. Jack would never know the truth because the jerkoff had killed himself.

Of course, Jack was no longer on the job, so he wasn't privy to the investigation. Even though Ray was still on the job, his best

SLAUGHTERHOUSE
BY
K.A. Lugo

Tirgearr Publishing

Published by Tirgearr Publishing
Ireland
www.tirgearrpublishing.com

ISBN 978-1-910234-65-5

A CIP catalogue record for this book is
available from the British Library.

10 9 8 7 6 5 4 3 2 1

DEDICATION

Always for Peter

ACKNOWLEDGEMENTS

There are so many people I want to thank for making this book possible.

My biggest thanks goes out to my husband, Peter. He supports and encourages me throughout each project. He listens to me rant about plotting issues and cheers with me when I find my way over stumbling blocks. And he makes sure I'm fed when I get so busy I forget to eat. I love him to the moon and back, infinite times.

My family also gets a huge thank you. Without their faith in me through the years and belief in my writing abilities, I wouldn't be here today and welcoming another book into my Jack Slaughter series. They never doubted I could successfully transition from romance to thrillers and have cheered me on all the way.

A big thanks goes out to my Dad who helped with a plotting issue and who gave my biker gang their name: 666s, Triple Sixers, Sixers.

Thanks to my production team: editor, Lucy Felthouse; proofreader, Adrienne Rieck; and cover designer, Cora at Cora Graphics.

Of course, a huge thanks goes out to my cover model, Rocco Benedetto, lead singer for the Italian group Oraillegale. Search him out on YouTube www.youtube.com/@oraillegaleligabue. Trust me on this!

I can't close this without recognizing the help and support from two fantastic guys:

Detective Adam Richardson of the Writers Detective Bureau. Adam is a technical consultant for writers and screenwriters, and he runs a podcast where he answers writers' questions. For more details on the podcast and courses, check out: www.writersdetective.com. You can join his group on Facebook at: https://www.facebook.com/groups/writersdetective

Retired police sergeant for the City of Milwaukee, Patrick O'Donnell, who runs Cops and Writers. Patrick has published two books for writers focusing on police procedure. Check out the Cops and Writers series where you normally buy books. Links on Patrick's website - https://www.copsandwriters.com. You can join his group on Facebook: https://www.facebook.com/groups/copsandwriters

Finally, to my readers: To my new readers, thank you for giving my books a chance. And to those following me over to thrillers . . . welcome to the dark side!

CONTENT WARNING

This book discusses suicidal feelings.

friend was being unusually tightlipped. Probably on Haniford's orders. So was Cutter. Jack understood, but it didn't mean he was happy about any of it.

His phone vibrated again. He didn't know who was trying to reach him and he didn't care. Why hadn't he just turned off the damn phone completely? Why couldn't he do it now?

He gazed past the phone to the opposite end of the dining table. Zoë's highchair had been moved into the living room so investigators could examine the crime scene before the coroner removed the man's body. The table had been pushed out of the way too, but Jack had moved it back before sitting down.

I should have moved the highchair back too.

He considered going to get it but didn't. Would it have made a difference or changed things? Probably not.

He inhaled long and slow, then closed his eyes again and let his memories replace everything that had been taken from him—the light from the evening sun filtering through the front window and moving across the living room to brighten the dining area; the sound of Leah singing in the kitchen while she cooked and the smell of her marinara; Trax rushing to meet Jack at the door and stuffing his nose in his hand, wanting to be petted; and Zoë in her booster chair at the end of the table, clapping her hands and trying to sing along with Leah. He smiled and let the feelings of love and joy fill him. This was the final vision he wanted in his mind . . . when it was time.

Abruptly, in his mind, he stood in the center of the kitchen and the horror of that night flooded back. He started shaking again.

He'd had to push Trax's lifeless body across the floor and step over a pool of his blood to get into the kitchen. He couldn't find Leah anywhere, but he knew she'd just been there as her marinara was burning on the stove. And Zoë—

In a blink, he stood beside her. She was in the highchair with her head cradled in his hands. Blood soaked her clothing and spilled over the dining table and onto the floor. He checked her carotid artery and felt the still-warm, sticky liquid ooze between his fingers.

He squeezed his eyelids tighter against the horrific images in his mind, but it only made them worse.

His phone vibrated again. Reluctantly, he opened his eyes and the reality of the cold, abandoned house punched him in the gut. He couldn't suppress a howl of anguish.

He gazed from the bloody table stain, past his phone, to the items in front of him:

Nick's bottle of Jameson and both crystal tumblers he'd poured measures into.

His Beretta and the magazine with the single 9mm Parabellum round he had yet to chamber.

And a note—*his* confession—explaining his actions. He'd propped it against the small urn containing Zoë's ashes.

He'd agonized over his confession for the last two days. How could he put into words the torture living inside him for so long? His struggle went beyond sadness, melancholy, and despair—into a realm of the inexplicable. He'd crossed the line in his depression and couldn't see a way back.

It was painful enough not knowing where Leah was or if she was still alive. After so long without any leads, he'd begun conceding *she* had been the one who killed Zoë and Trax. But why? And if she had, where was *her* note, dammit?

Since then, he struggled the most during birthdays, anniversaries, the holidays and other special events. He'd already started losing his shit at Thanksgiving. Playing happy families at the Navarros' and pre-Christmas bullshit were just some of the reasons he wound up in the Castro and finding Pepper Mint, aka Bob Johnson, dying in the driveway of the Majestic Lounge.

He'd thought he was coming out of his funk with Zelda's birth, but finding a dead man in his house threw him sideways again. Knowing he'd taken his life here, and the only note *he'd* left behind simply said *I'm sorry*, ate away at whatever rationality Jack used just to function day-to-day until there was nothing left inside him. He was sure the man's suicide had been the catalyst for what he was about to do.

Sleep eluded him. All he thought about was trying to rationalize what the man had done. He obsessed about it until he finally just shut everyone out.

He turned away clients and distanced himself from his friends so he could try rationalizing the man's motives and how they may have related to the loss of his own family.

It didn't take long for Jack to realize he was spiraling. No one needed to see that shit. He even made excuses every Thursday why he couldn't show up at the Navarros' for dinner.

At first, he'd told Ray he needed time to process what had happened in his house, but, in reality, it went much deeper. Jack was ashamed to admit he was starting to hate Ray's happy family.

Ever since Zelda and Dewayne had entered the Navarros' lives, Jack couldn't imagine a more perfect family. Zelda was an angel, with her chubby cheeks always framing a smile, and her tiny hands reaching out for him whenever she saw him. Her new baby scent filled him with memories of Zoë and reignited feelings of love he thought were long gone.

Then there was Dewayne. Any family he had seemed to stop with his mother, Denise Watkins. The space where his father's name should have been on his birth certificate had been left blank, and there were too many Denise Watkinses to determine which one was Dewayne's mother. Dewayne had given inspectors the names of a couple of his mother's past boyfriends, but only one had come through by giving inspectors information on Denise's preferred shooting gallery—a place where junkies went to get high.

But when a patrol car pulled up outside the known flop house in the Tenderloin, those who were able to, ran. The few junkies officers had managed to corral denied knowing Denise or said they hadn't seen her in a long time. Like Leah, Denise seemed to have vanished into thin air.

Despite the way Dewayne's mother had left him, the teen had really stepped up once he became part of the Navarro family. He was a caring and attentive young man who fell in love with Zelda the instant she was in his arms. He'd even agreed to go back to school where he was getting decent grades as he fought to catch up to the other kids his age.

Jack also found it harder than he'd expected, knowing Ray's career was on the same trajectory as his own had once been. Only his friend's was racing along like a bullet train after being credited with solving two serial killer cases last year—ones Jack had actually solved but had been unable to take the credit for, because he was no longer on the force. His name barely got a footnote on the reports. He wasn't angry or jealous of Ray, just disappointed with himself, which made him feel even more useless and insignificant.

Adding insult to injury, Jack's neighbors no longer referred to the house as the Slaughters' House, or Violet Cottage, but simply as *the slaughterhouse*. And why not? Corpses were piling up and his own would add to the body count, thus reinforcing the house's moniker. It would have been hard enough trying to sell the place with potential buyers knowing a child, and her dog, had been murdered here. But adding two suicides . . . . The best anyone could do was burn the place to the ground, get a priest to bless the ash-filled earth, then start over.

What made Jack struggle the most was losing his friend and confidant, Father Nick. The old priest would have been able to talk him down from this. Nick had been part of Jack's life since he and Leah had bought this little house in the Sunset District. Back then, Nick had been assigned to St. Gabriel's just up the street before being reassigned to St. Frank's. Jack and Leah attended St. Gabriel's and had planned on enrolling Zoë in the adjoining elementary school.

Now? They were all gone.

Jack's heart thudded hard at the thought. He needed his friend now more than ever.

You've only to think of me and I'll be listening, Nick had written in his letter before he passed before Christmas.

"Nick, are you listening?" Jack asked aloud. He tilted his head and listened for the faintest reply, but silence filled the room.

He took deep breaths to steady himself, scrubbing the moisture from his eyes with the back of a fist.

Knowing what was coming, it seemed as if the world stood still. The house was as quiet as a tomb—no kids played on the street, no cars drove by, not even the sound of the ocean two blocks over. Just eerie silence. Except for the pounding in his chest echoing in his ears.

He looked at his note propped against the urn filled with his daughter's ashes. After two days of trying to put his feelings into words, he had really wanted to take the easy way out with the same two words in the dead man's note: *I'm sorry.*

But sorry for what? *Everything.* What did it even mean? That was the issue. How could he explain the *everything* he felt inside? There was too much, and most people probably wouldn't understand. And frankly, he was too tired to even want to try explaining it all, so he'd made it as brief as possible.

He also explained why he'd chosen today to accept his fate; it was the four-year anniversary of losing his family. As it didn't seem like he'd ever find those responsible for destroying his life, today seemed like the right time to check out.

The phone vibrated again. He let it ring out, but almost immediately, it started again.

Jack gazed at the Beretta's magazine. He'd expected to spend the single round once he found Leah, but after all this time, there still weren't any clues as to where she was, alive or dead. The trail had gone cold. Or maybe the trail never existed.

Jack was spinning his wheels and getting nowhere, other than sinking deeper into the mire that had become his life. He was too far gone now. Could Nick really have pulled him out of it?

Nick, do you hear me? screamed inside Jack's brain.

He realized his thumb and index finger hurt; he'd been twisting his wedding ring. The skin beneath the gold band burned from the friction. He gazed at the ring. It wasn't anything fancy, but it symbolized his absolute devotion and dedication to his wife and family. That was worth more than any fancy design, but he still hadn't managed to take off the ring in all these years. He ached knowing when his corpse ended up on Cutter's table, the ring would come off then. The first time since Leah had slid it onto his finger at their wedding.

He wondered just then, if Leah was alive, did she still wear her ring? Or if she was dead, had her abductors killed her for the sake of the gold?

Jack wiped his eyes again before lifting the bullet magazine. He tapped it against the Beretta's hilt to ensure the rounds were settled before inserting it. He heard the familiar click as it locked in place. He pulled back the slide, chambering a round, then let it click back into position.

"Nick, if you're listening," he said, his voice raspy and weak. "It's now or never."

The Beretta wavered in his hand. He inhaled deeply and held his breath, hoping to calm his racing heart, but it wasn't enough.

"Please, Nick," he pleaded, but the room . . . the house . . . remained still and soundless. Nick wasn't here. Maybe he never was nor would be.

Jack eyed the Beretta. Was there really an afterlife? Would he see his family again, or was he doing this because he wanted the pain to end? He thought it was mostly the latter. In reality, what he was about to do was against his religion and he was undoubtedly going to Hell. No, he'd never see his family again. But he couldn't live like this anymore. The pain was too great.

It was time.

His gaze settled on the tumbler of Jameson.

The tradition.

Lifting the glass, he watched the fading afternoon light catch the facets in the crystal. The depth of the whiskey's color seemed otherworldly—deep and mysterious, beckoning.

He'd poured a large measure, but he downed it in one. It burned all the way to his stomach. He didn't remember the last time he'd eaten, so the heat of the alcohol burned in his gut and the faint buzz hit his brain simultaneously. His body started relaxing and he felt his strength evaporate.

A moment later, his tears ceased, and his heart stopped racing. Somehow, he felt resigned to his fate and waited for the blissful end to his torture. Was this acceptance, or was he just that numb?

It was now or never.

Jack lifted the Beretta and slid the barrel into his mouth. His teeth grazing the metal felt like nails on a chalkboard. The cold steel was a shock to his lips, and the shape of the barrel was almost phallic, but he held his hand steady.

He forced happy memories to the front of his mind, the coming home, the singing before he even opened the door, the joy on their faces upon seeing him, Trax's nose snuffling in the palm of his hand . . .

With a deep breath, Jack thumbed the trigger.

His body jerked with the loud bang.

CHAPTER TWO

Jack's eyes snapped open as the Beretta fell out of his hands and clattered onto the table. His heart slammed against his ribs as he shot backward.

He exhaled hard to catch the breath he'd been holding and scrubbed his face with his fists. His gun had never misfired before. *I pulled the trigger. Why didn't it fire?* He checked the safety. *Off.*

"Jack! I know you're here."

Jack jerked his head toward the open stairwell leading down to the garage. The kitchen door hadn't been replaced after the investigators had taken the man's body away. He heard Ray moving through the garage, knowing he would take advantage of the missing door.

The Harley's horn beeped. "I found your Jeep and bike. I thought you said your garage was too small for both of them."

Jack realized then, the loud bang he'd heard was the garage door slamming closed, not his Beretta discharging.

Goddammit!

Bolting to his feet, Jack looked around. Did he really want Ray seeing what had very nearly gone down here?

Quickly, he grabbed his note and slid it into his jacket's side pocket. At the same time with his other hand, he flipped on the Beretta's safety and stuffed it into the waistband at the back of his jeans. He left the whiskey and glasses where they were, then slid the tiny urn behind the bottle, hoping Ray didn't see it.

"What are you doing?" Jack spun to see Ray stepping onto the landing at the top of the stairs. He continued into the house and walked over to stand beside the dining table. "Drinking?" He nodded to the bottle.

"So what?"

"So what? That's all you can say?" Ray threw his hands onto his hips and waited for Jack to continue. When he didn't, Ray asked, "Where've you been, *ese*?"

Jack saw the looks of both anger and worry on his friend's face. "What are you doing here?"

I haven't seen you in days. You're not answering your phone or replying to messages and no one has seen you. It's like you dropped off the face of the planet. You worried the hell out of me, so I asked Haniford to run a trace on your phone."

"You pinged my phone?" Jack asked in disbelief. "How dare you—" *Note to self: leave the phone behind when you try this again, asswipe.*

"GPS is a great thing."

"You had no right hunting me down just because I wasn't answering my phone," he spat.

"I'm your closest friend, so I absolutely have the right. You don't tell me you're going off-grid after what happened here," Ray waved a hand toward the bloody wall, "and I'm going to be concerned. So, you're goddamn right I pinged your phone. Now alarm bells are going off, finding you sitting *here* with a bottle." Jack didn't need to be chastised like a petulant child. He moved past Ray and into the living room long devoid of furnishings to put space between them. "Don't walk away from me."

Ray spun him around by the upper arm in the center of the room.

"Step off, man," Jack growled. Jerking out of Ray's grasp, he nearly fell into the blood-stained highchair. He pulled himself upright and stomped to the window. After taking a few deep breaths to compose himself, Jack finally gazed back at his friend. The instant he saw Ray's genuine look of concern, he regretted his tone. "Sorry. It's just . . . . Everything's gotten on top of me the last few months and I needed some down time."

"I get it, but you need to keep me in the loop."

Jack looked out the window and saw the fading day had already turned the sky a pale yellow—the golden hour—so he knew it would be dark soon.

"You don't need to worry about me. I'm fine." He would have been finer if Ray had been five minutes later. *Or I'd been five minutes earlier.*

Ray moved beside him but didn't say anything for a long moment. When he did, his tone was restrained. "Jack, clearly you're not fine. You never come here. At least not to just sit in near darkness. And I haven't seen you hit the bottle in nearly a year. Something's up. Talk to me."

The last thing Jack wanted to do was tell his best friend what he'd just interrupted. How the hell did he explain the real reasons why he'd ignored all the calls?

"I wasn't drinking."

"Explain the bottle and glasses on the table."

"I was—" Jack knew it would sound crazy but said it anyway. "I was talking to Nick." It wasn't a lie. "I only had a shot."

"I remember you told me about the tradition—talk, then drink?"

"Talk, then one shot before I left his office. I was just leaving when you arrived." That wasn't a lie either.

"What did Nick have to say?" Ray asked.

Did he want to tell Ray the priest had never answered?

"He said Heaven's great. God's a nice guy, and he and Jesus play golf every Sunday after services—"

"For Christ's sake, Jack. This is serious."

Jack looked into his friend's eyes for a long moment. Had Nick sent Ray to interrupt him? The thought the old priest may have shocked Jack. A chill raced up his spine remembering all the phone calls he ignored. Jack wasn't ready to process a divine intervention, if that's what it had been, so he changed the subject.

"Why are you here?" he asked again. "Do you have an ID on the guy who offed himself here?"

"You're deflecting."

"And?"

Ray inhaled deeply and took out his notebook. "That's why I've been trying to reach you." Jack watched him angle the pages toward the light coming in from the streetlamp and flip to the page he wanted. "We ran his prints against the AFIS database. He wasn't in the system, so we checked the DMV database for prints and got a hit. Tristan Rybak. He was a junior at San Francisco State University, where he was studying for a Master's in Humanities & Liberal Studies—good grades, clean record. Overall, a good student."

"He didn't look like any student I've ever seen. He looked and smelled pretty rough."

"For no apparent reason, he suddenly dropped off the map when he was twenty . . . about eight or nine years ago. He's probably been on the streets this whole time."

"Nine years? Did anyone report him missing?"

"Stacey Maguire. His girlfriend at the time. She alerted campus security when she couldn't locate him for a couple days and they performed a rudimentary investigation. When the parents arrived, city cops were brought in, and a missing persons report was filed at the department. He'd been MIA until he was found here."

"Has his family been notified?" Jack asked.

"Yeah, I sent Harry and Wash over to break the news once the ID had been made."

"Were Harry and Wash able to learn anything new about the kid? Had he ever contacted them for anything . . . money, food, to come home . . . ?"

Ray shook his head. "No, but Mrs. Rybak remembered seeing a strange man standing on the sidewalk across from the house a few years ago. She said she would have been scared by a vagrant in their neighborhood, but there was something familiar about him. She turned to call for her husband to come take a look at the man, but when she turned back, he was gone. They never saw him again."

"Any idea why he chose my house to off himself?"

"None that I can tell."

"Rybak, you said?"

"Yeah, why?"

"Sounds familiar, but I don't know why it would."

"I'm sure you'll remember eventually. You usually do."

Jack just grunted. "Did you get a copy of the missing persons report . . . investigator's report . . . anything?"

"*Homes*, you know I did."

"Let's see what you have."

"Why don't we go back to your apartment? There's more room to spread out there. And it has power." Ray flicked his gaze toward the dark ceiling light.

Why pay for electricity and gas when no one is using it?

Was he ready to go? He'd come here for one purpose, and it hadn't included leaving. At least not vertically. He could tell Ray he'd follow him over to his place then sit back down and try eating the bullet again. Or was he curious enough now to dig into who Tristan Rybak was and why he killed himself in this house?

"Yeah, alright. I'll meet you there," Jack finally said, curiosity winning.

Ray glanced toward the darkened dining area. "You've been drinking. I'll take you home."

"I only had the one. I'm fine. I'll meet you at my place. I want to get the kitchen door back on its hinges then I need to lock up." Dealing with the door would give him an extra barrier for next time. When he returned to complete his task, he didn't want another surprise visit like the one he'd just had.

"I'll give you a hand."

Jack didn't need the help. "I got it," he said, walking toward the kitchen. Ray followed.

Jack retrieved the door from the garage while Ray grabbed the pins from a kitchen drawer where Jack had put them for safekeeping when the door came down.

Holding the door in place while Jack maneuvered it into the hinges, Ray asked, "Were you ignoring all your calls or just mine?"

"I wasn't ignoring you specifically. I just turned off the ringer for some peace and quiet." Jack fitted the first pin into the hinge then gave it a sharp tap with a hammer, sliding it into place.

"Yeah, well, you had me worried shitless. Haniford too when I told him you were MIA."

"Sorry."

14

"Is that all you have to say . . . sorry?"

"Sorry, *Dad*, I won't do it again?"

"Be serious. You need to tell me the next time you want to go to ground."

Under his breath, Jack said, "Yeah, fine."

Jack moved to hammer in the second pin, then the last. Ray's deep breathing told him his friend was still upset.

"Jack," Ray started.

Jack stood up, task completed, and tested the door's swing. No squeaks.

"Jack," Ray said in a softened voice. "You know you can talk to me."

He couldn't face Ray for more than a moment before turning away. "I know. Thanks." He felt Ray's gaze on him as he sneaked the tiny urn into an inside pocket before grasping the tumblers and whiskey bottle off the table and taking them to the kitchen. *Waste not, want not.* He downed the whiskey meant for Nick then rinsed out the glasses and put them on the drainboard near the bottle.

He took his time making sure the back and front doors were secure.

"Ready?" he asked from the door he'd just hung.

"Just waiting on you."

In the garage, Ray lifted the big door while Jack went to his Harley. He rolled it out to the small driveway and leaned it back on the kickstand. Ray pulled the door back down as Jack slid on his helmet. Lifting the visor, he pushed the automatic starter and the bike rumbled to life.

"Before I forget." Ray pulled out a folded piece of paper from his pocket and handed it to Jack.

"What's this?" Jack gazed at the paper, simply scrawled with *Mayes* and a phone number.

"Number for a lawyer."

"Lawyer?" What the hell did a lawyer want with him? He'd sorted out his affairs before coming here. Did his estate lawyer need something? He looked at the name but didn't recognize it.

"Did they say what they wanted?"

"To talk with you. She didn't give me specifics. Just that you needed to call at your convenience. By the sound of her voice, convenience meant as soon as possible."

"Why call you?" He looked at the paper again before stuffing it in his pocket. If it was important, they'd call him back.

"Couldn't reach you either. I guess she had my number as backup."

Jack threw a leg over the saddle and gloved up. "I'll meet you at my place."

He flipped down the visor and was on the road before Ray had opened the door of his old red Silverado truck.

Thoughts of Tristan Rybak spun in Jack's head; what did his house or his family have to do with his suicide?

CHAPTER THREE

The Harley gave Jack the advantage in heavy city traffic and he arrived at his apartment well before Ray. He was grateful for the extra time as he needed it to put away the things he'd left on his desk—things his friend would need to sort out the Slaughter estate, if it could be called that: the envelope containing the deed to the Sunset house, pink slips to his vehicles, a copy of his last will and testament, other official documents, and sets of keys.

He took a couple deep breaths and forced down the worst of the blackness living inside him. He knew his friend was worried and was no doubt still trying to understand why he'd found Jack sitting at the table in his house with a bottle of whiskey and talking to a dead man.

If Jack could deflect the conversation enough, maybe Ray would forget about his concern, or at least push it to the back of his mind, so they could discuss the reason they were back in the apartment—Tristan Rybak.

Jack grasped the Beretta from the small of his back and ejected the magazine. He pulled back the slide and ejected the single Parabellum round from the chamber. Once everything was safely returned to the Beretta's lockbox and in the desk drawer, he set the envelope on top of the box. Then Zoë's tiny urn beside it.

Ray let himself in just as Jack was locking the drawer.

"You need to find a place with better parking," Ray complained as he closed the door behind him then made his way across the room. Jack was grateful his friend seemed oblivious to the changes in the apartment. "I had to park up near Washington Square. Winter might be over, but it's still *muy frío* out there."

17

"Karl always brings the cold with him," Jack said, referring to the nickname San Franciscans had given the blanket fog that was as synonymous with the city as the Golden Gate Bridge and Rice-A-Roni.

Ray dropped onto the sofa and extracted a folder from inside a jacket pocket. The folder was folded in a U and held together with a thick rubber band. Ray set it on the cushion beside him.

"Got any coffee going? This place is freezing. You leave a window open or something?" Ray asked, drawing his jacket lapels together.

Jack pulled his chair around the desk and sat facing his friend. "No. I just got here. Rybak file?"

Ray handed Jack the folder. "Yeah. Copies of everything are in there—missing persons report, investigator's report, copy of his driver's license, fingerprints, previous records, ME's report, photos . . . . The usual stuff."

Jack removed the rubber band, flipped open the folder and slid out the photographs he assumed the parents had supplied when they filed the missing persons report. The most recent seemed to be Rybak's class picture. The feeling hit him again that he should know the man. He stared at the picture for a long moment and wondered what had happened to drive him underground.

A moment later and without looking up, Jack asked, "You hungry? I'll call downstairs and order us something." He couldn't remember the last time he'd eaten. The last few days had been a blur of activity and sorting out his affairs. The mere mention of food made his stomach grumble, even as the stress of what he'd very nearly done at his house made him want to puke.

"Sure, fried rice would be great," Ray said as he rose. "I'll give Maria a call and let her know I found you. She's been worried sick about you, man."

Guilt rushed through Jack. Ray's wife had cornered Jack over the holidays and told him she knew he struggled. Like anyone else who asked, he let her know her concern was appreciated but he was okay. Of course, he'd never tell her, or anyone, just how bad things really were. Not even Ray, who was his closest friend.

"Tell her I'm sorry to have worried her. I'm fine. Just needed some—"

"Downtime," Ray finished for him. "I get it. Don't forget eggrolls."

As Jack made the call downstairs for food, he watched Ray walk out onto the landing and close the door behind him. He wondered why his friend needed so much secrecy for a call home.

When Ray returned, he carried a bag with Tommy Wong's logo on the side. "I met the delivery guy on the stairs."

"Set it on the desk," Jack said, moving the folder he'd been thumbing through.

Ray set the bag on the small table beside the sofa. "I'll grab those little folding tables from the back room. Least we can do is dine in relative comfort before hitting the files." Before Jack could stop him, Ray was through the door. A moment later, he reappeared. Thumbing over his shoulder, he asked, "Hey, bro. Wanna tell me what that's all about?"

"What's what all about?"

"All the boxes. You moving or something?"

Jack folded his arms over his chest. "No, why?"

"Everything is packed back there. Even the coffee pot. What gives?" Ray set the tables in front of the sofa and unfolded them. When Jack didn't reply, Ray looked up at him with a piercing gaze. He crossed his arms, mimicking Jack's posture, as if he were squaring up for a fight. "Well?"

Jack hadn't rehearsed this. If things had gone to plan, Ray would already know why he'd packed up the apartment.

"Well, what?"

"If you're not moving, why is everything packed back there?" Ray slowly scanned the room and spotted the other packed boxes before meeting Jack's gaze again. "You *are* moving!" He dropped a hand to his hip and slapped Jack's upper arm with the other. "Why didn't I notice before? Some inspector I am. You finally decided to move in with us for a while?"

Shaking his head, Jack said, "I'm not moving in with you, brother. Where would you put me anyway? You barely have room for the menagerie already living there."

"We'll find space." Suddenly, Ray's tone became serious. "You're moving back to Sunset." It wasn't a question. "It makes sense now."

"How so?" Jack was definitely curious about how his friend came to the conclusion.

"It's obvious now that I see it. I found you at the house. Your Jeep is in the garage and so was your Harley. Everything is packed here. Even your computer." Ray clapped Jack again on the upper arm and said, "Come on. You can tell me what changed your mind while we eat."

Ray emptied the contents of the paper restaurant bag onto the folding tables: traditional takeout boxes filled to bursting with fried rice, containers of eggrolls, and a six pack of cold beer.

In his wildest dreams, Jack never thought today would end up like it had. He'd fully expected to either be in the first stages of rigor at his house, or by some fluke he'd already been found and laid out on a slab in Cutter's fridge. Yet, here he was, sitting down to a meal with his best friend. The scent of the food filled the small room, making Jack's stomach squelch.

Oddly, he wasn't actually hungry. He was ravenous.

"So, let me get this straight," Ray said, his mouth full of eggroll. "Your Jeep is in the garage at the Sunset house, but you're not moving there. And all your stuff is packed up here and you're still not moving? Is that right?"

Jack nodded. "Pretty much." He took a long draw on the beer, trying to wash down the lump sticking in his throat. It wasn't food. He'd been trying to think of something to tell his friend that made sense.

"I have to tell you, *ese*, I'm confused, because it sure looks like a move to me."

It would have confused Jack too if he were in Ray's shoes. "It's pretty simple. You don't have room in your garage for the Jeep since you converted it for the new room for Dewayne. Since selling Lea— the Mustang . . . I can now get the Jeep into the garage. It makes sense keeping it there."

Ray groaned through a mouthful of rice. He didn't look convinced. "Why was your bike in the garage too? If you aren't moving in, why put it inside?"

Good point, Jack thought. Jack used another swig of beer to give him time to think of an answer. "There were kids on the street playing ball. It was safer inside."

Yeah, that sounds plausible.

"Mmm-hmm." Ray still wasn't convinced. "What's up with packing up the apartment?"

The answer to that one wasn't as easy. "You're a nosey Nellie tonight. Can't we just eat in peace?"

"Nuh-uh. What gives? You're moving and I want to know where to," Ray demanded.

Jack pushed his table away and leaned back on the sofa with the remainder of his beer. *Think, dammit!* Whatever he told Ray, he'd have to commit to. Right now, he only wanted to find out who Tristan Rybak was, then go back to his house and be done with it all.

"Painting," Jack finally said.

"Painting."

"I've been here four years and the place needs it."

"You can paint without boxing everything up," Ray pointed out.

Nodding, Jack said, "True, but I'm doing the floors too." Shit! He didn't want to commit to that project any more than he wanted to paint the walls.

Ray looked deep in thought as he gazed around the room. Jack could practically smell the grease burning from the cogs whirring in his friend's head as he digested what he'd been told.

A long moment later, Ray turned back to him. "Is that what you've really been doing the last couple days? Packing to fix up the apartment?" Jack nodded. "Tommy owns the place. Why are you doing all the work?"

Here was proof positive, when you told the truth, there was less to keep track of when forming a lie. Especially a big one. *Think, think!*

21

"Tommy's paying. I'm just arranging everything since my schedule is flexible." Just to dig himself deeper in the lie, he added, "I'll take this stuff over to the house while the work is being done, get a hotel for a couple nights until it's finished."

"Don't do that. You can sleep on our sofa."

"Thanks, but I don't know how long it'll take. I don't want to become a fixture."

"Worse things could happen. When are you going to start?"

In his head, Jack chanted leave it alone. "I don't know, but for now, you've brought over the files on Rybak. Let's talk about that." *Good save, Slaughter.*

"Okay, okay," Ray capitulated. "Tell me one thing before we dig into those files. Does your refurb include getting a new sofa? Because one of the springs in this piece of shit is tapping my *culo* like it's drilling for oil." Ray shifted in his seat and leaned over to rub his ass cheek.

Jack chuckled. "Yeah, new sofa. You can help me pick one out."

CHAPTER FOUR

Jack cleaned up after their meal while Ray went to Washington Square to move his vehicle closer to the apartment. By the time he let himself back in, Jack had grabbed a couple large coffees from Wong's and placed his old banker's lamp back on the desk where he now sat.

"I got us some coffee and fortune cookies," Jack said without looking up.

Two folders were laid out in front of him—one containing copies of old missing persons reports he'd pulled out of one of his packed boxes, and the other was the one Ray had brought with him.

When Jack had become a private investigator nearly four years ago, he soon realized a lot of his work would come from locating missing people. He'd ended up developing a relationship with officers working in the Special Victims Unit which kept copies of the MPRs on all open cases. While it had been nearly six months since he'd updated his file, he found the old report on Tristan Rybak deep within the folder.

He compared the two reports. They were identical printouts, except Jack's was older and had a few brief notes in the margin, including, had anyone questioned the girlfriend or family about the known associates listed on the report only as Kyle and Logan?

The air shifted when Ray sat before the desk and reached for his cup. The coffee aroma wafted in Jack's direction, instantly pulling him away from his too-much-food drowsiness compounding the after-effects of coming down off so much adrenaline and eating way too much on an empty stomach.

Curiously, he'd found a new appreciation for the simple dish of house special fried rice and beer, and now coffee and sweet fortune cookies. He wasn't sure if he should attribute his awakened taste buds to having not eaten for so long or to what Ray had interrupted at the Sunset house.

He sipped the hot liquid then cracked open a fortune cookie— *Lean on your friends in time of need.*

Jack's heart thumped against his ribs. Where were the funny quotes like *The fortune you seek is in another cookie* and *Help! I'm being held hostage in a fortune cookie factory.*

He pushed the fortune aside and stuffed the half cookie in his mouth. He spun the MPRs to face Ray. "I found my old missing persons folder. Rybak was in it. That's why his name sounded familiar. Other than the girlfriend, there were only two names listed as known contacts, Kyle and Logan. Do we know if either were located and if they've been questioned?"

Ray set down his cup and went through his folder. "The investigator's report is . . ." he rifled through the contents, "here." He slid the page in Jack's direction. "Based on this, the only reason the officers spoke with dorm residents and teachers at all was to appease the mother who was in hysterics."

"Understandable."

"Of the few who were questioned, the consensus was, aside from classes, Rybak spent a lot of time alone in his dorm room playing video games. Beyond that, most people only knew *of* him but weren't friends *with* him. His teachers couldn't speak to the gaming, only that he'd regularly attended classes and was getting decent grades, at least until a couple months before his disappearance. His grades started falling and his attendance became spotty. Then he just stopped attending class at all. Soon after, he was reported as a missing person."

"And Kyle and Logan?"

"Nothing indicates they'd been located or spoken with."

Jack scanned the document as Ray spoke. What he said matched the investigating officers' report. "Doesn't seem like much of an effort was put into this."

"You know how it is. Most adults eventually turn up. Unless it's a kid or an adult with special needs, or there's a ransom demand, not a lot of energy is invested in a search."

"It's a fucked-up system, but I suppose it keeps guys like me in business," Jack said, looking down to the investigating officers' names. "Officers Stewart Minter and Brian Davis. We should have a talk with them and see what they remember."

"No can do unless you want to call them. They both transferred out a couple years ago. I don't know where to, but Haniford may."

"Let's leave it as a last resort, if it comes to that." Jack looked up at Ray. "You seem to know a lot about this."

"Not really. I just remember the case. Nothing made sense. Including a strange call Rybak's parents received telling them to stop looking for their son because he was dead. The parents hadn't been convinced—they wanted his body. Every year, on the anniversary of his disappearance, the parents ran another appeal in the papers, but until he turned up in your house, he'd been assumed either hiding or dead."

"Now it seems maybe it was a little of both." After a moment, Jack continued, "What about Rybak's girlfriend, Stacey Maguire? Was she questioned?"

"Briefly. She told investigators Rybak had started hanging out with a couple guys."

"Kyle and Logan?" Ray nodded. "If Rybak was an avid gamer, how did he hook up with Maguire?"

"I don't know, but apparently she was angry with him leading up to his disappearance because he'd been spending more time with his new gaming friends than her."

"Sounds like she was jealous. Did she ever meet the friends?"

Ray shook his head. "Maguire said she'd never met them, but they were also gamers."

"With names like those, if they were attending the university with Rybak, they should have been easy enough to look up in school records. How many Kyles and Logans could there be? I wonder why that wasn't investigated while officers were on campus."

"Got me. Now that we know something about Rybak, I can go back to the school and see if they'll open class records."

"You need to get a warrant. Even though Rybak was an adult at the time, the school probably won't want to dole out information without being compelled, especially since he hasn't legally been declared dead," Jack said.

"I'll take care of it in the morning," Ray said, "then head over to SFSU."

"Swing by here and pick me up." Ray just stared at him. "What?"

"Showing you the reports is one thing, but you can't get involved with this."

"Why not?"

Ray counted on his fingers. "You're not on the force. No one has hired you to investigate this. And, more importantly, you're too close. Let the department do their job."

Jack sat back in his chair and folded his arms across his chest. "You can either take me with you, or I'll go on my own. I don't need a warrant as a private investigator."

"You wouldn't diss me like that, would you?" Jack remained motionless, staring at his friend. "Come on. If I take you with me, Haniford will have my *culo*."

"Tell him what I told you. I either tag along or I'll fly solo."

"Jack—"

"Don't *Jack* me. You expected me to get in on this or you wouldn't have brought over the folder. Don't expect me to stand down now."

Rybak had committed suicide in his house, and goddammit he was going to find out why.

CHAPTER FIVE

Friday – March 26

9a.m. sharp, Ray was on the street below Jack's apartment, honking from a department-issued vehicle—his usual nondescript black sedan. Ray rarely honked from the street, so Jack knew his friend was not in a good mood.

He slid into his leather jacket then pocketed his notebook, phone, and keys before closing the apartment door behind him.

Ray pulled into traffic before Jack had his seatbelt clipped into place. Horns blared around them.

"Good morning to you, too. Wake up on the wrong side of the bed?" When his friend ignored him, Jack said, "I'm guessing Haniford is the reason you look like you want to tear off my head."

Ray kept his gaze on the traffic. "Ya think?"

"Tell me what happened."

On the twenty-minute drive over to the university on Holloway Avenue on the west side of the peninsula, Ray went into detail about what Haniford thought about Jack's insertion into the Rybak case. Jack knew his former lieutenant liked him, but he'd like Jack better if he got back on the job. What he'd said to Ray hadn't been encouraging.

"I expected as much," Jack admitted.

"Maybe so, but I rather he'd yelled at you instead." After finding parking in the small lot beside the university admin building, Ray shut off the ignition and finally turned to Jack. "I've got the warrant in my pocket, so we shouldn't have any trouble getting what we need from school records. With any luck, some

27

of Rybak's teachers are still here and we can speak with them too."

Jack nodded. "Might make better use of our time if we split up."

"Maybe. Let's see where we get with Admin first."

Once inside the building, Ray took point and went to the reception desk where a middle-aged, casually dressed, dyed-blonde woman sat. Her name tag said Nancy.

Ray withdrew his badge and showed it to the woman. "I'm Inspector Ray Navarro with SFPD. This is private investigator Jack Slaughter. We're working a case involving a former student… possibly three students. Is there someone here we can speak with?"

"Just a moment, Inspector. I'll see if Ms. Fong is available. She's in charge of Student Services." Nancy lifted the phone handset and punched in a series of numbers. "Ms. Fong, a couple of police inspectors are here and have questions about some students. Yes, ma'am. All right, I'll let them know." Replacing the handset, Nancy said, "Ms. Fong said she's quite busy today, but if you'd like to make an appointment, she'll be happy to speak with you then."

"Please get her back on the phone and let her know we have a warrant. She can make the time now to help us, or we'll help ourselves."

Jack nearly laughed at the innocent smile Ray gave Nancy.

Nancy didn't bother with formalities. "They have a warrant. Yes, ma'am." Hanging up, she said, "Ms. Fong will be right down. If you'd like to have a seat—" Nancy motioned to a waiting area across the lobby, but before she could finish her sentence, a voice came from the nearby stairs.

"Inspectors." Jack looked up to see an attractive Asian woman descending the stairs. Her dark hair was up-styled over a heart-shaped face. Her smart two-piece dress suit was a shade of beige that complimented her complexion. Her matching heels clicked on the marble tiles as she strode toward them. "I am Ms. Fong. I understand you have questions about our students…and a warrant? What's this about?"

Ray flipped open his wallet to show the woman his badge and credentials. "We're investigating the disappearance of one of your students. We have some questions, and we'd like to take a look at your records. Hence the warrant." He handed it to her next.

"I see," she said, eyes widening. "Who are we talking about? A missing student has not been brought to my attention."

"His name was Tristan Rybak." Ray gave her a copy of the MPR.

"That was some time ago. Why are you just now looking into it?"

"We're following up, Ms. Fong," Jack said. "Some new evidence has come to light since Mr. Rybak's disappearance."

Looking up at Jack, she asked, "What kind of new evidence?"

"His body," Jack flatly said.

A hand flew to Fong's mouth as she gasped. "Oh my. After all this time . . ."

"We'd like to take a look at his school records," Ray continued. "Maybe there's something there that could tell us more about his disappearance. We'd also like to speak with his teachers, if any of them are still with the school."

"Certainly. Please, come up to my office and we will go through it all there." Fong spun on her heel and returned the way she'd come, Jack and Ray behind her.

In her office, Jack shifted uncomfortably on the narrow chair.

"You'll see the warrant covers records for Rybak as well as two other possible students who Rybak may have been associated with prior to his disappearance," Ray said.

Fong pulled her keyboard toward her. "Let's start with the known student." A moment later, she continued. "I have his records here. Major studies in Humanities and Liberal Studies with a special focus on the arts . . . graphic design and creative writing. Notes here say he wanted a career in writing gaming scripts and designing the graphics."

Ray scribbled in his notebook. "His girlfriend at the time said he was a gamer, so his major makes sense."

"Was she a student here too?" Fong asked.

"We think so," Ray said. "Stacey Maguire. She's not on the warrant, but if you would be kind enough to look—"

Fong tapped her keyboard a few times and said, "Yes, she was.

She was in the same year as Mr. Rybak and graduated the year following his disappearance." She pressed a few more keys. "Similar areas of study as Mr. Rybak, but her focus was marketing."

"I need to get a copy of Mr. Rybak's records," Ray said.

"Is that really necessary?"

"Yes, Ms. Fong," Jack cut in. "They'll give us a better idea of the type of student he was, particularly if he was written up by any of his teachers or if he had any trouble outside of classes. Also, attendance and the like."

"It will all help in filling out the details of who Rybak was, which may help us discover why he disappeared. And why he's only reappeared now, albeit deceased," Ray added.

"Are any of their teachers still at the school?" Jack asked. "Perhaps they know something not in the official records."

"Yes. They are in class now though." Fong rose and went to a side table with stacks of paper and pulled a few pages before returning to her desk. She made a few marks with a pen before handing them to Ray. "We have a large campus. It is set up in quadrants. The first page is a map to the Humanities and Creative Arts buildings. And here is some information on those classes." She pointed to the notes she'd made. "These are the names of the instructors and their classrooms."

"Thank you," Ray said, then flipped pages in his notebook. "We also need to see if we can find any friends he might have had on campus. When his girlfriend was interviewed, she indicated Rybak had recently met a couple new gaming friends. She only had first names, so we're not sure if they were students or just people he met online. If you could search those names, it would be a great help. They're included on our warrant," Ray reminded her.

"You only have first names?" Fong asked. Ray nodded. "It will not be an easy search. So many students have the same name."

"How many students do you know called Kyle or Logan?" Jack asked.

Fong typed the first name into her computer. "Kyle. Hmm . . . Looks like there were two at the time Mr. Rybak was here." She clicked a few more keys, then looked between Jack and Ray, serious again. "Kyle Warren might be the young man you are looking for. The records show he had a similar interest of study as Mr. Rybak and attended the same classes."

Jack asked, "What about the other Kyle?"

"Kyle Jenner was a freshman that year and his notes show he had regular attendance in his classes and graduated on schedule. It is possible he knew Mr. Rybak, but they did not attend any of the same classes. As well, Mr. Warren stopped attending classes just before Mr. Rybak."

"Jack, do you remember a Kyle Warren in the MPRs?" Jack shook his head. "Ms. Fong, do you know who reported Warren missing?"

"There is nothing in the record to show he was missing. Only that he stopped attending classes. You might visit the Financial Aid office as he was attending the university on a full ride scholarship. I see here there are no next of kin listed and no emergency contact. Maybe Financial Aid has something more for you. What I can tell you is he had almost perfect attendance until a few weeks before he stopped attending classes altogether."

Jack sat forward. "And the school didn't find it odd that two students went MIA around the same time?"

Fong remained cool. "I can only tell you what I see on their records. It was a long time ago."

"Surely their disappearance would have alerted someone on campus, and an investigation would have been carried out," Jack continued.

Fong wrote something on a slip of paper and slid it toward Jack. "This is the name of our head of security. You may ask him your questions." She looked at Ray. "What was the other name?"

"Logan," Ray said.

After a few taps on her keyboard, Fong said, "We had one Logan . . . Logan Armstrong. Mr. Rybak and Mr. Warren were both juniors; Mr. Armstrong was a senior. He was a chemistry major with good attendance. Nothing obvious here linking him with Misters Rybak and Warren, but looking at the dates, his normally good attendance seemed to drop off at the same time.

Hmm . . . it looks like he had a strong 3.8 GPA, but it dropped around the same time as the others. He graduated by the skin of his teeth."

"That's good enough for me," Ray said. "I need printouts of everything you have on those three, as well as Stacey Maguire, if you don't mind. And I'll need the names and contact info on each of their parents or emergency contacts." Fong nodded. She set her printer up and it quickly started ejecting pages.

CHAPTER SIX

After speaking with Rybak's university lecturers, a woman in Financial Services, and the head of Campus Security, Ray drove Jack over to Beep's Burgers on Ocean Avenue in the Ingleside District, about a five-minute drive from the university. Neither spoke on the drive.

Beep's was a Mel's Drive-In style diner but without indoor seating and movie tie-ins. Above the wraparound exterior counter, the surrounding glass allowed diners to watch their meals being prepared.

The place attracted classic car enthusiasts, including an annual '50s night. On those nights, many dressed in period garb and bought their freshly detailed, souped-up and cherried-out hotrods to show off. And the diner played music from the likes of Elvis, The Del-Vikings, The Cadillacs, Debbie Reynolds and others popular at the time.

Jack hadn't been here since he and Leah lived in the Sunset house. Initially, they rode over on his Harley Fatboy—the same bike he had now—and when Zoë was born, they came over in Leah's pale-yellow 1965 Mustang. Back then, while it wasn't cherried-out, it was in good condition. Jack more so than Leah enjoyed those events, but they both loved the burgers and root beer floats.

Ray pulled the department vehicle into a space beside the building. They got out and placed their orders at the window then took two of the three stools at the side of the building nearest the car. From here, Jack had a one-eighty view from Lee Avenue to the junction on Ocean Avenue, as well as the Muni's electric buses.

Ray quietly watched the cook making their lunch. When it was apparent he wasn't in any rush to say anything, Jack broke the silence. "Ms. Fong and the teachers were accommodating, but they didn't tell us much that we didn't already know about Rybak."

Ray nodded.

"We did get IDs on the other two though."

"Uh-huh."

"Based on what the woman in Financial Aid told us about Kyle Warren being raised in foster care, I don't think there's much more we can learn about him unless we want to track down his foster parents. Sounds like once he aged out of the system, he was on his own. Doesn't look like he bonded with any of his foster siblings either—none of them were listed as emergency contacts or known associates." When Ray didn't say anything, Jack continued, "It's amazing that he managed to keep up his grades and earn a full ride scholarship, especially to SFSU. Definitely not an easy thing to do. That takes a lot of hard work and determination. Why throw it away, especially when he only had a year left to go?"

"Dunno."

Jack glanced at Ray, who sat motionless, staring into the restaurant kitchen. "Something bothering you?"

"Nope. I'm fine," Ray muttered.

Something was up. "Would you say it's safe to assume the three men were friends? Or at least Rybak and Warren were since they had the most in common." Ray shrugged. "Let's assume they were. Since they disappeared around the same time, do you think they went to ground together? I know it's a couple weeks since Rybak took his life, but if they've been together, do you think Warren is still there and waiting for Rybak to come back?"

"Anything's possible."

"And since we have the vehicle information on both of them, get someone to run the plates and see if anything pops." Jack's brain kicked into gear, trying to put the pieces together. "Hey, now that I think of it, we know what happened to Rybak, but has anyone found his vehicle? If he drove over to my place, is it still parked nearby, or has it been impounded? Run both of their names through the FBI's IAFIS system and see if something hits there too."

"Already on it," Ray grumbled.

"Maybe Armstrong's still around. Fong said he was a senior at the time and finished out the year, even though Rybak and Warren had disappeared. We need to find out what their connection was since nothing popped on Fong's records. And see if Maguire is still in the city and ask her about the three."

"Yes, boss," Ray said with a mock salute. "I'll get right on that too." Sarcasm dripped from his friend's words–or was it annoyance? Jack let it go.

Just then, a man inside the kitchen tapped on the glass, indicating their order was ready for pick-up. Jack rose. "I'll get it."

For old times' sake, Jack ordered the same meal he always did when he'd come here with Leah—a double burger with cheddar and swiss with bacon and jalapenos. Leah had preferred the veggie burger with avocado. They always shared onion rings but they each had their own float.

The instant the float's sugary vanilla and spicy flavors hit his tongue, emotions awakened of the times spent here with his family. For once, he wasn't being dragged into his sorrow. He felt only love for his wife and daughter and smiled at the memories of being here in this place with them.

A few minutes later, after tucking into his burger and Ray still giving him the silent treatment, he asked, "You pissed at me again or is this from before?"

"Why can't it be a little of both?" Ray asked without looking up from his meal.

Jack took a long swallow from his float, forcing more sugar into his system, before stuffing a salty onion ring in his mouth. Something was off with his friend, and he couldn't figure it out. He ate his meal in silence and let Ray do the same.

Over the years, they'd developed a routine. If Jack's job crossed over into official territory, as it had over the holidays with the drag queen murders, Jack brought Ray in immediately. What was different this time?

35

His burger finished, Jack wiped his mouth and tossed down the napkin before spinning to face Ray, who still wasn't looking at him.

"Haniford didn't agree to let me tag along today, did he?" Ray huffed, telling Jack he was right. "Why did you pick me up if he wasn't on board?"

Ray took a long, slow breath then calmly said, "Like I said last night. We both know, whether he agreed or not, you would have gone on your own anyway."

"Yeah, so? I'm an investigator. I investigate things."

"You're a *private* investigator, Jack." Ray finally looked up. "No one has hired you to look into Rybak."

"He killed himself in my house. That's the only invitation I need."

"And the reason why you're too close to this. Haniford put *me* on this case. You have to let the department do its job . . . let *me* do my job."

"I know you're a thorough investigator, Ray, but some guy offed himself in my house and no one's said shit to me about it. Not even you," Jack snapped. "So, you bet I have a vested interest. If Rybak knew *anything* about what happened in my house . . . to my family . . . I need to find out."

"That's why I let you tag along. Even knowing if . . . *when* Haniford finds out, I'll probably be fired. Or worse, lose my promotion and get busted down to desk duty. Jesus, they'll probably have me cataloguing evidence in the basement," Ray groaned. "At least taking you with me, I can keep an eye on you—"

CHAPTER SEVEN

Promotion?

"What do you mean by keeping an eye on me?" Jack asked, his hackles rising.

Ray stared at him for a long moment. "Jack, something's up with you. You keep telling me you're fine, but I know you. You're hiding something from me and it's pissing me off."

Jack sat back and crossed his arms. He absolutely didn't want Ray knowing how fucked up he really was. "I don't know what it is you think I'm hiding from you, but I'm good," he lied. "I appreciate you worrying about me, but you don't need to."

"Then explain your disappearance. You *forced* me to ping your phone so I could find you, then you got mad because I cared enough to go that far. Do you really think I wanted to invade your privacy like that?" Ray asked, his voice hitching up as he spoke. "It made me feel like shit, but you were avoiding me. Then I walk in with a fifty-pound sack of worry strapped to my back and find you in near darkness with a bottle of whiskey. Tell me how you think that should have looked to me. *Tell me, goddammit!*" he demanded through clenched teeth.

Tension-filled silence fell between them as they glared at each other. Neither blinked. Jack didn't know how to convince his best friend he didn't have cause to worry, even when he knew Ray really should be scared shitless.

Under his breath so the gathering lunch crowd didn't hear him, Jack said, "I don't know what else to say, brother, other than what I've already said. Tell me what you want to hear and I'll say it."

"What I want is for you to talk with someone. A professional. You should be able to move on by now. If you won't talk with me, you need to talk with *someone*. You need help."

Jack refolded his arms and huffed. "When you and I went to the house to gut the kitchen, I felt good. I was ready to move on. Starting with selling the house."

"I get it."

"Do you really? I don't know how you can. You didn't walk in just minutes after your daughter had her throat cut and was left to bleed to death. Your wife hasn't disappeared and left you wondering all these years where she is and what happened to her, or even if she's still alive. Or if she's the one who actually orchestrated it all." Jack felt his eyes well up but refused to succumb to the emotion. Not in front of Ray.

"You're right. None of those things happened to Maria or Zelda, but it doesn't mean we didn't feel the losses too."

"I know, but this is something I have to work through. It's why I left the house as it was after that night. What if the investigators missed something? But after three years, it was obvious I wasn't going to find anything new either, so I was ready to let the house go and try moving on," he insisted.

Ray nodded. "I know you were, and I was happy to help you however I could."

"Yeah, but then I realized Zoë...she'd been put in the highchair. She hadn't used a chair in months. It had been in the garage, so someone had to have brought it up and put her in it. Why? And if I'd missed that, what else had I missed?"

"Maybe it was the only thing, Jack. What if the only reason she was in the chair was to . . ."

Jack glared at Ray. "What?"

"Just to hold her in place. Nothing else."

"I thought of that too. When I couldn't find anything else, I decided again it was time to move on. I was ready, man. But then, like a pan of hot acid being thrown on me, suddenly there's a corpse in my dining room. His note . . . *I'm sorry* . . . was that because he'd been the one who killed my daughter? Because he took my wife to God only knows where and did God only knows what to her? And I'll probably never know because he's fucking dead." Jack's voice rose as he spoke, but now, he took a breath and vowed, "But if his friends know anything about it, you can be sure as shit I'm going to find out."

"Let me help you. I'm here for you. We're family, dammit. You and I are more than *amigos*. We're *hermanos de otra madre*—brothers from another mother. You know you can talk to me, tell me anything. Let me help you," Ray insisted.

Jack heard the passion in his friend's voice and saw the truth in his eyes. "Then why won't you believe me when I tell you I'm fine, and I don't need a babysitter? I just needed some time on my own to work through things."

"You've been working through things for four years now. You need help."

Jack looked into Ray's eyes for a long moment and knew his friend wasn't wrong. Jack just wanted to do things on his own terms.

He rose and grabbed the packaging from his lunch and walked it over to the garbage can provided for Beep's customers. He tossed it in then turned toward Ocean Avenue and started walking.

"Jack," Ray called, but he ignored his friend and kept going. A moment later, a hand on his arm spun him around, stopping him in his tracks.

"What?" he snapped.

"Come on, Jack. What's this all about?" Ray spread his arms out in a pleading gesture.

"I'm going home." Something punched Jack in the gut. It was the first time he'd referred to his apartment as home. "That's what all this is about."

"Get in the car. I'll take you."

"No thanks. I'll find my own way." Jack turned again, but Ray's hand was still on his arm, stopping him. He looked at his friend, willing him to let go.

"Is this because you think I'm babysitting you?" Ray asked. "Or because I want you to get some professional help?"

Jack put on a false smile and repeated Ray's own words. "Why can't it be both?" He jerked his arm free and started walking again. The Metro line was just across the street. He'd get on and take it into North Beach, then walk the rest of the way to his apartment.

"Seriously, you're going to throw a hissy because I'm worried about you? This—this isn't you, Jack. Why are you fighting me?"

Jack's heart thumped hard. Moments ago, he'd been enjoying the memories that came with revisiting an old haunt he'd shared with his family, and now he was ready to throw a punch at his best friend. All because of . . . what? His promotion? Why would he be angry? Ray was a great investigator. He deserved a raise. Jack didn't understand his friend's anger. Right now, all he knew was he was pissed off and just wanted some space.

Jack spun on his heel to a halt and stomped back to Ray. "This is why I wanted to be alone. I can't get it out of my head that this Rybak character killed himself . . . in *my* house . . . without telling me where Leah is. *I'm sorry* isn't good enough," he said. "I really was ready to move on, but I never expected something like this would ever happen. Now, I've got even more shit to work out and I don't need you or anyone else harping on me."

"Look," Ray started, stepping back and obviously forcing himself to calm down. When he spoke, his voice was lowered and more controlled. "I'm sorry if you think I'm harping on you. That's not my intention. The truth is, we both want answers, so I need your help on this investigation, but—"

"I know, I know," Jack cut in, holding up his hand. "If I want to work the case . . . any case . . . I need to get back on the job. I'm not ready."

Ray shook his head. "I know you better than anyone, and at times probably better than you know yourself. Thing is, I don't think you'll ever be ready to come back to work, and that scares me. You said you won't come back until you find Leah, or at least the person who killed Zoë. I'm as hopeful as you are that something will finally turn up to give you peace, but I have to agree with Haniford about the job. Shit or get off the pot."

"He said that?"

"Pretty much. He wants you back as much as I do, but all of this isn't just about not letting you shadow a few cases. The fact is, the longer you're away, the harder it's going to be for you to get back in the game."

"You think I haven't thought about that? I already see new faces starting to fill the department. Jesus," Jack swore, running his fingers through his hair. "I was nearly arrested for murder last year because Massie didn't know who I was. Not even when I played the *don't you know who I am card*. And *Imura Revolvers . . .* what the fuck is that all about?"

"Exactly my point. In the last four years, you've become more tech savvy than anyone I know. Combined with your years of investigative experience and it makes you one fucking hell of an inspector. But you're spending so much time following cheating spouses, serving subpoenas, and doing background checks that you're losing track of how the real bad guys are finding ways around the system, like the *Imura Revolver*. Getting back on the job now, you can bring all your new skills with you and teach the new recruits how to do their jobs better. God knows after the fuck up with Massie and James over the holidays, if we have more of that to look forward to, the department is going to need all the help it can get."

"Sounds like something that should be handled at academy level," Jack said. No fucking way. He'd feel like he was being busted down to street cop again and becoming some rookie's field training officer.

"You also need to consider you're starting to lose connections in the department simply because of rotation. As longtime officers age out, new recruits are coming on board, and none of the new cops know you. You come in looking for favors and they're going to send you packing."

"Are you saying you don't have my back anymore?"

A crease formed between Ray's eyes. "I will always have your back, and you'll always be a brother in blue. I'm just saying, we're not part of the new blood."

"Fuck 'em, then," Jack cursed before crossing Ocean Avenue to the Muni stop, as the Metro pulled up.

"Jack, listen to me," Ray called just before Jack stepped through the doors. "You need to get back on the horse while your ass still fits in the saddle."

CHAPTER EIGHT

Saturday – March 27

"Is it safe to come in?" Ray asked, standing at the threshold. Jack had been so entrenched in his work he didn't hear the door open.

"You've never waited for an invitation before. Why now?" Jack asked, only briefly glancing up from his computer screen.

Yesterday, after calming down, he'd unpacked his computer and set up the desk so he could get to work. He knew he couldn't go back to the Sunset house to finish his job there until he finished his job *here* . . . figuring out who Rybak was and why he'd killed himself in Jack's house.

"Maria and I talked, and she thought it was a good idea you and I should work things out."

"What did she have to say?"

Ray crossed the room and lowered himself onto the sofa. Jack spun his chair in his friend's direction, crossed an ankle over the opposite knee and leaned back with his fingers woven over his abdomen.

"Nothing I didn't already know but certainly seemed to need reminding of. Used to be a time I could read you like a book, but lately . . . I don't know."

"Nothing's changed," Jack said.

"No, something has, and I think we've both been ignoring it."

"Enlighten me."

Ray sat forward on the sofa, elbows on his knees, and squared his gaze with Jack's. "You've been keeping things from me."

Jack chuffed. "Because I didn't tell you I was taking a few days to myself?"

"Not just that, but that's part of it. I noticed you were keeping things from me before you took the case with the crazy lady."

Jack knew he meant Ginnie Whitney-Cummings, the former model who'd hired him to follow her husband before Christmas. "I told you everything about the case."

Ray shook his head. "No, you didn't."

"She was a socialite—"

"Don't go there. You've had other important clients and you've always told me about them. I tried brushing it off, but it made me realize it wasn't the only time." Ray counted on his fingers as he described three other instances in the last few months. He wasn't wrong.

"Maybe I didn't think you'd be interested. *I* was barely interested. Two of the cases were closed before the end of business the same day they signed my contract."

"That's not the point."

"Then what is the point?"

"The point is, it's becoming common practice. You only tell me anything when you need my help. Or need something from the department you can't get on your own."

"Are you saying I'm using you?"

Ray inhaled slowly, then said, "Sometimes, yeah."

"I'm sorry you feel that way, Ray. I—I didn't realize you thought I was withholding things from you. I'm certainly not using you. Well, sometimes, but you've always been involved in those investigations. And," he added, "you've always gotten credit for solving those cases. Hence your promotion . . . which you never mentioned." Ray's back straightened. "Look, I don't care that you're getting the credit. I expect it, but I'm sorry if you feel I'm using you."

"Maria—"

"Maria what?" he asked, scowling.

"She said you two had a talk before Christmas."

"And?"

"She's as worried about you as I am. You don't come to dinner anymore, you don't talk with me anymore, and . . . . We both feel like you're pulling away. That's how she put it. You're putting distance between us, and we don't understand why. Have we done something or said something that's making you walk away from us?"

Ray looked truly worried, and it came through in his voice.

"Absolutely not. It's not my intention to make you feel that way. I don't know what else to say." Of course it was his intention. If he hadn't pulled away from Ray, from the Navarros, he wouldn't have been able to go through with his plan to eat his gun. Little good it did him, because Ray had turned up anyway. *After pinging my damn phone.*

"Whether it was or not, I need to know where we stand. You had quite the blowout at Beep's yesterday."

"I'm sorry. I've been under a lot of pressure." The age-old response to everything.

"Over what? We used to talk through things like this. I know I've bitched enough at you about my problems."

"I didn't realize we were keeping score."

Ray sighed heavily. "We're not. You're missing the point."

Mimicking Ray's posture, elbows on his knees and leaning forward, he said, "I get it. Yeah, I probably should have told you I was taking a few days to myself. Maybe I assumed you had your hands full with a newborn and a new teenager, and I didn't think you'd notice I wasn't around for a couple days." Then he added, "And I'm sorry I got upset with you pinging my phone. I probably would have done the same thing if the situation were reversed."

"Wouldn't notice you weren't around for a couple days? What kind of *mierda de caballo* is that?" Ray sputtered.

"It's not horse shit, Ray. I don't know what else to say."

"I don't know either. Just tell me where we stand because yesterday made me feel like shit. I feel like—"

"Like what?"

Ray sat back and inhaled sharply. Without looking at Jack, he ran his palms down his thighs and said, "I feel like I'm losing you."

"You're not losing me." Tingles went up Jack's spine at the lie, but hadn't that been the point of not telling his friend what he was up to? "Trust me. We're fine."

"I'm growing to detest that word. Find another one."

Jack scowled. "How about we're all good? What else do you want to hear?"

"If we're good, tell me why you were huddled up in your house drinking." Ray leveled his gaze on Jack again.

"I had one drink. Just like I told you. The bottle and glasses were from Nick's office. We always had one shot after we'd talked."

"And you were at the house talking to Nick?"

Nodding, Jack said, "In a manner of speaking. I was doing all the talking. If he was there, he was only listening. When I was done, I drank my shot and was ready to leave." Just not the way Ray thought. "Then you showed up."

Ray's features seemed to harden. He looked around the room at the boxes then back at Jack. "You told me you weren't moving back to the house. Where were you going after your talk with Nick?"

"Home." Not a lie either. He had intended on going home to his family. Let Ray take it he was coming back to the apartment.

Ray stared at him for a long moment, making Jack wonder if his friend had twigged that he never called the apartment home.

"When are you going to tell me the rest, or do I have to drag it out of you?"

"I don't know what you mean."

"Maria reminded me it was the anniversary." After a short pause, Ray asked, "Do you want to talk about it?"

Just then, the wind went out of Jack and left him breathless. Neither of them flinched or even blinked as they looked at each other. He knew Ray was waiting for an answer, but he didn't want to talk about it.

"There's nothing to talk about. It is what it is," he finally said.

"You could have told me that's why you wanted to be alone for a few days. Not just drop off the face of the planet. I know Christmas was especially hard on you last year. Until Dewayne came along, we thought for sure we'd have you living with us for a while. We still want you to stay with us. We'll move Zelda into our room—"

"Stop. I'm fine here. Your house is more than full as it is. Besides, Christmas is over and now that my house has been released back to me, I can finally get over there and gut it so I can sell it," Jack said. "The place feels like an anchor around my neck. I need to sell it."

"I'll help you, if you'll still let me."

"Of course."

"So, are we good?" Ray asked.

"I keep telling you we are." Jack stood up and held out his hand. Ray reached out as he rose, but Jack pulled him into an embrace. "I'm sorry I worried you."

"I'm sorry I forgot about the anniversary."

"It wasn't yours to remember."

After a few slaps on the back, the men parted. Jack threw himself back into his chair. Ray remained standing, hands on his hips. He nodded at the sofa. "When are you going to start looking for a new sofa?"

Jack grinned. "Soon. Have you looked into those boys from the university?"

"I ran their names. Prior to the date of Rybak's and Warren's disappearances, they were pretty clean. Logan Armstrong is another story."

"How so?" Jack asked.

"Initially, he was busted for minor teenage stuff—weed, underage drinking. The reporting officers noted the joint and beer were taken off him and he was let go with a warning, but it got his name into the system."

"I feel a *but* coming."

"But after college, he's been busted a few times for possession with intent to sell or distribute which earned him some time in county lockup. Seems he's become quite the hophead," Ray said.

"I bet his parents are so proud they invested all that money sending him to SFSU for him to become a drug addict."

"Don't forget his major was chemistry . . ." Ray left the rest hanging.

"Were you able to track down Rybak's girlfriend?" Jack asked, grateful the conversation had taken off in another direction.

He didn't like that he'd hurt his friend, but he'd make a better effort at being more open with Ray until it was time for Jack to go back to his house. Maybe if he told Ray he was going out of town for a couple days, he'd have the privacy he needed to get the job done, and without interruptions this time.

Ray nodded. "Her last known address is her parents' house over on Wawona Street near the Irish Center."

"Are you going over to see if she's still there?"

Ray nodded, then checked his watch. "It's still early enough. Wanna take a ride?"

"You bet. You'll have to drive—unless you want to go on my bike." Jack remembered the last time Ray had been on the back of his bike and smiled. He'd taken them over to a vehicle dismantlers last spring when they'd got a lead on a victim's car.

Ray glared. "That's gonna be a hard no, *ese*. I'll drive."

CHAPTER NINE

The Maguire residence was on Wawona Street, kitty corner from the United Irish Cultural Center.

Ray parked the department vehicle in front of the garage.

From the street, the house appeared to be little more than a pair of boxes, one set on top of the other. Below the flat roof, a timber clapboard first floor was set above the red brick single car garage. The only architectural features included a large upstairs window that was the same size as the garage door below, and long, narrow red brick planters on either side of the driveway containing a few struggling geraniums. To one side of the house, narrow red brick stairs led to the front door, which Jack and Ray headed for.

The Maguires must have seen them pull up, as they were met at the open front door by a clean-shaven, round-faced man with prematurely gray hair. He wore a pair of dark-blue trousers, a long sleeve white shirt, no tie, and the collar was unbuttoned. A hint of tattooed Celtic motifs peeked out from his rolled-up cuffs on both forearms.

"What can I do for ye, fellas?" His accent was soft but recognizably Irish.

Ray flipped open his wallet and presented his badge and credentials. "I'm Inspector Ray Navarro and this is private investigator Jack Slaughter." The man eyed them both with suspicion but didn't say anything. "We're looking for Stacey Maguire. Does she still reside at this address?"

"What's this about?"

"It's a personal matter, sir. Is Stacey here?" Ray asked again.

Thanks to the man's slight stature, Jack saw over his head into the house. A pretty young woman with long, dark-blond hair stood against one side of what looked like a hallway.

"Sir," Jack said. "She's not in any trouble. We just have some questions about a college friend, Tristan Rybak."

The young woman stepped toward them, saying, "It's okay, Da. I'll speak with the officers." Her voice didn't bear a hint of an accent like her father's, telling Jack she was probably either born in the States or had come over very young. Her father let Jack and Ray inside, before closing the door behind them. "This is about Tristan?" She folded her arms in front of her and looked between Jack and Ray with worried curiosity.

Her father remained by the door, crossed his arms too, but with a stiffened back and puffed out chest.

"We understand Mr. Rybak disappeared in his junior year at SFSU," Ray said. "You reported it to campus police who in turn notified his parents. A formal missing persons report was filed by them."

Stacey nodded. "That's right."

"Have you been in contact with Mr. Rybak since then?" Ray continued.

"No. I haven't talked with him since the day before his disappearance." Stacey shifted on her feet and recrossed her arms. "It's been a long time. Why are you digging it all up again?"

"Can you tell us how you met?" Jack asked, deflecting her question. "According to the school, you didn't have any of the same friends or classes."

"I was working at the Irish Center." She flicked her head in the general direction of the cultural center across the street. "There was a party or some sort of event—I can't remember what it was. He came with friends. Then we met up on campus and eventually started seeing each other. He was really sweet."

"You told officers you and Mr. Rybak had been fighting. Can you tell me what that was about?" Ray asked. He'd pulled out his notebook and took notes.

"Does any of this really matter anymore?" Mr. Maguire asked. "It was a long time ago."

"Please bear with us," Jack said to both father and daughter. "We'll get to our reason for being here in a moment."

Stacey sniffled, then nodded. "We weren't really fighting. I was just jealous because he'd stopped coming around as much. Stupid, I know, but sometimes days would go by without seeing him, especially the weekends. That was really the only chance we had to spend time together. During the week, we both had school and homework or whatever. I started taking it personal."

"I don't blame you," Jack said. "What did he say when you confronted him about ignoring you?"

"Nothing really. He apologized, of course, but the behavior continued until one day he just disappeared. Literally. I haven't seen him since that last argument."

Ray asked, "Do you think he was seeing someone else?"

Stacey shook her head. "No, not another girl. He met a couple guys and started spending his free time gaming with them."

"Do you remember their names?" Jack asked.

"Umm . . . Logan and Kyle, I think. He knew Kyle from one of his classes, but when he met Logan, that's when things started changing."

"What do you mean things started changing?" Ray folded his arms in front of him as he concentrated on her explanation.

"Like I said, spending more time with them than with me."

"His school records showed he was taking classes to get into the gaming field." Stacey nodded. "I guess that means he was a gamer. Do you know what they were playing? *Super Mario . . . Grand Theft Auto . . . Halo . . . Call of Duty . . .*?" Jack threw Ray a questioning look. How did his friend know about all those games? "The kid," Ray simply said with a shrug. Right. Jack nearly chuckled. When he'd taken Dewayne into protective custody, the only reason the teen agreed to leave his own house was if he could bring his Xbox and big screen TV.

"None of those. Tristan and Kyle played one called *Fortnite*. When Logan came on the scene, suddenly all they wanted to play was *Head Shop Heist*. It was the dumbest thing I'd ever heard of if you ask me."

"How so?" Ray asked.

"Most kids who game play ones like you mentioned. Those guys? It was all about *Head Shop Heist*. I tried it once. Boring as hell."

"What was the gist of the game?" Ray continued.

"Just like the title says . . . stealing from head shops. Points are scored based on the type of gear and pot you collect in the game. If you find a shop selling harder stuff under the counter, you get more points. When your money runs out, the winner is determined by how much you collect, or steal, without getting caught. The more exotic the brand, the more points."

"That's where the heist part of the name comes from," Jack remarked.

Stacey nodded. "Yeah. Literally, players are encouraged to steal from the shops. Tristan and his friends were really into it though, because they played it all . . . the . . . time," she said for effect. "I saw how it changed him. Either the game or his new friends, or both, but it didn't take long."

"What do you mean, changed him?" Jack asked.

"Tristan started smelling like pot." Her nose wrinkled. "When we'd meet up, he was always stoned. Sometimes stoned *and* drunk. If I wanted to date a waster, there were plenty to choose from. But I liked Tristan. He seemed serious about his education and got good grades. We got on great—"

"Until Logan," Ray finished for her. Stacey nodded. "Were you aware Kyle had also gone missing just before Tristan?"

"Not until later. Everyone seemed focused on Tristan. His mother had to push campus police to do anything at all. They said Tristan was an adult, it wasn't a school-related incident, blah blah, but eventually the real police were called. They questioned me, then I never heard anything about it again. I rang his mother a few times to see if there had been any news, but eventually she told me to stop calling, so I did."

"When were you made aware Kyle had disappeared?" Ray asked.

"No one said anything to me. It was just talk around school."

"Did anyone from the school or the police question you about him?" Jack asked.

Stacey shook her head. "Some of the other students said he didn't have any family, so maybe there wasn't anyone looking for him. Sad, if you ask me."

"What do you think happened to Tristan and Kyle?" Ray asked.

Stacey looked between Jack and Ray, her gaze matter of fact. "I don't know, but I figured whatever happened to Tristan had to have been because of those other guys. And if Kyle disappeared, whatever those guys were up to, it couldn't have been good."

"Ye still haven't told us what this is all about, officers," Mr. Maguire said, still standing beside the closed front door.

Jack looked at Ray. He knew his friend hated delivering bad news, so he let him off the hook. "We're here because there has been a development in this case."

"Did you find him?" Stacey wiped the tears from her cheeks that had started falling.

Jack nodded. "Yes. It seems he had been alive since his disappearance, probably living on the streets."

"Had been?" Mr. Maguire asked.

"His body was found—" Jack didn't get a chance to finish.

"I knew it!" Stacey shrieked. "I knew those guys were trouble." As soon as her tears started, her father was at her side, embracing her.

"Do you know what happened to him?" her father asked.

"We're not at liberty to share the details with non-family members," Ray said. "But it's clear it was quick, and he didn't suffer."

"Thank Christ fer that," her father said, crossing himself.

CHAPTER TEN

Sunday – March 28

Jack sat across from Ray at the Navarros' dining table. Zelda was bundled like a burrito in her soft, pink blanket and nestled in the crook of his arm.

"I don't know how you do it, Jack," Maria said as she set two cups on the table along with milk and sugar. "She cried so much today. No matter what I did, she wouldn't settle. You pick her up and she goes right to sleep."

Jack smiled. "I wouldn't be much of an uncle if I didn't have the magic touch."

Maria gave Ray *the eye* at the spluttering sound he made before reaching down to take the sleeping baby.

"Leave her with me," Jack said. "Get some rest while you can."

"Are you sure?" she asked. Her features noticeably relaxed.

Jack knew how hard it was raising a newborn. "Absolutely."

"Thank you so much." Maria leant down to kiss Jack on the cheek before scurrying into the kitchen to where Dewayne was rinsing dishes in the sink before putting them into the dishwasher.

The teen looked happy. CPS normally didn't foster kids with cops, but Ray's reputation was exemplary, especially after the two major busts last year—discovering and stopping The Butcher and The Drag Queen Killer.

What clinched the deal in letting Dewayne stay with the Navarros was the boy's promise to the social worker that if the Navarros, or Jack, couldn't take him, he'd run away from anywhere he was fostered, which included state care. He'd already proven he could take care of himself, so they let him stay where he wanted.

The cherry on top for CPS was the Navarros refused the usual foster care payment and were supporting Dewayne as if he were one of their own. Maybe Dewayne realized the Navarros weren't taking him in for the money; maybe they did care about him. Whatever it was, it was clear he was happy and not going anywhere.

A moment later, Jack heard the dishwasher switch on, pulling him out of his thoughts. Maria and Dewayne headed out of the kitchen. Maria placed a hot pot of coffee on the table and muttered, "*¡Un largo baño de burbujas está llamando mi nombre!*" She disappeared down the hallway.

Dewayne stopped on his way to the living room and said, "If you still want me to show you that game, I'll be in the living room with Choo Choo." Choo Choo, the dog formerly known as Butch and who'd belonged to Ginnie Whitney-Cummings, had also been taken in by the Navarros.

"We'll be in after we have our coffee," Ray told him. Dewayne nodded and headed for the sofa. "You don't have to do this," Ray said, nodding at Zelda as he poured their coffees.

"Maybe I want to. I'm telling you now, though, if she needs her diaper changed, I'll be passing her over to you." Jack grinned at his friend's glare. "Tell me what you found on Rybak. Or was this just a ploy to get me out of my cave?"

Chuckling, Ray said, "Maybe a little of both." A moment later, he had pulled out the pages from the folder they'd been in and spread them across the table in front of him in purposeful stacks.

"You've been busy," Jack said.

"You have no idea. Okay." Ray took a deep breath. "Last week at lunch, you suggested Rybak might have driven to your house. I looked through his school records and found a photo of a 1977 Pontiac Firebird Trans Am. I ran the plate number and confirmed the car was registered to Rybak. From the photo in his class records, the vehicle looked well-maintained and had one of those special gold-on-black paint jobs like in that movie."

"What movie?"

Ray scratched his head. "I can't remember what it was called.

It had a guy in it from that movie where some friends go into the woods to hunt, and the kid playing a banjo—"

"You mean *Deliverance*?"

Nodding, Ray said, "That's the one. He was one of the hunters."

"There wasn't a Trans Am in *Deliverance*, my friend." Jack lightly laughed.

"I know that, *vato*. He was in another movie that had one. He was being chased by the *poli gordo* with the big white hat. Come on, you're the car guy. You know what I'm talking about."

Jack did love his classic cars and he knew exactly what movie Ray was talking about, but it was fun watching him flounder. "You mean Burt Reynolds. He drove a black Trans Am in *Smokey and the Bandit*."

"Yes! Finally."

Smiling, Jack said, "Let me see the photo." Ray found it in his stack of papers and slid it across the table. "Sweet ride. It does look like Rybak took good care of it. This is what they call Bandit Style—black car with gold pinstriping, brushed gold aluminum snowflake rims, and a big gold Laughing Phoenix on the hood. Just like in the movie." Jack slid the photo back across the table to Ray. "FYI, the decal was also called a Laughing Chicken, Screaming Chicken, and Fire Chicken."

"Yeah, yeah, whatever. Showoff. DMV records also confirmed the vehicle has remained registered, despite Rybak's disappearance."

"Really?" Jack exclaimed. "Do you suppose his parents kept it registered on the off chance he'd come home one day?"

"That's the thing. It's not registered at his parents' address. It's registered to Rybak at an address on Geary Boulevard in the Sutro Heights District. I sent officers to canvas the streets around your house to look for the vehicle, but they came back with nothing, so I'm going over to Geary in the morning."

"Maybe that's where Rybak's been hiding all this time," Jack suggested.

"Anything's possible. I can tell you one thing."

"What?" Jack's exclamation stirred Zelda but she settled quickly in his arms.

"I don't think Rybak had the car in his possession. You won't believe this."

"Try me."

"I think the car's with Logan Armstrong."

"What the— how did you link Rybak's vehicle to Armstrong?"

"The address on Geary matches the address in Armstrong's school records."

"Do you think Rybak has been staying with Armstrong all this time?"

Ray shook his head. "Based on the condition of Rybak's remains, I'm sure he was living on the street."

"I wonder what Armstrong is doing with the Trans Am. If Rybak sold it to Armstrong, wouldn't he have registered it in his own name?"

Ray shook his head again. "I'll ask him when I question him tomorrow."

"Wasn't Armstrong the one who was a year ahead of Rybak and Warren? What's he doing back at the school?"

Ray shrugged. "I'll ask him about that too. In the meantime, I put out a BOLO on the vehicle in case it's spotted before tomorrow. It's out on the street so we should find it soon enough. Not many '77 Trans Ams on the road anymore."

"What about Armstrong's own vehicle?"

Ray scanned Armstrong's paperwork. "School records show he drove a silver 2005 Mazda 3 hatchback registered to the same Geary Boulevard address. I ran the plates and it came back to an Edith Armstrong. Based on her date of birth, she must be Armstrong's *abuela*."

"When was the Trans Am last seen?"

Ray thumbed through the pages. "At the university just after you found Rybak."

"I don't suppose there's any indication he's made any attempt at paying any of the citations?" Jack asked.

"Nope. Now the vehicle has an order of impound. The next time it's spotted on the road, it'll be impounded until the tickets have been paid. Of course, Armstrong probably knows since the car is registered in Rybak's name, he won't be held responsible for paying them. The vehicle will probably end up at auction."

The hairs on the back of Jack's neck stood up at the mention of auctioning the Trans Am. It could be one sweet ride again if there wasn't too much restoration in it.

Jack shook himself. Didn't that defeat the purpose of having a bullet with your name on it?

"Before that happens, let's put a lien on it. And let's get campus security to keep an eye open for us. Have them call you directly the next time it's seen on campus and we'll go over ourselves to see what's what."

"Good idea," Ray said. "There's more. Since graduating, Armstrong has earned himself a record."

Jack frowned. "I thought Fong said he was a good student?"

"They all were, until they hooked up. Armstrong only graduated by the skin of his teeth, as Fong said."

Jack remembered. "Good students can still have a police record."

"Of course, but Armstrong's record had been clean until after graduation, even if his grades had slipped."

"What happened after graduation?" Jack asked.

"Apparently, he has a history of giving—" Ray said the word giving with finger quotes "—his friends weed. Not a big deal since it was legalized, but the two times he was arrested, he was in possession of cannabis over the limit allowed by law, along with a pocketful of cash."

"With drugs and cash, how was he not cited?"

"What was on him wasn't sufficient enough to prove he'd been selling."

"Doesn't mean he wasn't. If it was enough to detain him, why not arrest him?"

"The incident reports both said he was cited for possession over the legal limit permitted in a public place. There's also a note here that says he'd bought the dope at Dragon's Lair over in Chinatown."

"Isn't that one of the places owned by the Jade Dragons gang?"

"Yeah. They have a few shops around town—the Dragon's Head, Dragon's Claw, Dragon's Tail—but the Dragon's Lair is the main shop that handles distribution to the other shops. Why?"

"You know Amy Chin at the department, right? She normally works up in SVU. She helped us over at the Majestic at Christmas."

"Right. You two have history, don't you?"

"Not exactly. She wants to make history and I'd rather not. Anyway, her brother, Daniel, was the antithesis of the law-abiding Officer Amy Chin. He was a Jade Dragon."

The statement hung in the air for a long moment before Ray said, "*¡Meirda!* Does Haniford know? I mean, he must, right?"

"You can bet your ass he's been keeping a close eye on her. As far as I know, her record has been spotless. It wouldn't matter what her brother did or who he associated with. Chin wasn't responsible for him. As long as *she* wasn't involved with the gang or aiding and abetting him, she was as eligible as the next person to become a cop. Since her brother went missing a while back, I'm guessing the spotlight on her has been turned off."

Ray whistled low. "When did her brother disappear?"

"I can't remember if it was just before or just after I took sabbatical. A few years ago anyway."

"A lot of people went missing right around the same time. Think there's a connection?"

"Possibly." Jack nodded, then finished off his coffee. The cold bitterness hit the back of his throat like tepid sink water. He swallowed hard to stifle the cough he felt scratching his esophagus. Zelda must have exhausted herself earlier in the day, as she still slept like the proverbial baby when he cleared his throat. "Do you have anything else on Armstrong?"

"Remember he was a chem major?" Ray asked.

"Yeah, what about it?"

Ray went back to his paperwork. "A couple years ago, a citizen reported a man on the beach."

Jack chuffed. "That's not against the law."

"No, but wandering aimlessly while *desnudo* is." Jack chuckled. "Reports said he'd been wandering naked up and down the beach, muttering to himself, talking to the sun, accosting sunbathers and swimmers with wild ramblings. A surfer had to pull him out of the water before he drowned himself. He said Armstrong was staring into the sky and didn't know he was walking into the water," Ray said.

"He was tripping."

Ray nodded. "From the time the first call came in before noon and the time when officers were finally sent down there in the evening, he must have been tripping for as many as nine or ten hours."

"Shit, that's a long trip," Jack exclaimed. "Why didn't officers respond to the calls earlier in the day?"

"No idea, but even when they took him into custody, he wasn't immediately arrested. He was taken to the ER for his own safety. The doctors said he didn't know where he was until he came back to earth, and when he did, he couldn't remember where he'd been all day."

"Did they run a tox panel to see what he was on?"

Ray sifted through the paperwork. "Tox screen came back with a cocktail of drugs . . . lysergic acid diethylamide—"

"LSD," Jack said.

"Right. Also cocaine—"

Jack sat up. "What? He was on both LSD and coke? Fuuuck! He's lucky he didn't stroke out right there."

Ray nodded. "That's not all. He also had fentanyl in him and something called trimethyl . . . trymethoxen . . . damn it!"

"Trymethoxphenethylamine . . . or in layman's terms, mescaline."

"You know too much, *ese*."

"Any of those drugs could knock you on your ass," Jack said. "Combining them is a death wish. After a ten-hour high like that, I wonder how fucked up he is since then."

Ray shifted in his chair then pulled another sheet of paper out of the folder he'd set aside and laid it in front of him. "I have a theory."

"I'm all ears," Jack said as he carefully moved Zelda into the bend of his other arm. He felt a familiar ache tracking up his arm to his shoulder from holding the baby in the same position for so long. He looked down at the tiny bundle. She fussed only a little before settling again. Her smile just then made him want to lean down and kiss her forehead, but the serious look on Ray's face refocused his attention.

"Hear me out before you tell me it's bullshit."

"When have I ever—" Ray glared at him. "Let's have it."

"This is what we know. Rybak was friends with both Warren and Armstrong, even though they'd only known each other a few months, according to Stacey Maguire."

"Agreed."

"They all met while playing that online game, *Head Shop Heist.* As it was an online game, let's assume the guys didn't actually know each other in person, not at first. But they eventually met face-to-face." Ray looked at his notes. "I've got our computer geeks looking into all three of their accounts to see when they each started playing the game and when they started playing together. We obtained a warrant for the game company's server which holds all the data. The game also has a chat facility which we'll scan too."

Nodding, Jack said, "Awesome. What else?"

"For shits and giggles, and because of Armstrong's possessions record, I went over to Robbery Division and talked with Bud Schuman about any unusual cases they'd been on in the last ten years—had he seen any new trends in burglary or theft, anything unusual that stood out to him. What he told me probably won't surprise you, but until he mentioned it and not knowing about this game, I don't know if I would have even considered it."

"Get on with it. You're such a drama queen."

"Maybe I like drama, and maybe I like knowing it annoys you." Ray grinned. "Just do me a favor and don't drop my daughter when I tell you."

"I promise. Spit it out. What did Schuman tell you?"

"He asked me if I'd ever heard of *Head Shop Heist.* When I said no, he told me about it and the sharp spike in robberies in the city's head shops. Largely grab and goes, but also smash and grabs after hours."

"What were they taking after hours?"

"Anything they could get their hands on within a minute or so—bongs, pipes, grinders, even edibles, shit for vaping—"

"What about the pot itself?" Jack asked.

"It gets better. Schuman said he'd have someone do a deep dive into the archives for the older cases, but he gave me copies of what he had from when they went digital. There were only a few records but enough to compare the dates of those robberies from around the time Rybak and Warren went missing."

"I'll be damned. By the look on your face, I know you have more."

"Of course. What do you take me for, a rookie?"

"Absolutely not. Lay it on me."

"His team spotted a pattern with the same three perps—same clothes, same strategy, like they had it down to a science. Their faces were always covered but they were sure it was the same knock-off group. Witnesses who saw the getaways all confirmed it was the same vehicle—an old gray Mazda."

"Really?" Jack said with surprise.

"There's more. After one of the shops had been hit three times, they finally decided to upgrade their security and added outside video surveillance. They caught the car pulling up to the shop. Once inside, they destroyed the surveillance hardware, but there had been enough time for the video software to save to the cloud." Ray folded his arms in front of him and sat back with a smug grin.

"Are you shitting me? Tell me you got a plate number."

"It's only a partial, but get this. The partial matches a vehicle already under investigation. A silver Mazda 3, last registered to—"

"Logan Armstrong," Jack finished. He nearly laughed at Ray's shit-eating grin. "You need to get someone to trace that vehicle. He might be driving Rybak's Trans Am, but if he's still knocking over head shops, it won't be in that car."

"Agreed. And if Armstrong was the last person to see his friends, maybe he can tell us where Rybak's been and what happened to Warren."

"Great stuff, Ray." Ray laughed. "What?"

"You thought I was done. That's funny."

"Don't keep me hanging, brother."

"Guess which head shop got robbed the most?" Jack shrugged. "Dragon's Lair."

"No shit."

Ray put up a finger, telling Jack he still wasn't done. "Guess where Chin's brother worked."

"Dragon's Lair?"

Ray nodded. "Guess who was working the night at Dragon's Lair when it got robbed—" Jack opened his mouth to speak, but Ray was quick on the draw. "And guess who went missing that same night."

Almost under his breath, Jack said, "Daniel Chin." Ray touched his nose then pointed the finger at Jack, telling him he was spot on. What did Chin's disappearance have to do with the college boys? Had he been some sort of lookout for the trio? Things were moving quickly. Almost too quickly. "Is it just me or does it feel like this investigation is moving way too fast? I don't want us missing anything."

"Jack," Ray calmly said, "a man killed himself in your house. Haniford pulled in every available cop and has prioritized this. When I told you the other day at Beep's that you're still a brother in blue, I meant it. No matter what, you will always be *my brother*. I will always have your back. So does the department. Everyone wants a piece of this so you can finally get some closure. We'll figure out why Rybak killed himself in your house, and if it ties into what happened to Leah and Zoë. I promise."

"Hey," Dewayne called from the living room. "You still want me to show you how to play this game? If not, I got homework."

Just then, Zelda jolted in Jack's arms. When he looked down, Jack saw her big eyes were open and looking directly into his. She smiled for a moment before yawning. Then her face screwed up before a tiny squeak. Zelda smiled as the aroma rose.

Jack stood and passed the infant across the table. "Sorry, brother, but this one has your name written all over it."

For the next hour, Dewayne showed Jack and Ray how to play *Head Shop Heist*, including built-in game features. The three of them huddled around Dewayne's games console with Jack in the driver's seat, playing an anonymous user.

"There's a lot going on here. I thought this was supposed to be an older game," Jack said.

"Games are updated all the time. When this one was released, players mostly stole what they wanted. Like most games, it was about racking up credits. Credits are game money you use to buy—" using finger quotes around buy "—stuff within the game. Let's say you only have enough credits to buy some really cheap weed, but if you stole something like an expensive bong, you can sell it to another player, or pawn it, and use that money to buy more expensive weed."

Ray scratched his head. "What's the point if you couldn't actually smoke it?"

Dewayne chuckled. "It's just a game, Dad. It was probably designed for stoners. What makes sense to stoners?"

Dad.

When had Dewayne started calling Ray Dad? He smiled to himself, remembering the first time Zoë had called him Daddy.

"What else?"

Dewayne turned to Jack. "Remember when I showed you how to play *Grand Theft Auto*?" Jack nodded. "In that game, players are given point-earning tasks by the game's crime bosses. Things like stealing cars, kidnapping someone, assassinating someone, etcetera. The more heinous the crime, the more points you earn. Like shooting a cop earns more points than shooting an innocent bystander."

Jack remembered watching Dewayne's character shoot a cop in cold blood. It had turned his stomach then as it did now.

If it wasn't bad enough, these types of games also promoted racism, violent assaults against women, torture, and outright murder. They were teaching users, usually teens, to commit Class A misdemeanors. And now this game was teaching players breaking and entering. Not just any structure, but ones now specifically selling drugs.

"Great. Juuust great," Jack muttered.

Dewayne had helped Jack create his character. Once in, he was given a basic list of common types of cannabis, a restrictive budget, and a cheap handgun—some sort of six-shooter that came with only six bullets.

"If you run out of ammo, you have to buy more with your credits or steal something you can sell to buy more bullets." Jack nodded his understanding. "If you get shot while carrying out a heist and survive," Dewayne continued, "you earn street credits for surviving, but your character's lifeblood, your game energy, is reduced. Lose too much blood and you're dead. Game over. Survival money goes into game credits. With credits, you can buy more lifeblood, or paraphernalia to smoke what you steal . . . you can make your character smoke it."

"Who the hell comes up with this shit?" Jack asked.

Ray grumbled. "I'm not sure I like you playing this game, *hijo*."

"Don't worry," Dewayne said. "I'm only showing Uncle Jack how to play it."

"What else do I need to know about this game?" Jack asked.

"When you're out of money and street credits, you steal what you want. The more expensive the item, the more points you earn."

"Thank goodness it's just a game," Ray said.

Dewayne looked at Ray. "It's more than just a game these days. Now it includes a real online shop selling CBD products and edibles, and they'll mail it to you."

"Welcome to the 21st century. Everything can be yours at the tap of a key," Jack said on a long sigh.

"No kidding. For lazy people, right? You can also order online and choose the shop closest to you to pick it up yourself."

Jack clicked a few more links on the site then sat back in disbelief. Dewayne was right about the new site options. The shop was full of marijuana and smoking-related items.

Jack clicked the link marked *Store Locator*. He typed in *San Francisco* and watched an interactive city map pop up with pins where all the city's head shops were located and their contact information.

A flashing graphic on the screen that said *Plan your route* drew his attention to a link for an interactive game option for the city.

It wasn't uncommon for games to be based in real cities—*Grand Theft Auto: San Andreas* was based on San Francisco—but to tie locations within the game itself to *real* shops . . .

"What the absolute fuck?" Jack grumbled. His stomach tightened as his overactive investigative mind went into high gear. Anyone who really wanted to rob head shops could plan it through this game. With the interactive map, especially in cities like San Francisco, with its somewhat complicated road scheme, players could plan a real crime *and* figure out the best getaway route. The game also gave them the estimated travel times, based on the method of travel, such as by car, foot, or even bicycle.

Why would a gaming company create something like this? Surely, they were promoting real crime and targeting high income shops. It was as if the creators were saying, *We give you all the tools you need to plan the perfect crime. You only need to get out there and do it!*

He clicked on the *About* page and read:
Our mission at Head Shop Locator
is to help tokers find head shops in their area.
We believe cannabis in all of its forms should be universally accessible.
Groovy Games is a subsidiary of Head Shop Locator
and is intended for casual entertainment purposes only.

"Casual entertainment, my ass!"

CHAPTER ELEVEN

Monday – March 29

The house on Geary Boulevard was easily located on the western side of the peninsula at 46th Avenue. It was set on a corner lot near Sutro Heights Park and built in a vague Art Deco style. The three-story dwelling was painted off-white with contrasting dark-gray horizontal bands drawing the eye upward and away from the small and awkwardly placed windows of the lower floors. The cloudless blue sky revealed the sharp corners of the flat-topped roof, accentuating the squareness of the structure.

Ray parked his department vehicle beside the short driveway on 46th Avenue and followed the white picket fence around the corner to the front walkway on Geary. The fence was quaint but uncharacteristic to the design of the house.

The front garden also contrasted with the house's architecture. The once manicured lawn seemed to only have an occasional mow and was dotted with yellow dry patches and tufts of weeds. The footpath to the front door was cracked, with grass coming through. Framing the space along the inside of the fence, short California lilac was overgrown and dead in places and mixed with taller weeds that had been missed by the lawnmower. The only thing growing against the house were short Monterey pines that may have once been manicured, but it was hard to tell.

At the front door, Ray pushed the doorbell. An old-fashioned buzzer sounded inside. Just as Ray reached for the bell again, two clicks came from inside the door as the locks were disengaged, then the door slowly opened.

A small, thin woman appeared from behind the door. Jack guessed she was in her early eighties. Short, curling, white-gray hair framed her delicate wrinkled face. She pulled her light-pink sweater around her pale-blue dress with arthritic hands. On her feet were matching pink slippers.

The old woman didn't look comfortable seeing two men on her doorstep. Her grey-blue gaze darted quickly between Jack and Ray.

"Yes?" she croaked.

Ray presented his credentials and calmly said, "My name is Inspector Ray Navarro. I'm with the San Francisco Police Department. This is private investigator, Jack Slaughter. Are you Mrs. Armstrong?"

"Police?" Her hands noticeably shook. "What's this about?"

After pocketing his wallet, Ray gave the woman his business card. "Is Logan Armstrong your son?"

"He's my grandson."

"Does he reside with you?" Ray pressed.

"Yes, ever since his parents passed. What do you want with him?"

Jack spoke up, keeping his voice soft. "Mrs. Armstrong, we're following up on a case and your grandson's name came up as a possible witness. We'd like to speak with him and get his side of the story."

"He . . . ." Her gaze darted to one side for an instant before she said, "He's not here right now."

"Can you tell us when he'll be home or where he is?" Ray asked. "It would help our investigation if we could speak with him as soon as possible."

"He comes and goes. He doesn't tell me what he's doing." She sounded nervous. By the way her gaze kept darting to one side, Jack wondered if she had something wrong with her eyes, or was her grandson standing nearby and listening?

"Can you tell us where he works? We'll speak with him there," Jack suggested.

"I-I really don't know. He never tells me anything."

When she tried closing the door, Jack put up his hand. "I'm sorry, madam. Please. Would you have a cell number for him?"

She paused for a moment as if thinking about it. Her eyes darted to the side again and lingered before looking back at the men. She was definitely rattled.

Finally, she said, "You wait right there, and I'll get it."

"We will," Jack promised with a smile. Then she closed and relocked the door.

"Suppose she'll be back?" Ray asked.

"I'm sure she's just being cautious," Jack said. "She doesn't look comfortable with us being here."

A moment later, the door opened again. This time it was on a chain latch. The old woman's hand shook as she handed Ray a piece of paper through the narrow opening. Once Ray had it in hand, she closed the door again and locked it.

"*Now* I think she's done with us," Jack said.

"*¡Vieja loca!*"

Standing on the sidewalk beside the car, Ray said, "Let me give Armstrong a call and see where he is." He dialed the number and waited.

Jack cocked his head toward the house and listened. Below a narrow balcony, the single car garage had an old style pull up door and it was open about a foot. A cell phone rang somewhere inside. "Hear that?" Jack whispered.

Ray pulled his cell away from his ear and listened. "Yeah." He disconnected the call and the ringing stopped. "To be sure it's not just a coincidence—" He redialed.

"There it is again. I bet he's here. It's no wonder the old lady seemed cagey." Jack quietly edged toward the garage door. The phone rang from the back of the space.

Ray didn't have a warrant allowing him to raise the door and go inside, but there was nothing saying Jack couldn't poke his head in. Had he been alone, he would have gone inside. Worst case, he would have been arrested for trespassing. For Ray, it would mean much worse, not to mention blowing the case.

Jack dropped and rolled toward the opening. The door was

lifted just enough for him to squeeze his head under. The back of the garage was dark, but the light coming through the partial opening illuminated enough of the front of the space for Jack to see a car had been backed in. Clutter along the walls gave someone just enough space to get in and out of the car. All he saw of the vehicle was a black spoiler under a dark car cover.

Jack heard Ray leave a message. "Hello. Mr. Armstrong, my name is Inspector Ray Navarro. I'm with the San Francisco Police Department. Your name was given to us as a witness to a recent incident. I wanted to have a chat with you to see if you can corroborate what happened at the scene. You can reach me at this number at any time."

Just then, a door into the house opened and light from the interior filtered across the back section of the concrete floor. Two pairs of feet came into view—those of Mrs. Armstrong in her pink slippers and some belonging to a male, based on the heavy boots and jeans the man wore. Jack heard voices at the very back of the garage.

"Why were they here . . . why were the *cops* at my house? Did *you* call them? Tell me!" the man demanded.

His house?

"No, I didn't call them."

Jack was sure he heard fear in the woman's voice, so she probably wasn't about to correct him. Given the man's presence and tone, Jack was sure this was Logan Armstrong.

"What did they want?"

"They said you witnessed something and wanted to talk to you about it."

"What was it I was supposed to have seen?"

"They didn't say," she whimpered.

"What did you tell them?"

"I didn't tell them anything." Mrs. Armstrong's voice began shaking. "Logan . . . let me go." So it *was* him.

"They were here long enough."

"Stop shaking me. You're hurting me."

"Tell me, old woman," Logan all but shouted.

"Logan, stop this. You're hurting me," she repeated, then cried out.

That's it. Jack shimmied through the door opening as quietly as he could, stood, then stole along the side of the car toward the back of the garage. Light from the open door cast a faint glow on the man's face.

Mrs. Armstrong gasped when she saw Jack. Considering the inconsistent shadows, she probably didn't recognize him. When Jack reached out to grab Armstrong, the man turned and immediately threw a punch at him. He quickly flinched backward but Armstrong's fist caught him square in the chest, winding him. Armstrong rushed past. He threw open the garage door and high tailed it down 46th Avenue.

Jack looked out and saw Ray's stunned expression. "Get him!" he shouted.

Ray took off after Armstrong.

Jack righted himself and turned to the woman. "Are you okay?" When she nodded, he rushed out of the garage. As he moved, he removed and tossed his heavy leather jacket through the still open car door then headed after Ray.

Jack hit 46th Avenue at a full run. At the corner, he saw Ray turning west onto Point Lobos Avenue. Ray raced across the median then north up Alta Mar Way. Jack darted between cars and followed Ray onto Seal Rock Drive at the top of the short block. In front of him was a long row of houses, all built side-by-side as if they were one long structure. Ray and Armstrong could only go west or east. Jack looked west and saw Ray following Armstrong down Seal Rock Drive.

Jack's heart pumped hard, making his ribs ache. His thigh muscles protested at the sudden and prolonged demand on them, but he ignored his discomfort and kept going, breathing fully through his mouth in big gulps.

At the junction, Armstrong must have turned north onto El Camino Del Mar and into the Fort Miley Military Reservation as Ray moved in that direction.

The fort had originally been designated as the Point Lobos

Military Reservation back in the 1880s. In 1903, a battery of sixteen 12-inch mortars were installed, including two 12-inch rifled guns mounted on disappearing carriages along with several supporting buildings, making the site a formal military installation. At the time, the fort had been renamed in honor of the late Lieutenant Colonel John D. Miley.

By the 1930s, the barracks were already being razed to make way for the Fort Miley Veterans Hospital, now known as the San Francisco VA Medical Center and one of the top VA facilities in the state.

Once past the Fort Miley entrance sign, Ray diverted into the forest and headed toward the VA grounds. Jack saw his friend struggling with the terrain and reached over to pull him along when he caught up.

Ray waved him off. Indicating for Jack to keep moving, he gasped hard. "Don't lose him. I'll go this way and . . . try heading . . . him off."

As Jack passed, he side-ran while looking back at Ray, "You gonna be OK? Too many tacos are slowing you down."

"Fuck you," Ray shouted as he forced himself upright again and took a path toward the facility.

Jack stopped chuckling once Ray was out of view. Too many tacos were slowing him down too. Or maybe he was getting too old for this shit. He couldn't let it get to him now though. Armstrong was still within view, and as long as he was, Jack was sticking to his tail. He wasn't going to let himself be bested by a junkie with an attitude problem.

Armstrong stuck to the trees at Battery Chester. Long gone were the mounted guns on their disappearing carriages, but the concrete sunken foundations were still in place.

Just then, Armstrong ducked under some branches and into the shadows of the tall cypress trees. Jack followed but lost him when a flash of sunlight blinded him. He blinked hard to clear the glare in his vision, and when he looked back, Armstrong was gone. Jack kept moving forward.

He suddenly skidded to a halt, kicking up loose dirt and gravel when the path gave way to a sharp drop-off on the hillside. He struggled for balance as he fought to keep from going over the side. At the sound of running behind him, he spun in place, gasping for breath, preparing to take off again.

Ray came to a stop beside him. He bent with his hands on his knees and took in long gulps of air. Sweat dripped off his face. "Where . . . where is he?"

Jack slowly turned again in a full circle, scanning the trees and dense hillside, but it was peacefully quiet except for the echo of the waves surrounding the Battery Lobos coastline.

He ran his fingers through his sweat dampened hair. "I—I don't know. I was following him past the battery and then he disappeared into the trees." Jack kicked the graveled path in frustration. "Goddammit!"

Ray straightened and clapped Jack on the shoulder. "Come on." Ray turned back the way they'd come. "We know where he lives. I'll set up plain-clothed officers in an unmarked vehicle across the street from his house. When he comes back, they'll take him into custody and bring him in for questioning."

"When we get back to the house, we need to have another chat with the old lady," Jack said. "She should get her locks changed while we're there so she can protect herself from her grandson."

"Do you think that's necessary?"

"I caught Armstrong manhandling her in the garage. I think her behavior at the front door was because she knew he was home, and she was more scared of him than a couple cops at her door who may have been able to help her."

Ray gave Jack a sly sideways grin. "A couple cops, eh? Does this mean you're coming back to work?"

Jack chuckled. "You know what I mean. We're working the case together so of course it's *we*. I just don't want you getting the impression again that I'm questioning your ability to handle the case or overstepping your authority." Jack referred to the discussion they'd had at Beep's last week. "You know how I get on cases."

"Full charge. I get it. Doesn't mean I can't like the sound of *we*."

CHAPTER TWELVE

B ack at the house, the garage door was still fully open. The only thing showing under the heavy car cover was the license plate.

Ray ran the plates then handed Jack his phone before going around to knock on the front door to speak with Mrs. Armstrong again. The plate information wouldn't take long to come back.

Jack leaned against the rear fender of Ray's unmarked vehicle. From where he stood, he had a near perfect view of the garage's interior, as well as both ends of the block in case Armstrong decided to come home while he and Ray were still there.

The radio squelched. "Ray, I have the information you requested." He recognized Amy Chin's voice and kept his replies short.

"I'm listening." Dispatch confirmed what Jack already knew, but he wrote it in his notebook anyway. "Copy."

"Is that you, Jack?" He didn't have the patience for her. Without saying anything, he turned down the volume, tossed the radio on the passenger seat of the car, and concentrated his focus back toward the garage.

If anyone asked why he'd entered the garage without a warrant, he'd claim exigent circumstances— Armstrong was manhandling his grandmother and Jack thought she was in danger.

Now that the threat of danger had been eliminated, he was obliged to remain outside and off the property. Or would have been obliged if he'd still been on the force. As it was, he was no longer a cop, and in his mind, cop rules no longer applied to him. With Ray around the front of the residence, Jack took advantage of the quiet and went into the garage. He peeled the cover from

74

the front of the vehicle and stood back with a low whistle.

The car had obviously seen better days, but Jack would stake his life on whose car it had been. He didn't need to see the gold decal of the Laughing Phoenix on the hood to tell him what he was looking at.

This was the late Tristan Rybak's missing 1977 Trans Am.

"That *abuela está* loca. If she's afraid of her grandson, why wouldn't she let us help her?" Ray asked, pulling his seatbelt around him then snapping it in place.

Jack shook his head. "Maybe I read more into the situation in the garage than was there."

"You're rarely wrong."

"There's always a first time. Like I said earlier, she's probably too afraid of him to let anyone help her. I just wish she would've let us look in the car."

"You did though, didn't you?" Ray said, nodding toward the still open garage door.

Jack grinned. "What do you think?"

"I think you should tell me what you saw."

Jack chuffed under his breath. "Someone would have to get into the vehicle to find anything significant. The blacked-out windows didn't make it easy to look inside, especially in a relatively dark garage."

"But?"

"What I could see were dozens of fast food wrappers and Coke cans. The ashtray is full of cigarette butts and what looked like roaches; there certainly was a strong smell of cannabis and tobacco, even with the windows up. Whatever Armstrong has been doing with the vehicle, he certainly hasn't taken care of it. It looks like the back seat is still in good condition, but it's hard to tell under so much trash. The front seats are definitely torn up. There are tears in the driver's seat where the foam cushion is either visible or completely missing. There's no doubt he's been using the hell out of the vehicle. I've been in stakeout vehicles that were cleaner."

Ray chuckled. "¡Eso es asqueroso!"

"Just one more reason not to go back on the job—takeout trash and the smell of greasy fast food."

"And another reason why I'm working alone until you come back."

Avoiding Ray's bait, Jack said, "Hey, Armstrong dropped this on his way out of the garage." He handed Ray the phone. He'd put it into one of Ray's clean evidence bags to protect any evidence on it and prevent from contaminating it with his own fingerprints.

"I didn't see him drop anything."

"It fell out of his pocket as he passed you. I found it in the weeds beside the curb." Ray lifted an eyebrow at Jack's explanation. "That's my story and I'm sticking to it." He sure as hell wasn't going to admit he'd taken it off the toolbox in the garage. That would make anything they found on the phone inadmissible in court if this ended up going any further. "There might be something in it telling us where he's been and with who."

"Uh-huh," Ray said, sounding unconvinced as he pocketed the phone. "Good find. I'll get it into Evidence so we can take a look."

"Since we're done here, are you heading back to the department?"

"Maybe, why?"

"If you are, drop me back at the apartment. I've got an errand to run. If not, drop me over on California Street and I'll get the bus over to Chinatown. I've got a craving for a mooncake."

"For a guy who says he's tired of Chinese food, you sure eat a lot of mooncakes." Jack chuckled. "You need help with anything?"

"I'm just picking up my bike. I need to go over and talk to Cutter."

Ray started the car, checked for traffic then pulled onto Geary Blvd. "I'll take you."

"Howzit, brah?" Cutter greeted when he saw Jack at his office door. He rose to move some files off a chair in front of his desk. When Ray entered behind Jack, Cutter looked surprised but repeated the Hawaiian word for *brother* in greeting. "Brah."

"Don't bother with the chairs. We're only stopping for a minute," Jack said.

Cutter straightened and folded his arms. "What do you need?"

"I need to see if the PM is ready for Tristan Rybak," Jack said.

Cutter glanced at Ray. "Is this PD official or personal official?"

"Rybak is the guy who committed suicide at Jack's house, so a little of both, but mostly PD official," Ray said. "I'm lead on the investigation."

"Sure. Give me a sec." Cutter sat behind his desk and tapped his keyboard. A moment later, the printer whirred to life.

"There are a couple other names associated with Rybak," Ray went on. "One we know is still walking the planet."

Jack huffed. "Walking? The guy's like a cheetah." When Cutter cast a confused look, Jack added, "We went to speak with him this morning and he rabbited into Fort Miley and disappeared. He was there one second and the next he was gone in the shadows."

Cutter chuckled. "What's the other name you need run?"

Ray pulled out his notebook. "Kyle Warren. He ran with Rybak and another guy called Armstrong . . . our rabbit. Warren disappeared around the same time as Rybak."

"Was his body recovered?" Cutter asked.

Jack shook his head. "We don't know if he's dead or alive and in hiding as it appears Rybak was. Just chancing an arm here. If he's in the system as deceased, it's one more name we can cross off our list."

Cutter went back to his computer. A moment later, he said, "There's nothing in the system under that name, though he could have been a John Doe. Or maybe he's still alive."

"If he is," Ray said, "he certainly hasn't had feelings of remorse like Rybak had. If the pair have been together all this time, with Rybak gone, maybe Warren will eventually come out of the woodwork too."

CHAPTER THIRTEEN

Thursday – April Fools' Day

Jack checked the time on his phone. Again.

She was late.

He expected after years of hounding him for a date, the least Amy Chin could do was show up on time, goddammit.

He wasn't angry about her tardiness. He was still pissed six ways from Sunday because of her blackmail.

After speaking with Bud Schuman in Robbery last week, Ray had finally received copies of the archived reports he'd asked for. He'd planned on spending Wednesday morning going through them, then visiting some of the shops after lunch. It was a long shot, but maybe something had been missed when the reports had originally been written. As they were now technically cold cases, it wouldn't hurt to go back and re-interview witnesses and shop owners.

Ray had called Jack and asked if he wanted to tag along. Of course, he did. If any of this helped him learn more about Rybak and why he'd chosen Jack's house to off himself, he wanted to be the first to know.

When Jack entered Ray's office yesterday morning, the angry look on his friend's face was the last thing he'd expected. Ray told him he'd called down to Reception and asked them to let him know when Chin arrived for work. As soon as he got the call, he went up to SVU to speak with her about her missing brother. Anyone in their right mind would have wanted to help and give Ray what he needed. Especially the sister of a missing man. Neither Jack nor

Ray had expected her to throw them a curveball.

She was happy to help, but she'd only talk with Jack.

Angry heat flashed through his body as he immediately turned on his heel and left Ray's office. Not waiting for the elevator, he took the stairs by twos to SVU. By the time he mounted the last stair and stomped over to the Missing Persons desk, he was spitting nails.

What really sent him over the edge was when she told him she'd be happy to help in any way she could, but only over dinner. Hence his sitting here on the patio at the Hog Island Oyster Co. at the Ferry Building and staring at the Bay Bridge. The bridge lights had come on moments ago, as had the patio lights and heaters, and the deepening blue sky behind told Jack the sun was setting on the west side of the peninsula.

His jaw ached from grinding his teeth. He forced his hand to relax around the bottle of Bette Jane's Ginger Beer he'd been nursing since his arrival nearly an hour ago. The last thing he needed was broken glass in his palm and a trip to the hospital. Lord knew he'd had more than his share of those over the years.

Bitch!

Blackmail was bad enough, and possibly actionable within the department—coercion and impeding an investigation—but now she had the audacity to be late.

Frankly, if he didn't feel that her brother's disappearance was somehow tied into the Rybak investigation, he wouldn't have waited *this* long. Hell. He wouldn't have even agreed to dinner. Did she think he'd wait around all night for her? If she did, she had another thing coming. It had taken her four years to get him to take her out, so maybe making him wait was her payback. He was almost sure it didn't have anything to do with today being April Fools' Day and this whole situation being a set-up at his expense.

He checked the time again.

"Fuck it," he grumbled.

The chair's metal legs screeched across the concrete as he rose. He pulled out his wallet and extracted some money to pay for his drink and the time he'd wasted taking up one of the tables. He knew the waitress was anxious to turn the table for paying diners, so he added a generous tip for the inconvenience and dropped a twenty onto the table, setting the bottle on top so it didn't blow away.

"Jack!" The sound of her voice grated on him and made the hairs on the back of his neck rise. When he looked up, the sight of her kicked him in the gut as he watched her step through the restaurant door and walk across the patio.

Amy Chin was a small woman. He guessed she only just met the department's height requirement of five feet, but geared up, she always appeared *more than*.

Right now, there was nothing of Officer Amy Chin about this woman. Everything about her made her look dainty and delicate, and her choice of attire screamed seduction. Many around them stopped what they were doing and stared at her too.

Jack knit his eyebrows together as he swept his gaze up his co-worker from toes to tits.

Her deep-pink stilettos clicked across the concrete as she approached him. His gaze followed her slim, shapely legs north to the hemline of her slinky deep-pink-almost-red silk dress, if it could be called that, to where it stopped at the top of her thighs. The fabric hugged her perfect hourglass-shaped body. He wasn't sure which was holding up the top of the dress, the micro-thin shoulder straps or her stiff nipples pressing hard against the sheer material.

He nearly laughed at the thought, if she pulled up the top of the dress to cover her breasts more, he might get a look at her panties. Pull the dress down to better conceal her crotch and her tits might pop out over the top.

As Chin moved, she pulled the long, pale-blue embroidered shawl she wore around her. The delicate peony and lotus blossoms matched the color of her dress.

He swallowed hard, embarrassed for her rather than being aroused. She was trying too hard to impress him. Little did she know it was the exact opposite he found sexy—a woman whose self-confidence and inner femininity radiated outward to enhance her natural beauty, regardless of what she wore. Someone like Leah.

Jack suspected anyone else would have found Chin exciting, beautiful, and maybe even ready for a night doing the horizontal bop. To him, her attire was garish and made her look cheap.

Forcing himself not to stare, Jack threw himself into his chair and pocketed the twenty he'd set on the table for the waitress.

She stood beside her chair and looked down at him, no doubt waiting for him to pull it out for her. When he didn't, she yanked it out herself and dropped onto the metal seat, exclaiming, "Goddammit!" She tried adjusting her dress and shawl so she wasn't sitting directly on the cold metal.

He caught her glare then and noticed her makeup echoed the colors of her garments, but her natural brown eyes seemed to blacken as she scowled at him. She was angry about something, and he was sure it was something other than him not pulling out her chair.

She tossed her small matching pink purse onto the table then leaned back with her arms and legs crossed. Her foot immediately started bobbing up and down. The look on her face implied she wanted to tear off someone's head. Probably his.

"Nice of you to finally show up," he said.

"I don't know why you couldn't have picked me up. A real date would have."

"This isn't a date, Officer Chin." He used her title to drive home the point.

"Then what are we doing here?"

"This is nothing more than a business meeting. You said you'd only help us with our enquiries regarding your brother if I took you to dinner. That's the *only* reason why we're here—talk, eat, then go our separate ways."

She huffed. "You still could have picked me up."

"And you could have called to say you'd be late."

"I would have been on time, but—" He didn't really care why she was late. He just wanted to get this over with. "I took a Fast-

Fast Cars because it should have been faster than the Muni."

"And probably a better idea not to take public transport in that get-up." Chin's scowl darkened. *Play nice, Jack, or you won't get what you came here for.* "What happened? Did the vehicle blow a tire?"

"I wish." She sat up and arched her back to look over the other patrons. Her shawl fell off her shoulders, forcing Jack to look away from the sight of her nipples pressing against the sheer fabric. It was chilly here, overlooking the Bay, and the reason why he hadn't removed his leather jacket. *She should have dressed more appropriately.* "Where's the waiter? I need a drink."

"Tell me what happened."

"The asshole dropped me off at Fisherman's Grotto down on the Wharf." Chin threw herself back again and refolded her arms.

"You did tell him the Ferry Building, didn't you?"

Chin glared at him. "Of course I did, Jack."

"Then why did he drop you at the opposite end of the Embarcadero, nearly two miles away?"

Chin huffed and glanced away. "When he picked me up, he had boxes in the back seat and asked if I minded sitting up front. The last thing I expected was for him to put his hand on my leg."

"He what?" Jack wasn't happy sitting here with Chin, but it did make him angry hearing anyone would put their hands on a woman without her consent.

"Yeah. He pulled up to a traffic light and looked over, said my dress looked really soft and could he touch it. Then his hand landed on my thigh."

"So, you got out and . . ."

"I reached into my purse and pulled out my badge. I told him he was lucky I didn't have my weapon on me, or I'd have blown off his balls!"

Jack didn't know if he should laugh or be angry because she didn't get out of the vehicle. "Then you got out." She looked away. "Amy . . ."

"I know, I know. I was reaching for the handle when he turned onto a side road. I thought he was going to drop me off right there, but he kept driving. The one time I want to get out and walk and all the lights are green. When he finally stopped, I found he'd driven to the other end of the Embarcadero. I reminded him I wanted the Ferry Building. He said he knew and to just get out. I asked for his license and Fast-Fast Cars credentials, but he reached across me to open the door and started pushing me. I'm not exactly dressed for an altercation, so I got out. I did get his plate number and called it into the department, then waited for a responding officer. By the time I'd given my statement, another patrol car pulled up with the asshole in the back. After I IDd him, they let me go."

"By the tone of your voice, that's not all."

"You'd think the car would have been enough—I prepaid the fare when I booked. When he threw me out at the Grotto, I didn't have any money on me to get another Fast-Fast Cars, so I had to either walk or get a streetcar." She lifted a stiletto-clad foot. "I'm not exactly dressed for walking."

"The reporting cop didn't offer you a ride down here?"

Chin shook her head. "He probably assumed I was going into the Grotto and left. I didn't have any money and didn't realize until it was too late that I didn't have my Clipper card on me either. I know I was taking a chance getting on the streetcar without paying but I was hoping to just get here and forget about the last hour. But of course, that's when the Muni cops thought it was a good time to spring a surprise inspection. I was ticketed for failure to pay the fare, even after I explained who I was and the horrible start to my evening. I swear, it would have been quicker walking."

Jack wanted to laugh at the string of misadventures she'd suffered but didn't dare. What else could he say but, "I'm sorry."

Chin recrossed her legs and looked at Jack for a long moment before she added, "You know, this is all your fault. You should be the one paying this fine."

"How do you reckon?"

"You should have picked me up," she said for the third time. Jack wasn't going to repeat himself, so he said nothing. "It's not like it was out of your way," she grumbled.

"You live over in the Richmond District. That's the other side of the peninsula."

"I did, but I moved to be closer to . . . work," she finished awkwardly.

"Makes sense. Where's your new place?" he calmly asked. He didn't want to know, but her pause made him shift anxiously in his seat. When she didn't reply right away, he asked again, "Amy, where's your new place? Or is it a secret?"

"Nottingham," she said under her breath.

Jack knew exactly where she was. Nottingham Place was little more than a short alleyway located about a block over from Tommy Wong's. She hadn't moved to be closer to work, but to be closer to *him*. "You're right. It would have been quicker to walk. When did you move?"

Just as quietly, she said, "About a year ago."

If he thought he was pissed about her blackmail and her late arrival, knowing she moved so close to him, and a fucking year ago, was infuriating. Had getting information about her brother not been so important, he would have left her where she sat and walked out on her. Instead, he took long, deep breaths to calm his rage. She had always had a way of getting his blood pressure up, but this was over the top.

He pushed his anger down and, calmly as he could muster, asked, "Why didn't you tell me?"

"Why should I? It's not like you'd ever come over. Every time I've invited you, you turned me down."

She wasn't wrong, but she had an unhealthy attraction to him, and discovering she was practically living on his doorstep for the last year without knowing disturbed him. Had she been spying on him? Just then he wanted to go back to his apartment, get up on the roof to see how much of her place was visible, and potentially how much she might be able to see from there. *Could she see into his apartment?* His insides shook at the thought.

He couldn't force her to move, and she hadn't done anything illegal, so he tried shifting the conversation. He needed to focus on her brother.

"I hope it's a nice place."

"Where's that damn waitress? I need a drink and I'm hungry."

Jack spotted their waitress and motioned to her. A moment later, she appeared with menus and took their drinks order. As much as Jack wanted to order something stronger, he settled for another Bette Jane's Ginger Beer since he was on his bike. He didn't need to be inebriated on the ride home. Chin ordered a G&T with extra G.

"Not drinking, Jack? Come on, lighten up. Let's have a nice time together."

"I drove."

"Great. You can give me a ride home after. It's the least you can do considering the trouble I had getting here."

"Not gonna happen, Amy."

"But we're neighbors. If you drop me off on Nottingham, you can come up to see my new place," she coyly suggested.

Jack shook his head. He really hated lying to people, but sometimes a little white one couldn't be helped. "I'm going to Ray's after. Opposite direction. Sorry. Besides, I'm on my bike. You're not exactly dressed for it."

Chin shyly smiled. "You noticed. What do you think?" She let the shawl fall from around her shoulders. The chilly air instantly stiffened her nipples again under the silky fabric. Her brown eyes darkened the longer she gazed at him. When she coyly dipped her head, her short black hair framed her face and made her look both innocent and tempting. She knew exactly what she was doing.

"I think you forgot to finish dressing before you left your apartment." Jack picked up a menu and blocked her scowl from view. He breathed deeply. He wasn't a man of steel. Any red-blooded male would be turned on by her scantily clad body and overt seduction. But he wasn't just any red-blooded male. He was a married one, even if he didn't know where his wife was, or if she was still alive.

He heard Chin grumble and glanced over the top of his menu. She'd wrapped the shawl back around her shoulders and was now scowling at her menu.

85

"What the fuck?" she said under her breath.

"Problem?"

"It's all seafood." Her gaze scanned back and forth across the offerings.

"And your point? We live in San Francisco. What did you expect in a place like this?" He waved to the sign over the door. *Hog Island Oyster Co.*

"It also says hog, Jack. As in pig, as in pork, as in meat. Let's go somewhere else."

"When the waitress comes back, ask her what the specials of the day are. Maybe they have something you'll like." Jack scanned his menu. "Look, there's pork belly. Happy now?" If she hadn't just blindsided him with her new apartment location, he would have laughed at the childish look she gave him. He knew it well because Zoë had given it to him more than once. It said, *don't like it, can't make me.*

The waitress arrived with their drinks and a forced smile. "Have you decided on your meals?" Jack looked at Chin. She finally sat up and asked for the day's specials. It was a short list, most of which revolved around oysters, but the last item was chicken, so she ordered that and tossed down the menu. "Would you like something to start? I can recommend the Kilpatrick appetizer. Four oysters per order, cooked with bacon, shallots—"

"If I wanted oysters," Chin snapped, "I would have ordered oysters."

The waitress, who Jack knew from his arrival was called Jenny, did her best not to show her hurt at Chin's rudeness and turned to Jack. "For you, sir?"

"I'll start with the Kilpatrick and have the steamers with pasta for my main meal. You can bring them together. Thank you, Jenny. And I'm sorry for keeping you waiting. My friend," he said, swallowing hard, "had trouble with traffic." Jack gave Jenny a sincere smile and saw her expression soften.

Jenny gazed between Jack and Chin. "I'm glad she finally arrived safely." Jenny's tone lacked sincerity. "I'll bring your meals as soon as they're ready." She turned on her heel and quickly walked away.

"You know," Jack said as he settled back. "You should have been nicer to her. She could spit in your food, and you'd never know."

CHAPTER FOURTEEN

When Jack returned from the bathroom, Chin and Jenny were laughing together like long-time friends. He forced the frown off his face as he sat.

"Everything all right here?"

Jenny had just delivered the food and was tucking the food tray under her arm as she looked at him. "Amy's right. You should have picked her up." She gave Chin a wink before striding away.

Jack's scowl deepened. "What was that all about?"

Chin put a smug look on her face and sat back. "When she brought our food, I apologized for my behavior. All the shitty stuff that happened to me tonight wasn't her fault."

"No, it wasn't. That was a nice thing to do. What was all the giggling about?"

"She asked what happened, so I told her. She agreed with me. It was all your fault. You should have—"

Jack glared. He was tired of her blaming him for her own stupidity. He was beginning to wonder how she'd made it through the academy. Nothing about her, especially tonight, screamed professionalism, or that she was a responsible adult. If anything, she came over as a spoiled child, and one he thought needed a good spanking . . . if he thought she wouldn't enjoy it.

He unfolded his napkin and placed it across his lap. "This isn't a date, no matter what you told the waitress, but there's no reason we can't have a nice meal together. And talk shop, like you agreed. Are you good with that?" He gazed across the table for a long moment while she considered the unspoken options. Behave or else.

Nodding, Chin capitulated and softly said, "Yeah, fine."

Jack gave her a curt nod. "Would you like to try the Kilpatrick? It smells great."

She wrinkled up her nose. "Thanks, but no thanks."

Jack didn't feel any guilt or discomfort about eating in front of someone who wasn't. It was her choice not ordering an appetizer, and if she was waiting for him to finish his before she started her entrée, she could damn well eat it cold. He was hungry and he was the one paying. There was no reason for him not to appreciate the meal, even if he wasn't enjoying the company.

With the first bite, he felt his tension ease. For a moment, he let himself enjoy the savory flavors and Chin's silence as she poked at her meal with her fork.

Between bites, Jack pulled out his phone, switched on the audio record app, and set the device in the center of the table. "I hope you don't mind. This is easier for taking notes while I'm eating, and I can refer back to our conversation later." The jerk of Chin's head told him she was okay with it, or that she didn't care. Either way, he took it as her giving him permission. "Tell me about Daniel."

Chin's expression darkened at the mention of her missing brother. "Tell me what you want to know. I can't read your mind."

"Fair enough. Were you close as kids?" he prompted.

She shook her head. "Not really. We didn't hang out together if that's what you mean. We're four years apart, so I had my friends, and he had his."

"You became a cop, and he became . . ."

"He was still in high school when I joined the academy."

"When did he join the Jade Dragons?" He got right to the point.

Chin recrossed her arms and legs and avoided Jack's eyes. "I don't know." She wasn't making this easy. They both knew the drill—question and short answer, and don't say anything that could be misconstrued or used against you.

"Come on, Amy. You know he has a record."

She shot him a glare. "If you know, why ask me?"

"Because, you should know why he joined the Jade Dragons, and when. I'm giving you the opportunity to help me out. Us. Ray and me. We know he was with the gang when he disappeared. It would be helpful to know why he joined in the first place. Why does one sibling go into law enforcement while another chooses a life of crime? The more we learn about Daniel and his motives, the more likely it is we can find out what happened to him. Has he made contact at all?"

Chin shook her head. "No. He just . . . Like, one moment he was there and the next," she snapped her fingers, "poof. Gone."

"Do you think the gang had anything to do with his disappearance?"

"Probably. Maybe. I don't know. Nothing good ever comes from being in a gang. I told him that, but you know how kids are. They think they know everything."

Jack nodded. He thought he knew it all too when he was a teen. He'd been smart enough to stay out of gangs, though, even if some of his friends hadn't. "Everyone makes choices in their lives. Do you know what his reason was for choosing gang life?"

"I really don't know. He was always a good kid growing up. There were only the two of us and I remember him shadowing me when I was home. Drove me crazy, especially when I had friends over. When I became interested in law enforcement, I thought he'd keep shadowing me and join the force when he was eligible."

"But?"

"By the time I graduated from the academy, he was out of high school and didn't seem to have a direction yet. He should have been thinking about college and his future. Our father wanted him to take over the family business. We used to have an imports store in Chinatown. Mostly tourist crap, but Father said it was honorable work, and it provided a good income to raise his family. He wanted the same for Danny. He and I are the first-generation Chinese Americans in our family."

"Your father was living the American dream—immigrate to America, open a business, start a family, and enjoy everything that came with hard work?"

90

Chin nodded. "Something like that."

"Why didn't your brother want to be involved in the family business?"

"You have to understand, the Chinese are proud people. We work hard, not for riches, but to provide for our families. Losing the shop in the recession was a great humiliation to my father. He took it as a personal failure which deeply affected him. Even more so when the bank grew impatient for debts and threatened foreclosure."

"I understand. Italians are similar."

"One day Danny told Father he didn't have to reopen the shop if he didn't want to. He said he got a job that paid well so he could pay the bills. They didn't need the shop anymore. Father didn't want Danny's money and insisted he go to college to make something of himself, but Danny said he didn't need college to get something he already had—money. Father argued that Danny needed an education to take over the family business. Father was sure he would reopen the shop someday, but we all knew it was gone."

"Why wouldn't your father take the money? If the shop was closed and the property was being foreclosed on . . ."

"Danny was secretive about where he worked and how he came by so much money, which made Father distrustful. He was sure it was bad money and didn't want any part of it. My parents said I'd dishonored the family by becoming a cop, but now Danny was disgracing the family with his secretive behavior."

Chin's revelation gave Jack pause. "Why would they have objected to your joining the force? Did they want you to become a lawyer or doctor?"

"No, in a traditional family, the eldest son is meant to follow the father's lead. In our case, it was just the two of us, so Danny was expected to take over the shop when Father retired. For me, I should have been looking for a good husband who would provide for me and concentrate on making babies. Not chasing down bad guys with a gun and putting myself in danger every day."

"You've always been upstairs at SVU though."

"Didn't matter. The point was I wasn't married and raising a family. One day maybe . . ." Chin softened her gaze toward Jack, but he ignored it.

"When did you find out Danny had joined the Jade Dragons?"

"The first time he was arrested. When we learned Danny was in the gang and accused of selling drugs, it destroyed my parents. Losing the shop was humiliating, but they were close to losing the apartment too. The apartment was over the shop, so if the shop was foreclosed on—"

"So was their home. I get it."

"Now their son had chosen a life among demons. If that wasn't enough, I was put under a spotlight at the department. Even now that my brother is . . . gone, I still feel like someone is always looking over my shoulder."

"I'm sorry, Amy." What more could he say? Sometimes bad things happened to good people. Some recovered, but many didn't. Some did whatever it took to keep food on the table and a roof over their heads. Maybe that was how Danny saw it at the time. "How did Danny get involved with the Jade Dragons in the first place? If he was a nice kid growing up, I'd assume he had nice friends and he wouldn't travel far from his comfort zone."

Chin's eyebrows scrunched together in a tight line. Anger flashed in her eyes. "My guess is Kenny Chang."

"Who is Kenny Chang?"

"They were attached at the hip and had a lot of energy, so they got up to a lot of mischief. If one was caught up to no good, you could bet they were both in on it."

Jack chuckled. He'd had a friend like that growing up. "What happened? It doesn't sound like the relationship followed them into adulthood."

"Father caught the boys smoking in Danny's bedroom. Kenny confessed to having brought the cigarettes into our house, but my brother had equal blame in letting it happen. After telling Kenny to leave, Father spent an hour admonishing Danny . . . Kenny was a troublemaker, he was an instigator, he didn't come from an honorable family . . . blah, blah. He was banished from our home, and he forbade Danny from seeing Kenny again."

"Over cigarettes?" Surely her father was a little over the top. "Sounds severe. Why didn't he just ground your brother as penance?"

"Like I said, Father was an honorable man, and if someone dishonored him, it was a great shame. Defiling someone's home, even with cigarettes, was an insult to the family, and the perpetrator should be ashamed and never be allowed to show his face again." Chin's foot started bobbing up and down again. "Trust me. We all paid the price for Danny's indiscretion."

"Tell me about the gang. How did Danny go from shadowing you to the gang?"

"I lost track of his daily comings and goings when I entered the academy. I only saw him when I was home. One day, he let it slip that he'd been in touch with Kenny. Father was right about him being a troublemaker. Some of Kenny's friends were involved with the gang, many being brought up by the gang from a very young age. I'm sure it was Kenny who convinced Danny to join the gang and not tell Father. We only knew Danny suddenly had money and used it to help pay the bills. After Danny's first arrest and we learned the truth of the money, Father refused to accept Danny's help again. He had now dishonored the family."

Jack sat back, inhaled deeply and let the breath out again on an audible hiss through his teeth as he scrubbed his fingers through his beard. "Damn, Amy. I really don't know what to say."

"You don't have to say anything. It was a long time ago."

"How are your parents now? Has the shop reopened?"

She shook her head again. "The shop is long gone, and now so are my parents. Not long after all this, my father died. I think losing the shop and all the rest of it was too much for him. Mother took his ashes back home to China to be buried with his family. She never returned. The doctors there say she died from a broken heart. For a while, it was just Danny and me."

"And now it's just you."

Chin nodded. "Before the bank could foreclose, we sold the building and everything in it. When the estate was settled and the bills paid, we divided the little that was left equally. I bought a small apartment over in the Richmond on 14th near the park—I had to get out of Chinatown—and Danny rented a place in the Tenderloin."

"He didn't buy a place of his own too?" Jack asked.

"No. I don't know what he did with his money, but about six months later, he started coming to me for loans." She said the word loans with finger quotes. "The last time I heard from him, he called me to bail him out of jail. I told him I didn't have the money—I was literally tapped out. We argued and I explained I could lose my job if I kept getting involved in the life he'd chosen for himself." Chin sniffed and used the corner of her napkin to dab her eyes.

"What did he say to that?"

"He accused me of not loving him and said I chose the department over flesh and blood. I didn't, but he didn't get it. Afterward, I didn't hear from him for almost a year."

"What happened?"

"He called me. Asked me to meet him. Said he'd turned over a new leaf and was getting clean. He just needed a few bucks . . . Same old story. I asked him if he was still in the gang, and when he said he was, I told him to call me back when he'd gotten out. That was the last time I spoke to him."

"What can you tell me about Danny's disappearance?" Jack asked.

"Not much. I hadn't heard from Danny since that last call—weeks. Then I got a call from the department asking me to come down—they had some questions about my brother. I had no idea what was going on. When I got down there, I was told he was missing."

"With your parents gone and you two being out of touch, how did the department know Danny was missing?"

"Apparently, he was dating some girl, Lian Chang. Kenny's sister. She said he'd been working in one of the head shops owned by the Jade Dragons and hadn't come home one night after work. He hasn't been seen since. I tried calling him a million times, but the phone rang out, and after a while I couldn't leave messages because his voice mailbox was full, so I stopped trying."

"That was eight or nine years ago?"

Chin nodded. "About that."

"Did investigators turn up anything at all?"

"Not to my knowledge. I know it's not allowed, but I looked into the case files and there's really nothing there I didn't already know. Honestly, it seems like they didn't even try finding him. Forget he was my brother. To them, he was a drug dealer. Which, you know as well as I do, are considered scum and not worth the air they breathe. Right?"

"They're still human beings. A lot of people do the wrong things for the right reasons. You say Danny took the job to help out the family. Right reason, wrong choice." Chin was quiet a moment before nodding. "I'll get Ray to look into it for you, talk to the reporting officers and see why it wasn't followed up on."

"Thanks."

Jack pushed his plate away from him and asked, "Do the names Rybak, Warren, or Armstrong ring a bell with you? Did Danny ever talk about them?"

A crease formed between Chin's thin eyebrows as she thought about his question. "I don't think so. Wasn't Rybak the man who—"

"Yeah," Jack said. "It looks like Rybak and Warren disappeared around the same time as Danny and I'm wondering if they knew each other or had some other connection."

"What about Armstrong?" she asked.

"He's still around. He's selling drugs now, but we don't know for whom. When his friends went missing, they were all at SFSU. By all accounts, they were good kids until they got mixed up in gaming."

"Gaming?" Chin looked directly at him, as if recalling something.

He hesitated a moment, then slowly said, "Yeah. Why?"

"I remember Danny and Kenny getting into video games. There was one they played a lot. I think it was called Pot Store Raid or something like that."

"*Head Shop Heist*?" The hairs on the back of Jack's neck stood on end.

"Yeah, that's it. Why?"

"Just curious." It was a half-lie. "The name came up a while back and I was surprised to hear it again. It's been nearly a decade since it came out."

"Danny said all his friends were playing. Since Kenny wasn't allowed in our home anymore, Danny used to go over to his house to play." With a wistful smile, Chin said, "I remember he thought it was funny how he could rob all the shops in the city and his cop sister couldn't do anything about it."

Just then, Jenny returned to collect their plates and tidy the table. "How was everything?"

Jack noticed she'd relaxed a lot during their conversation. "We were so caught up in talking, I never stopped to ask how your chicken was."

Chin looked up at Jenny. "It was great. I loved the mushroom sauce. Thanks for the recommendation, Jenny."

The waitress smiled and turned to Jack.

"Everything was perfect," he said.

"I'll let the chef know. Can I get either of you dessert, coffee or tea, another round of drinks?" She told them the dessert specials from memory. Chin chose something warm and chocolaty while Jack opted for hot apple crumble and a coffee.

When he was done eating his dessert, Jack sat back with his coffee and gazed out to the Bay Bridge. The sun had set long ago, and the typical night fog had yet to encroach upon the city, so the bridge lights looked crisp against the dark, starry sky. Soft, jazzy music now filtered out from the restaurant into the patio space. It was nice sitting here with the warm cup in his hands on a pleasant evening, and forgetting it was actually April Fools' Day.

It was with some irony Jack thought this could have felt like a real date . . . had he been with Leah.

CHAPTER FIFTEEN

Friday – April 2

Ray agreed to meet Jack at the department early so he could play the recording with Chin from last night. When the playback was finished, Jack switched off the audio app on his phone and sat back in the chair he occupied on the visitors' side of Ray's desk.

Ray leaned back, mimicking Jack's posture. "That's quite the story. Do you think she's telling the truth?"

"I don't see what she'd gain by lying."

"How do you feel about her living so close to you?"

"Honestly, I don't know. She said it was to be closer to work, but I'm pretty sure it was at least a partial lie. You know how she's behaved since she joined the department; she's been relentless over the years about wanting me to take her out, even before what happened with Leah and Zoe. You have to admit, at times, her behavior has been unprofessional at best."

"It's just a crush, Jack. You're still a good-looking *hombre* . . . considering your age," he added, straight faced.

Jack glared but didn't take the bait. "Crushes don't last years. I think it's safe to say she's obsessed. This long? It's not healthy. Of all the places in the city she could've moved, I wouldn't have expected her to choose a place at the end of a dark alley in the red-light district, for Christ's sake."

"Call it Little Italy all you want, *amigo*, but your place is also in the red-light district."

"Big difference. At six-four and built like I'll send someone into next week for looking at me cross-eyed, no one is likely to bother me. Given how she was dressed last night . . . I'm not surprised her driver wanted a taste of her."

Ray shifted in his chair. "What was wrong with her outfit?" Jack gave him a quick rundown of Chin's barely there dress. Ray let out a soft whistle. "You shoulda got a picture."

Jack chuckled. "If you want one, pull the restaurant's surveillance video. You know, I don't think she realizes the impression she makes on people. You know me—everyone has their lives to live, however they choose. It's none of my business, but I try being supportive of others' choices. Last night, I was actually embarrassed for Amy. She knew it was just a business meeting, yet there was no getting around her dressing to seduce me. She was completely oblivious to everyone staring at her."

"Sounds like she put you in a difficult situation."

"If we didn't need the information on her brother, I would have left. I'd already been waiting an hour and was on my way out when she finally showed up." Jack felt himself getting worked up again. "I've been wondering if I should have a chat with Haniford about this."

"Are you sure you're not getting old and becoming a prude? She's young, single, and looking for fun," Ray said.

Jack ignored the *old* comment. "That's what her driver thought. She could have been raped. Or worse."

"Point taken. Let's focus on the case. If you go rushing to Haniford, he'll know you're poking around when he specifically told me to keep you out of it." Jack reluctantly agreed. "So, what was your takeaway from the discussion?"

"I learned a few things. Nothing mind blowing, but I'm sure you can agree we can use some of it." Jack pulled out his notebook and flipped it open to the page he'd made a list on earlier. He spun Ray's notepad around and, as he wrote on it, said, "I listened to the recording last night after I got back to my place and made some notes. I'd like to run a couple checks—"

"You mean you want *me* to run the checks," Ray corrected.

"Put it any way you like, but there are some people we need to know more about who could be relevant to the case. Since I can't do it, yeah, this falls on you."

When he was done copying the information, he spun the notepad back in Ray's direction. "Kenneth Chang, aka Kenny. Lian Chang reported Daniel Chin missing." He looked up at Jack. "Kenny's sister?"

Jack shrugged. "If Kenny had a sister, it's possible Danny got together with her."

Ray nodded his agreement and looked back at the notes. "And you want me to pull the files on Daniel Chin and run his history."

"Amy said he'd been arrested twice to her knowledge, but there could be more. I'd like to see what the system pulls up. It could give us a lead on why he disappeared," Jack said. "And I think we need to take another look at the MPR and any investigation Officers Davis and Minter performed back then."

"Do you think it's necessary? Sounds like a waste of time."

"Amy said she felt like no one took Danny's disappearance seriously. If she's right and there hadn't been an earnest search for her brother, I think we need to know what had or hadn't been done, and why Davis and Minter dropped the ball on a sister in blue. Might not hurt to run histories on those two as well to see if anything hinky pops up."

"So, you're saying you want a full workup on *all* of these people." He waved Jack's notes in front of him.

Jack nodded. "The Jade Dragons keep coming up in the conversation too, so I think we need to start following those threads and see where they lead, don't you?" By now, Jack had sat forward with his elbows on his knees. "Look up anything and everything on the gang, including the gang leader. He has to be on file, as well as any and all known associates."

Ray chuckled. "You don't ask for much, do you?"

"That's nothing compared to back in the day." He gave his friend a big, cheesy grin.

"Maybe so, *compinche*, but back in the day you were on the job and running your own checks." For a long moment, Jack didn't respond. "What? I know that look."

Jack shifted in his chair. "Hear me out. If we both go to Haniford, you can give him an update on the case. Explain to him how Amy would only talk about her brother if I took her out."

"He won't believe it."

"It's the truth and easily confirmed by letting him listen to the recording. I'll tell him I agreed to help facilitate *your* investigation. After listening to the recording, tell him you realized this goes deeper than you thought and would like his permission to bring me in to help run the checks on these people," Jack suggested.

Ray folded his arms in front of him. "Why wouldn't I just pull in someone else to run the checks? Andrews is riding a desk at the moment after pulling his ACL. I could give him the list."

"Because Rybak killed himself in *my* house. Like it or not, I'm investigating the guy and everyone he knew until I find out why he chose my house to off himself. I have a vested interest. Besides, Haniford hates when I'm investigating something relating to a department case and withhold intel. It makes his investigators work overtime to get it on their own. He'll bring me in just to keep me from doing that."

"You'd really withhold details from *me*?" Ray patted his chest over his heart and sniffed dramatically, as if he were about to cry. "*¿Mi hermano de otra madre me haría eso?*"

Jack smirked at Ray's failed attempt at sounding hurt. "Brother from another mother, eh?" Ray tapped his chest again; his pained expression took on a comedic look. Chuckling, Jack said, "I would never withhold from you. You know that. But look at this realistically. You need help and I'm available. More importantly, suggesting to Haniford that he let me in will protect your promotion."

"Screw that."

"You deserve it, and you know it. I don't want to be the one responsible if you lose it. Whatever you think of it, a promotion means more money. You have a growing family to think about. Especially since you refused money from Social Services for taking in Dewayne." From his friend's silence, he knew Ray was spinning things around in his head. Jack had known Ray long enough to recognize *the look*. "And while in Haniford's office, it would give me the opportunity to voice my concerns over Amy Chin's behavior."

"What do you expect him to do? He can't fire her for dressing like a hooker. She can do what she wants on her free time."

"True, but her infatuation with me has gone on long enough. She started hitting on me the moment she joined the department. Even when she was told I was married. And she barely waited a minute after I lost my family to kick it up a notch and hasn't let up. Now she's effectively moved in next door to me—a single woman in the red-light district—and only *now* tells me?" Jack took a breath and lowered the pitch of his voice back to normal. "Blackmailing me into taking her out before she'd help us with this case is *way* over the line. She should have been doing her job and giving you anything you need to help find Danny. Something's not right with her and I think Haniford needs to know. If he can give her a tap on the shoulder, maybe she'll back off."

Ray grumbled out an "I'll think about it" before shuffling through the papers on his desk. "Meantime, I've got the files from Bud over in Robbery on the head shop robberies." He shoved a copy in Jack's direction. "He gave me everything he had from around the time Rybak and Warren disappeared. There were a lot of very busy little *cacos* back then."

Jack skimmed the page before looking up. "Same guys from the university?"

"Not all of the robberies, but a lot of them. It sounds like you want to focus on the Jade Dragons, so let's concentrate our energies there."

"Thanks." Jack flipped to a blank page in his notebook.

Ray scanned the Robbery reports. "First, Li Zihao runs the Jade Dragons. According to Bud's notes, Li is a Chinese export who arrived in the city about fifteen years ago. He was thirty-eight on his last birthday and has a last known in Chinatown."

"Sounds pretty young to be a drug kingpin."

Ray nodded and continued. "He has a number of arrests since coming to the city, but he hasn't served any real jail time."

"Slick lawyer?" Jack asked.

"And deep pockets," Ray said with a nod. "According to Bud, Li runs five head shops around the city—Dragon's Claw down in the Mission District; Dragon's Tail in the Castro; Dragon's Heart in the Haight, Dragon's Head in Cow Hollow; and the parent shop, Dragon's Lair, is in Chinatown."

Jack rose and went to the city map on the office wall. He remembered putting it up when he'd shared this office with Ray. He'd used it so often—pinning and taping case details to it—he'd had to replace it several times. By the look of this one, it had probably been the last one he'd used before leaving the force four years ago. Pinholes and tears covered the paper, and it had faded over the years, but it hadn't served out its time yet.

"What's up, Jack?"

He scanned the map. "I want to get a visual of where the shops are located." He pulled a few tacks out of the corkboard beside the map and marked the locations of the head shops. When he was done, he stood back and folded his arms in front of him. Ray came up beside him. "Look at this. The shops appear in a sort of circle around the city. Jack used his pen and connected the tacks. "Here's the shop in Chinatown—Dragon's Lair." He circled it several times with the blue ink. "Using that for a point of reference—" He drew a line from one shop to the next.

"Hmm," Ray said as he scrutinized the map. "What do you think it means?"

Jack tapped the blunt end of the pen against the map. "The location of the shops are in a near-perfect circle around the city proper—the outer bounds of what's considered the main shopping and tourist districts. It looks like the shops were chosen strategically, as if they're marking territory."

"That's a stretch," Ray said, "but go on."

"If they have staked their territory, I think we need to talk to their competition before going into the Jade Dragons' shops. Maybe they know something that could help us."

"Any idea which you want to stop at first?"

Jack looked at his list and scrutinized the dates all of the shops had been robbed, marking each of the Dragon shops with a highlighter he pulled off his old desk—the one formerly occupied by Paul Travers and any number of partners Ray had scared off. "I think we need to visit the shops that had been robbed the most. Find out what made the shops so attractive to our thieves."

"Good idea."

As he contemplated the list, Jack's gaze kept going back to Dragon's Lair. "Hmm . . . ."

"Hmm what?"

"Did you notice Dragon's Lair had only been hit once? Other shops were hit multiple times but Dragon's Lair just the one time."

Ray looked closely at Jack's highlighted notes. "Looks like it."

"That shop was never hit again. In fact, the number of robberies around the city dropped way off after Dragon's Lair was hit."

"I think we need to have a chat with Li."

"Agreed, but after we talk with some of their competition," Jack said. "Do you think Haniford will approve a warrant for any surveillance video the shop may still have from back then? It's a long shot, I know."

Ray shook his head. "Too soon. Let's visit some of the independent shops and ask if they still have videos that far back. After talking with Li at Dragon's Lair, if we're met with any resistance, on *anything*, I'll take it to the LT and see if he'll agree to a search warrant."

Jack gave Ray a curt nod before returning to the desk. "Is Haniford in today?"

"Yeah, why?"

"There's no better time than now for you to bring him up to speed, and—"

"And ask him to bring you on board when he explicitly said no?" Ray went to his desk and collected the files. Jack followed Ray out of the office.

"Well, yeah," Jack said. "We still need the reports run, and there are a lot of head shops in the city to visit. You're a great investigator, but you're not Superman. You'll need help." *You* as in *we*, Jack meant.

"He'll probably pull in Harry and Wash."

"The more, the merrier. They're good investigators." If Jack knew his former partner as well as he thought he did, and he did, he knew Ray was running possible scenarios in his mind about how the conversation in the LT's office would go. By his friend's scowl, he'd bet Ray didn't think the conversation would end well. He stopped Ray just before they reached Haniford's office. "You know I'm right. Look, we can play it one of two ways. One, I can go in on my own and have that chat with Haniford about Amy's behavior. I'll let him listen to the recording from the restaurant and explain my concerns. She blackmailed us both into my meeting her, effectively forcing my hand to get involved. Now that I'm in the kitchen, why not let me cook?"

Ray huffed to disguise his chuckle. "And two?"

"Or two, you can go in and explain everything. Including how you were forced to bring me in for the non-date with Amy so you could get what you needed from her. Let him listen to the recording. Since she's forced me into the case, does Haniford want to avail of my help? It's not like it'll be the first time we've come to an arrangement like this," he reminded Ray.

"Is there a middle option?"

Jack shook his head. "I don't know. Maybe we both go in. You start, and when you get to the Amy bit I'll explain my involvement . . . explain my concerns about her . . . see what he says about the rest."

"You know, none of this makes me comfortable," Ray admitted.

"Me either, but I have a gut feeling we're onto something important. Not just why Rybak offed himself in my house. Just something . . . more. I can't explain it."

Ray took a couple steps back. "I know about your gut feelings ese."

"Stop being a drama queen. If I'm right, though, there's no way in hell Haniford or anyone will refuse you that promotion."

"I'm not worried about that."

"Maybe not, but I am. I have a feeling breaking this case will open a lot of doors for you, brother." Ray just laughed. "Come on. Let's go in. Whatever's going to happen will happen." Jack inhaled deeply when they reached Haniford's office door. "I just hope we don't ruin his lunch."

CHAPTER SIXTEEN

As it turned out, they had definitely ruined Haniford's lunch. Probably his dinner too.

Jack understood where the LT was coming from. He'd heard it before. Just not as loudly. In fact, the entire department had probably heard Haniford's rant. It still rang in Jack's ears over and above the roar of his Harley Fatboy as it screamed south across the city on the 280. At least he'd sent Ray back to his office before Haniford laid into him.

It was the same old crap, except this time there was no dancing around the subject—shit or get off the pot.

Haniford told him in no uncertain terms it was time to stop riding the fence. He was all for Jack getting back on the job. He'd even promised his same rank and a bump in salary, and a reinstatement of his partnership with Ray.

But if Jack chose the other side of the fence, it meant it was time for him to stop calling in favors because, after four years, they'd dried up.

He got it, loud and clear. He just didn't like hearing his LT—no, Haniford . . . the man was no longer his LT—talk to him like that. He wasn't wrong though. Neither was Ray the day he'd found Jack at the house.

Jack knew in his heart he'd never return to the department. Not after this long. He hadn't found Leah, nor had he found those responsible for killing Zoë and Trax.

Given he'd been ready to call it a day last week, did it mean he was giving up his search? Was that really why he'd pulled out his Beretta, or had he just wanted a break from the constant anguish he felt raging through his body for the last fifteen hundred and nineteen days? Not that he was counting.

His eyebrows pinched together until his eyes hurt; gritting his teeth made his jaw ache. Damn Haniford!

He gunned the motor and wove between cars. The speedometer edged toward a hundred miles per hour, but he didn't care. He made sure to stay as clear from other vehicles as possible in case he decided to do something stupid—he didn't want anyone else involved in his fallout.

Cold air whistled through the helmet visor and whispered across his hot cheeks. His skin burned because he was pissed off six ways from Sunday.

Haniford had been right.

Ray had been right.

He just hated knowing the two people he trusted most in the world were forcing him to acknowledge a truth he'd been denying for so long, and it made his blood boil.

Now he had to admit it—he was on his own.

What did that mean? Where did he go from here? Did he go back to his house with his Beretta and try again? Or, as Haniford and Ray had suggested many times—see a professional?

Before he could answer his own question, the exit for John Daly Boulevard came up. He slowed the Harley and signaled to cross to the far-right lane then exited the 280. Traffic forced him to slow as he merged right. He knew following this road would eventually take him to the Great Highway, the north-south route paralleling the Pacific Ocean. The same road just two streets over from his house—but that wasn't his destination.

As he approached the intersection where John Daly Boulevard met Skyline Boulevard, he merged right to join Skyline, and at Lake Merced, he merged left and turned onto Great Highway. He increased speed again and wove around slower traffic.

When he crossed Balboa Street, Great Highway became Point Lobos Avenue, and as he rounded Sutro Heights, he turned right on 46th Avenue. At the top of the block, he backed in beside Logan Armstrong's driveway, flipped down the kickstand with his heel, and cut the motor. The inside of his visor instantly steamed and blurred his vision. He was still huffing angrily, but he needed to calm down before he approached the house.

As he removed his helmet and gloves and hung them from the handlebars, the crisp sea breeze snapped Jack to attention.

He swung his leg over the saddle then casually walked toward Geary. The officers Ray had put on the house three days ago had been pulled from the job after twenty-four hours when Armstrong failed to return, but it didn't mean he hadn't come back. If the guy wasn't home now, Jack would sit on the place until he returned, however long it took.

At the corner of the house, Jack stopped at a tall juniper tree and watched a young man walk through the front yard toward a waiting car at the curbside. Food delivery by the looks of the insulated bag he carried. Jack doubted the old lady would have called for takeout.

He didn't have a plan in place other than he wanted to talk with Armstrong and he wasn't taking no for an answer. He certainly wasn't in the mood for chasing the little shit into Fort Miley again either.

Before heading to the front door, he went to the garage. Being tall had its benefits, as he was able to stand on his toes to look through the high glass windows across the top of the counterweight door. The space was dark but not so dark he couldn't make out Rybak's Trans Am. It didn't appear it had been moved; it was still covered, backed into the garage.

To ensure Armstrong wasn't going anywhere, Jack found a wedge-shaped piece of wood in the overgrown junipers and shoved it under the door. It should give Jack enough time to catch up with Armstrong if he decided to rabbit again.

At the front door, he knocked, rang the bell, then knocked again for good measure.

"Hold your horses, *goddammit!*" A male voice shouted from inside the house. "Did you forget part of my order?" When the door swung open, Armstrong stared at Jack for a long moment, gaping. The man looked like he was debating staying where he was or making a run for it. He chose the latter.

Jack wasn't a cop and didn't have to adhere to cop rules. While he hadn't been invited inside, the moment Armstrong turned on his heel, Jack shadowed him through the house. Armstrong moved surprisingly quickly through familiar territory. When he heard a door slam and lock, he figured his prey had gone into the garage and locked the door behind him.

He turned the knob; the door wouldn't budge. The locking mechanism was on the inside, so Jack assumed Armstrong had used a slide bolt or something similar. He rammed his shoulder into the wood once and the lock gave way.

Armstrong shoved at the garage door, trying to heave it up, but the wedge firmly held. Jack stopped just inside the space. There was nowhere for the guy to go.

"Why are you running, Logan?" Jack asked in an even tone. "I hate running."

Daylight shining through the garage door windows cast a pale light across Armstrong's face. His over-long, greasy hair had come out of its tie on the run through the house, and now strings of it hung over his face, but there was no denying the wide eyes staring at Jack. The guy was scared.

"Who are you? What do you want?" Armstrong asked, panting hard.

"I just want to talk to you." Jack remained cool, hoping the guy would relax a little.

"Who are you?" he asked again, his voice raised.

"If you calm down and let me explain, you can get back to your food delivery." Jack edged toward the open toolbox at the back of the Trans Am. It was covered in dust and junk; Armstrong certainly hadn't been working on the car. He removed a long, flat-edge screwdriver and moved along the passenger side of the car toward the garage door.

"What are you doing with that?" Armstrong back-walked around the front of the car to the driver's side in an obvious move to get away from Jack and move toward the house door so he could run again, but the old toolbox blocked his path.

"Look, Logan, I'm going to open the door to let in some light. Then we can talk." He shoved the screwdriver under the door and popped out the wedge he'd jammed in moments before. As he lifted the door on its creaking hinges, he said, "Please don't run. I'm not in the mood to chase you and just might shoot you instead." The last bit of information was enough to get Armstrong's head bobbing, agreeing he wouldn't run again. He didn't know Jack didn't have his weapon. As the door settled into the ceiling space, Armstrong tried bolting anyway. Jack had been prepared and body-slammed the guy into the hood of the car. "Come on, Logan! Talk means no running. You promised."

"How do you know my name? Did Li send you?"

So, he *was* involved with the Jade Dragons. "No, man. I'm here on my own. My name is Jack Slaughter. I'm a private investigator. I want to talk about your friend, Tristan Rybak, who—"

"Tris? What about him?" The tone of Armstrong's voice instantly changed, and he stopped fighting to get free.

"If I let you up, are you going to stay put this time?" Armstrong quickly nodded. Jack lifted himself up then grabbed the man by the front of his T-shirt and hauled him to his feet. He was rail thin and weighed almost nothing. "Come on. Let's go inside. You can eat while we talk." Jack didn't want to risk neighbors hearing what he had to say either.

At the kitchen table, Jack tossed Armstrong into a chair then grabbed a bowl and fork out of the drying rack beside the sink and sat them in front of Armstrong.

"Dude, you mind? Cokes are in the fridge. Help yourself." Armstrong indicated behind Jack with the fork before stabbing it into the pile of noodles he'd poured into the bowl.

Jack pulled two cans from the fridge—the second for him. He had a feeling he'd be here a while and would need the sugar and caffeine hit. He sat across from Armstrong and pulled out his phone, then hit record before setting it on the table.

"Tell me about your buddies, Rybak and Warren."

Between mouthfuls, Armstrong said, "I don't know anyone by those names."

"Funny. You were just sprawled across the hood of Rybak's Trans Am. Man, you should go to jail just for what you did to that car." Armstrong didn't raise his head when he looked up with a raised eyebrow. "Let's start again. Tell me about your friends, and how you came into possession of Rybak's ride."

"I don't know what you're looking for. Give me an idea."

The little shit wasn't going to volunteer anything. "Tell you what. I'll tell you what I know, and you fill in the blanks. Easier?" Armstrong nodded. "You three were friends at SFSU. You met while playing *Head Shop Heist*. For shits and giggles, you started playing out the game in real life by actually robbing head shops around the city. Am I right so far?" Armstrong gave him a noncommittal shrug while shoving more food into his mouth. "Something went wrong. You hit the wrong shop. After that, it gets sketchy. Your friends drop off the radar, and your once straight-A record tanks. You barely graduated, but even though you should be off starting your life with a career in chemistry—" Armstrong's head shot up. "Yeah, I know you."

"Fuck you."

"You're a brazen little fuck, I'll give you that, but it's all I'm giving you. Other than a chance to fill in the blanks like you agreed."

"Whatever, man."

"Tell me what happened to your friends," Jack urged.

Armstrong pushed his now-empty bowl to the side of the table and took a long swig of Coke before letting out a Chinese-scented belch that nearly turned Jack's stomach.

"Do that again and there'll be a chemistry project all over your grandmother's kitchen. Now tell me about your friends. What happened to them after that last hit?"

Armstrong threw himself back in his chair and crossed his arms. "What do you want me to say? Yeah, you're right. We started hitting the head shops. The game was fun, but it was more exciting doing it for real. What a rush, man." He grinned and chuckled.

"Until you hit the last shop. Dragon's Lair over in Chinatown."

His eyes widened. "How'd you know that?"

Jack grinned this time. "Because I know things. Don't test me."

"Yeah, it was the last shop. It went south. Fast."

"Your friends disappeared that night, didn't they?" Armstrong nodded. "Tell me what happened."

"Man, if I tell you, Li will kill me."

"If you don't tell me what I want to know, *I* might kill you," Jack warned.

"You a cop?"

"You have a short attention span. I told you I'm a private investigator, and I'm looking into the death of your friend, Rybak."

Armstrong sat forward in his chair and squared a surprised look in Jack's direction. "Tristan's dead? Can't be."

"When was the last time you saw him?"

"I don't know exactly. After New Year anyway. What happened to him?" There was genuine interest in Armstrong's voice.

"He killed himself. His body was found in mid-February."

"Wha—why? I mean, where . . . how?"

"*How?* He shot himself. Where? In *my* fucking house!" Jack spat. "I'm here so you can tell me why."

"Why would he kill himself in your house? Did you know Tris?"

Jack shook his head. "Nope. Never heard of him until I got home and found his brains splattered across my dining room wall." Armstrong flinched. "You want to tell me what happened that night . . . and how you ended up with his car?"

Armstrong took a long breath and leaned back again. "Yeah, I'll talk."

CHAPTER SEVENTEEN

"We'd hit a lot of head shops around the city. Some of them a few times . . . the easiest ones, ya know?"

"Any of them belong to the Jade Dragons?"

Armstrong nodded. "They were as easy as the other head shops, so we thought the one in Chinatown would be the same. By then, we had things dialed into perfection."

"So you thought."

"At the time, we didn't know anything about who ran the Dragon shops or who owned them, but since the others were easy in-and-outs . . ."

"Tell me what happened."

"From the moment we walked into the Chinatown shop, we knew we were in a whole other world. Everything we'd learned from knocking over the other shops went out the window and things went south fast. It was like the first place we'd robbed— back to square one, like we didn't know what we were doing."

Armstrong shifted in his chair and looked out the window. He tightened his arms around his chest. He was frazzled. When he finally looked back at Jack, he said, "We played it by the book . . . what we'd learned from robbing the other shops. Go in with masks on, all of us dressed in black. We each had different colored T-shirts on under the black shirts so when we took them off outside, no one could identify us on the street."

Jack nodded. "I get it. Go on."

"First, we cased the shop. When we knew there weren't any customers, we went in and fanned out. Tristan locked the door and turned the sign to closed. Kyle went to the counter, gun drawn, and got the counter guy under control. Then Tristan and I helped ourselves to the money in the register. Easy."

Jack rolled a hand, urging Armstrong to hurry up.

"The next thing was for Kyle to take the counter guy into the back office to get the heavier shit—most of those shops have an under-the-counter trade. And it's surprising how many shops keep large amounts of petty cash in little metal lockboxes in their desk drawer."

"But?"

"Normally, we'd take the stash and run, but when Kyle and the counter guy came back to the shop, they weren't alone. They'd seen us come in on the CCTV or some shit because as the office door opened they were all standing with guns drawn like some goddamn Bruce Lee movie. When one of the thugs pushed Kyle toward me and Tristan, he freaked and started shooting. He hit the counter guy and bullets started flying. Tristan and I ran for cover behind the displays, but Kyle took a bullet before he'd emptied his clip." Armstrong sat up straight and looked Jack square in the eye. "You have to understand. Until then, we'd never shot anyone. I don't know where Kyle got the gun or if it even actually worked. It was just meant for show. I didn't even know it was loaded."

"Warren's weapon was the only one? You and Rybak were unarmed?" Armstrong nodded. "Okay. Then what? You and Rybak obviously survived."

"Once Kyle was down and they saw we weren't carrying, some of the guys dragged us in front of some scary looking fucker with a scar across his face." Armstrong indicated the scar started at the side of the man's chin and traveled diagonally across his nose, eyebrow and forehead and disappeared into his hair. "The scar went halfway back. He tried covering it with his hair, but that scar was gnarly. That shit musta hurt!"

"I bet. Keep going."

"Kyle was still alive when they dragged him into the middle of the floor. Then they pulled over the counter guy and laid him next to Kyle. He wasn't moving. They made Tristan and me get on our knees, then the scar face guy walked over and looked down at all of us. I thought I was going to wet my pants."

"Did he say anything?"

"Yeah. He looked at each of us with his squinty eyes and said—
" Armstrong imitated the Chinese man's accent—"*'You have
dishonored your families, and mine. And you have insulted me with
what you have done here. For this, you must pay.'* We were scared
shitless and agreed to do anything he wanted; just don't shoot us."
Armstrong started wringing his hands together to keep them from
trembling.

"Obviously, he didn't."

"He said we would be paying him back, but neither of us had
any idea what he meant."

"Who was this guy with the scar?"

"Li Zihao, the leader of the Jade Dragons."

"Holy shit! You guys were robbing shops owned by the most
dangerous gang in the city and didn't know it?" Jack's voice hitched
up with disbelief.

"Believe me, we didn't know it at the time. We'd never heard of
the guy before, or who owned any of the shops," Armstrong said.
"If we had, we never would have hit any of the Dragon shops."

Jack took a breath and asked, "Okay, what happened next?"

"Li said Tristan and I had to work off our debt with him. We
hadn't even had the chance to pocket the money from the register,
so what debt did we have?"

"It was an honor debt." Armstrong nodded. "What did he
make you do?"

"He said he had a job for us. Some guy owed him money and
was late paying. He wanted us to either get the money and bring
it back, or bring back the guy and his men would collect on the
debt. It seemed like an easy task."

"What went wrong? Sounds like you guys were batting a
thousand for fuck ups that night."

"No shit. One of the thugs had Kyle's gun and handed it to
Tristan along with the address. If we stopped to call the cops,
they'd kill Kyle. If we didn't bring back the money or the guy,
they'd kill Kyle. They gave us an hour and if we got back late,

they'd kill Kyle. Honestly, I think they were just looking for any reason to kill him." Armstrong inhaled deeply and scrubbed his forehead. "I need another Coke."

"I'll get it. You finish your story." Jack rose and grabbed another Coke from the fridge before returning to his chair.

Armstrong popped open the can and took a long guzzle. He refrained from belching in Jack's face by directing it down the inside of his hoodie collar. "We did what he asked. We got in the car and raced like bats outta Hell to the address he gave us over in the Sunset District." Jack's heart thumped hard. Could have been anywhere, he kept telling himself. It was a big district. "On the way over, we formulated a plan—play it cool, talk to the guy, get the money."

"It didn't go down like that."

Armstrong shook his head. "The wife answered the door. We said we were there to pick up some money, but she said her husband wasn't home and didn't know anything about it. When she tried closing the door, we pushed our way in. Li had said to do anything necessary when he gave us Kyle's gun, so Tristan put it in the broad's face and told her to tell us where her husband was or give us the money. She runs through the house to the kitchen, screaming that her husband isn't home and to get out of her house or she'd call the cops. The dog is in the kitchen and starts barking. We were already jumpy as fuck and didn't need all the static. We just wanted the money or her husband so we could get the fuck outta there."

"He wasn't there, so what happened?"

"I swear, it all went down in a blur. I've tried forgetting it, but I still have nightmares, man."

"Tell me," Jack urged.

"The dog kept barking, she kept yelling, the kid started crying—"

"Kid?" The hairs stood up on the back of Jack's neck. This wasn't sitting well. Sunset District, wife, dog, and now a child?

"Yeah."

"And the husband definitely wasn't in the house?" Jack asked.

Armstrong shook his head. "Nah. Tristan kept the gun on the woman while I checked the house."

"Go on."

"I go back into the kitchen and the dog rushes us. Tristan fires a couple times, but we don't realize until then the gun doesn't have any bullets. The gun is just for show. Of course it is. There was no way Li was going to let us walk out of the shop with a loaded gun. What would have stopped us from turning around and shooting *him*? The wife must have realized it and rushed toward us. I grabbed her to keep her back and Tristan grabbed a knife off the counter. He stabs the dog to stop it from attacking us. The wife starts screaming, and the kid is screaming at the top of her lungs. Tristan shouted to shut the kid up. She tried quieting the kid, but she kept screaming."

Through clenched teeth, Jack growled, "Go on."

"The woman wouldn't tell us where her husband was, no matter how much we threatened her. I kept telling her to shut the kid up but nothing she did worked. Not even trying to rock the kid in her arms. I've never heard a kid scream like that, and the woman was yelling, and Tristan . . . He was about to lose it. He kept pacing and babbling, *What're we gonna do?* I looked at my watch and told him we had to do something. Our time was almost up, and if we didn't get out of there, Kyle was going to die, and the cops were going to come because of all the noise."

Jack slowly asked, "Next?" What he really wanted to say was, *Tell me which one of you killed my Zoë, and what did you do with my wife?*

"Tristan grabbed the kid out of the woman's arms and I held her back. He put the kid back in her highchair and before I could stop him, he'd slit the kid's throat."

"He did *what*?" Jack shouted, nearly coming out of his chair. By now, he was barely managing to restrain himself.

"I couldn't believe it either. When I asked why he did it, he said the situation was getting out of control and he just . . . panicked."

Rybak had been the man who'd killed his daughter? Was that why he'd left the *I'm sorry* note?

The revelation hit hard. After all this time, Jack finally discovered who killed his daughter and why she had to die. He wanted to puke and scream at the same time.

His forehead ached where his eyebrows had bunched together. His eyes burned with bottled emotion as he stared holes in the man in front of him. It took all his strength not to climb over the table and beat the shit out of Armstrong and demand to know where Leah was.

Instead, he asked, "What did you do with the woman?" When Armstrong stopped to guzzle more Coke, Jack snapped, "Tell me, goddammit. What did you do with the woman?"

"I'm getting there. Hold your horses! The car was just a two-door. We'd never get her in the back the way she was thrashing around—it took both of us just to get her out of the house. We knew just one of us would never be able to control her for the long drive back across the peninsula. The only place for her was the trunk. Tristan bound her hands and feet and I put a gag in her mouth. We took her to the shop for Li to deal with."

"What did he do to her?"

"He was pissed, man. What did we expect he was going to do with her, he wanted to know? She didn't have the money. He wanted the husband."

"Get to the point, and do it fast."

"He told two of his guys to take Tristan and deal with her."

"What did he mean?"

"I don't know, but I never saw her again. He made me stay in the shop and wait for them to get back. I sat with Kyle and tried to assure him everything would be okay. He was losing a lot of blood, but they refused to get him help. It was the longest hour of my life."

"So, they come back and then what happened?"

"Li and two thugs went into the back room. He had some other bad dudes watching us. Tristan was really freaking out by then. I thought he was going to run. Those bad dudes looked like they had itchy fingers and I didn't want Tristan getting shot too. I tried getting him talking, thought that maybe talking would calm him down a little. I asked him what happened, but he refused to talk about it. Just kept wringing his hands and looking at the front door."

Jack nodded. The kid was undoubtedly traumatized. "Then?"

"They weren't gone too long. When Li and his thugs came back into the shop, one walked over to Kyle and shot him. Just like that. Bang, right between the eyes." Armstrong choked on a breath. "They killed him, man. Like putting down an animal."

"If they wanted him dead, why not kill him earlier?" Jack asked.

"My guess? Leverage. With Kyle still alive, Li knew Tristan and I would be back. Once Tristan was back with Li's goons, there was no reason to keep Kyle around anymore. Li said one of our men had killed one of his men so one of us must also die."

"Harsh, but I get it. Equal justice. Maybe it was a mercy killing since Kyle was already bleeding out and Li was never going to get him help." Armstrong shrugged. "What happened to the bodies?"

Armstrong shook his head slowly. "I don't know, man. Li and his goons took Tristan and me in back and later when we came out, Kyle and the counter guy were gone."

Jack paused to get his rage under control. His heart felt like it was pounding a hole in his chest. Sweat dripped down his back under the leather jacket, and his body shook with anger.

"So let me get this straight. You got caught robbing Dragon's Lair. To repay Li, he sent you and Rybak to collect a debt. Since the husband wasn't home, you killed his daughter and the dog and kidnapped the wife." Armstrong hesitantly nodded. "And you never saw the wife again after Rybak and Li's goons took her away." The guy nodded again. "Did Rybak ever tell you what happened to the wife?"

"No. I asked but he said he couldn't talk about it. He never did. I don't know what happened to her."

"I can't imagine you'd paid back your debt to these people with one failed collection attempt."

"No, he put us to work for him."

"Doing what?"

"Mostly selling his drugs on campus and around the city. When he found out I was a chem major, he forced me to work in his lab."

"Doing what, exactly?"

"He's been trying to come up with a new party drug."

"Ecstasy's already widely available," Jack pointed out.

Armstrong nodded. "Li wants to up the game. He wants a drug that makes partiers high as kites, euphoric like never before, and in one tablet that keeps them going all night instead of having to pop another pill a few hours later. And he'll charge a premium for each tablet."

"That's a lot to ask. If it was possible to create something like that, wouldn't it have been done already?" Jack asked.

"Nothing like X, man, but Li seems to think I have it in me to create what he wants. Just because I majored in chemistry in college doesn't mean they taught me anything about party drugs."

"I'm guessing you haven't succeeded, since I haven't heard of a change in the market for party drugs," Jack said.

"No. I've tried dozens of formulas. Some were just amped up versions of X but didn't last long, or they made people really sick. The closest I've come to anything workable was just coating X in LSD, but it didn't last long, and the euphoria-hallucination balance was off. Trips were bad, man." Armstrong's face screwed up, making Jack wonder if he was remembering his trip on the beach Ray had told him about.

"So, back to square one?" Jack asked.

Armstrong nodded again. "Pretty much. It's been like that for years. Try something and it works but not exactly like Li wants it to, or people can't handle the side effects. Some even ended up in the hospital. Word got out, sales went down to nothing because people went back to the shit they knew and trusted, like X and Special K."

"Are you working on anything now?"

"It freaked me out the last time thinking I'd killed someone who'd been taken to the hospital. Li's not happy about it, but I need a break. You know. Go back with a fresh mind and shit."

Jack downed the last of his now-warm Coke and crushed the can in his hands. It didn't help how he was feeling—absolute rage.

Now Jack knew what had happened to his family, but according to Armstrong, it was all on Rybak. And *he* was too dead to find out what he'd done with Leah and where her remains were.

CHAPTER EIGHTEEN

Saturday – April 3

The slow rumble of the Harley vibrated through him as he backed it into a narrow space on Walter U Lum Place, the street in front of the Dragon's Lair head shop. After dropping down the kickstand, he cut the motor, removed his helmet and gloves, then ran fingers through his hair. He looked across the narrow street into Portsmouth Square—the place where the city began.

Long before today's city of San Francisco existed, Spain conquered South America in the early sixteenth century. Once they had their foothold, they tasked their Franciscan missionaries with establishing *congregacións*—congregations—up and down the coast of California. This included the construction of religious outposts—missions—as centers of learning for the native people already occupying the land. Invariably, this meant enslaving the natives and destroying their way of life in order to make them dependent on the church for their livelihoods.

By the early eighteenth century, just two months after the signing of the Declaration of Independence in the east and establishing the thirteen colonies as the United States of America, missionaries staked a claim on a large peninsula overlooking a large inland bay and called it *Yerba Buena*, or Good Herb, for the abundant wild mint growing there. And *Mission San Francisco de Asis* was erected.

Pueblos—towns—quickly sprang up outside of mission walls, built by *Californios*—Mexican natives of California. In typical tradition, a public gathering place had been allocated, called

The Grand Plaza, and Spanish style homes and buildings began emerging thanks to the influx of people and trade brought in through Yerba Buena Cove.

The nineteenth century saw a sudden expansion of the city. With growing sea trade, a customs house was erected beside the square. But soon, the Mexican American War broke out and by 1846, the USS Portsmouth, captained by John Berrien Montgomery, had seized Yerba Buena for the United States. Montgomery planted the American flag in the center of the plaza, proclaiming it now be called Portsmouth Square. He also declared Yerba Buena was no more. It was now San Francisco, paying respects to St. Francis for whom the mission had been built. Within the space of a few years, California's first public school opened opposite the customs house; and the United States' first Admissions Day was held in the square as California joined the Union as the thirty-first state.

The most significant event in Portsmouth Square had been the announcement in 1847 of the discovery of gold in the nearby mountains. News of the California Gold Rush spread like wildfire around the world and by 1849, California had become known as The Golden State.

Gold not only brought more city expansion, it also meant an even larger influx of humanity who built the city and laid track for the Trans-Continental Railroad. Soon clusters of people created their own communities, like Japantown, Koreatown, Little Saigon, and the largest Chinatown in the world, which Portsmouth Square was now at the heart of and became known as *Fa Yuhn Gok*, or the Garden Corner.

Yerba Buena Cove was now part of a larger shipping harbor that quickly earned the nickname of the Barbary Coast. Largely owned by the Chinese, brothels, dance halls, saloons, hotels and opium dens sprang up to give the newly minted gold panners places to spend their money.

When the Great Earthquake of 1906 struck, the square became a gathering place for survivors who hoped to find missing loved ones, and for medical attention in a new temporary hospital. A small tent city had been created for displaced city residents, as well as a corner of the square as a temporary graveyard.

The most recent renovations of the square began in the 1970s, when the park was paved over and modernized for twentieth century living. A Chinese-inspired gateway led to a new footbridge above Kearny Street connecting the park to the Chinese Cultural Center. And Walter U Lum, journalist and Asian rights activist, was honored with the street name where Jack had just parked his Harley.

Despite nearly two hundred and fifty years of history, the doors of *Mission San Francisco de Asis* were still open to the devout, and Portsmouth Square remained the beating heart of the original Yerba Buena that had blossomed into today's city of San Francisco, and was still growing into the twenty-first century.

Jack inhaled deeply as he admired a group of Asian women who moved as one as they practiced Tai Chi, the old men hunkering over tables playing Mahjong and checkers, and children laughing in the playground.

The city he loved had all begun right here on this very spot.

But for as much pride as he had in his city, he was also angry. His daughter would never know the city she'd been born into, and his family would never enjoy parks like this on fine spring days like today—the warm, blue sky above, and the scent of blooming cherry blossom trees. It made him furious after hearing Logan Armstrong's confession yesterday and knowing Tristan Rybak had taken his family from him. And because the bastard had killed himself, there was no possibility of retribution.

Frustration had coiled deep inside Jack since his discussion with Armstrong, so much so he'd barely slept last night. He literally felt like a raging storm in a bottle.

Before leaving the Armstrong house last night, Jack had devised a plan and put Armstrong right in the middle of it. Jack was going undercover, and Armstrong was his ticket into the Jade Dragons.

Jack looked at the time on his phone. If that shithead junkie stood him up today, he'd hunt him down and show him exactly how pissed off at Rybak he really was. Even if he didn't stand him up, he still might. Armstrong wasn't completely innocent of anything that had gone down in his house four years ago.

Jack knew he was on his own going undercover. Haniford had made it abundantly clear. And he wouldn't put Ray in danger by getting him involved. He had no choice but to do this alone.

With a deep breath, he pushed aside his anger and frustration and set his helmet on the upper part of the gas tank over the dials. He swung his leg over the saddle and straightened the leather cut he wore over his black fitted T-shirt instead of his leather jacket. The weight of the holstered Beretta tucked against his arm was heavy—physically and emotionally. He hated carrying the weapon—it was something he rarely did. It made his stomach sour knowing he'd been forced to use the weapon to kill Travers, the city's cannibal serial killer, and that he'd pulled it out again when he went looking for Ginnie Whitney-Cummings, who'd been killing drag queens over the previous holiday season.

His job as a private investigator rarely required a weapon, especially during interviews. But this was no ordinary interview. He wanted . . . no, needed . . . to infiltrate the Jade Dragons to get answers—what had they done with Leah?

Sliding on his dark sunglasses, he turned toward Dragon's Lair's doors. He caught his reflection in the glass. He looked every bit the biker he tried emulating. He'd dressed all in black—heavy boots, jeans, fitted T-shirt stretching over his biceps, the silver chain connecting his wallet in his back pocket to his black belt, fingerless leather gloves, and black sunglasses, and a dark *don't fuck with me* look on his face. Perfect.

Rampant jade-green Chinese dragons were painted on the building on each side of the glass door, and above it read DRAGON'S LAIR in bold gold lettering in both Chinese—龍之巢穴—and English.

A thick chemical fog overlaid with the pong of patchouli greeted him as soon as he stepped inside. Too many scents hung in the air and made him want to gag. He gazed around the shop while taking a moment to get his breath.

It wasn't what he expected, and certainly not like head shops he'd known from his time on the force. Typically, these shops were full of glass and ceramic pipes, bongs, hookahs, and bubblers, as well as papers, grinders, and roach clips. Many also doubled as smoke shops selling high-end cigarettes and cigars by the box. And some even sold jewelry and home décor, all with a marijuana theme, as well as incense, wind chimes, and anything else that aided in one getting high and staying there. Pot itself was normally sold under the counter.

Dragon's Lair sold all that and more. Now vaping was in fashion, and rows of shelves were full of various types, sizes, and colors of vaping pens, vaporizers, and dabs. Racks were full of vape juice and atomizers.

As Jack moved through the shop, he was surprised to see a long row of glass counters with shelves full of weapons—knives and daggers, folding blades, butterfly knives, throwing stars, nunchucks and tonfas, and even a few samurai swords. Jack guessed, if he were in the market and played his cards right, he could even obtain any number of firearms through this shop. Given the shop's gang affiliation, he had no doubt hardcore pharmaceuticals were being dealt from the back room as Armstrong had said.

As he moved through the store, Jack tried visualizing what Armstrong had told him happened that night. Where had the three hidden around the shop when bullets started flying? Where had Warren and the shop assistant lain when Warren was given the death shot? Were there security cameras? He didn't see anything obvious but it didn't mean they weren't there. If there had been footage, it had surely been deleted a long time ago.

As he moved through the space, he noticed two young men standing over a display case, pointing and whispering at the hand-blown glass pipes. Their behavior gave him the impression they were new to the game. When they saw Jack's gaze drawing down on them from over the top of the sunglasses he still wore, they turned and left. Good. If anything went down, he didn't want them getting hurt.

There was no one at the cash register and he didn't see anyone else in the shop, but he was certain whoever was out back knew he was there. He didn't have to wait long. A skinny Asian man appeared.

"What you want?" he asked.

"Armstrong."

"No Armstrong here. You go. You scaring the customers."

Jack folded his arms across his chest, casually slipped a hand inside the leather cut and palmed the butt of the Beretta. "What customers?" The skinny man side-walked to the register and started reaching for something there. "I wouldn't do that."

"You leave now. I don't want no trouble."

"Where's Armstrong?" he asked, giving him the same look he'd given the two young customers moments before.

The skinny guy quickly disappeared back through the door and a moment later two different men appeared, both dressed in a sort of uniform—white shirt with a mandarin collar, black sports suit, and black shoes.

The one to Jack's left spoke first. "What do you want?" His English was clearer, but there was a hint of an accent.

"Armstrong."

"What do you want with him?" asked the second man.

"If it were any of your business, I'd tell you. Is he here?"

The bell on the door tinkled, but Jack didn't turn to see who was coming in. This was a retail operation, and he hadn't turned the closed sign on his way in.

Armstrong stopped beside Jack and glanced between the two men behind the counter. "What's up, Kenny?" he asked casually. He cocked his head at the second guy. "Kai."

"Kenny Chang," Jack muttered.

"What's it to you?" The thin slits of Kenny's eyes pulled together and a faint crease formed between his equally thin eyebrows.

So, this was the Kenny Amy Chin had told him about—the one responsible for bringing her brother into the gang. Did he have any responsibility in Danny's disappearance too?

Jack ignored Kenny and gave Armstrong a side glance behind his dark shades. It didn't look like the guy had changed his clothes since yesterday. "You're late."

"So, sue me."

"Since when do you use the front door, loser?" Kenny asked.

"I want him to meet the boss."

Kai stepped forward. "That's not your place. Go around back like you're supposed to. Get your shit and leave."

Armstrong hesitated, but held his ground. "I'm not here for that. Mr. Li needs to meet this guy. He has a lucrative proposition."

Kenny and Kai gave Jack the once over, apparently not liking what they were seeing.

"Li makes his own deals, and he doesn't work with people he doesn't know. So, if you're not here for your shit, get out. Take your girlfriend with you." Kenny elbowed Kai and they chuckled before pulling back the edge of their jackets to expose the 9mm handguns tucked into the front of their waistbands.

"Why don't you let this Li tell me to my face he doesn't want my money?" Jack grumbled, stiffening his back to accentuate his height over the slight Asian men. His arms remained crossed and his palm on the Beretta in case the little fucks decided to get dirty. Kai moved his hand onto his 9mm but didn't draw it. Jack grinned. "That's a big weapon for a little guy like you."

Before Kai or Kenny had a chance to draw, the back room door opened. No one stepped through, but the tiny twins moved away from Jack and closed their jackets before returning inside.

"What's this shit?" Jack asked Armstrong with a lowered voice.

Armstrong ran his hands down his clothes, as if to rub out the wrinkles. "Looks like your wish is about to come true."

The man who stepped out of the back room was everything Armstrong had told him. Li Zihao was tall, maybe six feet, rail thin, and had a wicked scar across his face that gave him a permanent scowl. He wore a black sport suit similar to his thugs but with the first button undone. Jack knew Li had been in the city for at least the last fifteen years, but he still maintained his traditional hairstyle—long but pulled back into a braided queue that fell over his left shoulder. He didn't appear to be carrying a weapon.

"Logan," Li flatly greeted. "You have brought this man to meet me." It wasn't a question. His voice was slow and smooth and sounded more like he was about to invite them to tea. Knowing the Jade Dragons' reputation, and that of its leader, Jack remained wary.

Armstrong's nerves were apparent by his agitation. "Yeah, Mr. Li."

"Please explain."

Armstrong cleared his throat and fidgeted with his fingernails for a long moment. "Umm, he's . . . I mean, I umm—"

"I buy my shit from Logan," Jack said. If he waited for Armstrong to get his act together, they'd be here all day.

Li scrutinized Jack before refocusing his attention on Armstrong. "Is this so?"

Armstrong nodded vigorously. "Yeah. I've been selling him your stuff for a while now and he . . ."

"Has a complaint?" Again, Li lifted his gaze to Jack.

"No complaint. I want more."

"I see. You come into my establishment and want to make a deal. Yet you won't do me the courtesy of showing me the whites of your eyes. Most interesting," Li said with a curious undertone.

Jack slid off his sunglasses and stuffed them in his pocket, all while continuing to stare into Li's eyes. "Better?"

Li stepped closer and gazed more deeply, like he was looking for something. Whatever it was, Jack wasn't going to give him a chance to find it.

After a long moment, Li said over his shoulder, "*Guānbì shāngdiàn.*"

Kenny rushed from the back room to the front door. Behind him, Jack heard the lock click and a shade being rolled down over the glass. Kenny rushed past him again and disappeared into the back room.

Jack remained on guard, especially now he'd been forced to remove his hand from the Beretta. He knew without doubt he could take all three men—Li, Kenny, and Kai . . . and if necessary, the clerk—if it came down to a fight, but he wasn't as sure if they all drew down on him with their nine mils from behind the counter. He certainly didn't want Armstrong hurt in the crossfire. And he had no idea if anyone remained in the back room.

Li squinted at Jack. The scar didn't allow one eye to do more than blink, but the uninjured eye narrowed sharply. "Tell me what you really want." His previously relaxed demeanor turned serious.

"You don't appear to be the type of man who needs anything repeated," Jack told Li. "So, let's cut the shit and get down to business. If you're good with that, we can send Mr. Armstrong on his way, and you and I can make a deal."

"I think we will keep Mr. Armstrong a while longer." Li called out again. "*Yǐzi.*" Kenny and Kai brought out a pair of chairs and sat them facing each other a few feet apart. "Please, Mr. . . . I'm afraid Logan has forgotten his manners."

"Jack."

"Mr. Jack, please, have a seat and we will talk." Li stood beside the chair opposite the one he'd indicated for Jack and waited.

"Where's the chair for my friend here?" He cocked his head toward Armstrong.

"You and I will talk business. There is no formality with Logan. He may sit wherever he wishes."

"But he can't leave," Jack said.

"Correct. I don't know you. If anything were to happen, Logan and I would need to discuss his error in bringing you here. Are we understood?" Li's gaze bored into Jack.

Nodding, Jack took the indicated chair and sat carefully. Instant familiarity hit him. He always seemed to engulf the little chairs in Zoë's bedroom. As he did then, he sat still and took care he didn't break this man's delicate furniture.

"Sure. Whatever."

CHAPTER NINETEEN

Li sat with his legs crossed in a feminine style and his bony hands clasped atop an equally bony knee. His calm demeanor belied his disposition. It was clear Li could snap his fingers and his crew would fall into action.

Kenny and Kai stood behind Li with their arms folded in front of them like bouncers and glared at Jack. He knew the positions of their hands were within easy reach of their weapons. Kai seemed to have an itchy trigger finger by the way he kept rubbing his thumb across the tips of his fingers.

Jack sat quietly with his palms on his thighs and gazed directly at Li, careful not to make any sudden moves that might set off the thugs without waiting for their boss' encouragement.

After a long moment of silence, Li said, "Tell me what you want."

"I've been buying weed, coke, and some heroin off Armstrong for a while, but I find I'm in need of a lot more," Jack said.

"What is the reason for your sudden decision?"

"A little is fun to play with, but my crew needs a new supplier if we're going to stay in business."

Li's chin lifted slightly. "Your crew?"

"Yeah, *my* gang."

"Hmm. I'm intrigued. Tell me more of *your* gang."

Jack slowly rose and turned his back to Li, showing the gang patch on the back of his cut—the grim reaper riding a hyper-stylized Harley and brandishing a scythe. The bike seemed to be riding the waves with the Golden Gate Bridge in the background. The numbers *666* were above the design and *San Francisco* below it.

When he sat again, Li said, "6-6-6. I have heard of this gang."

The 666 gang, sometimes called the Triple Sixers or just the Sixers, was a police department creation and only brought out of mothballs when officers went undercover for cases relating to bike gangs. Had Rod worn his cut in the Majestic Lounge over Christmas, Jack would have instantly recognized him as an undercover cop. Though, as the Majestic was a gay nightclub, posing as a real biker probably wasn't the vibe Rod had been going for.

When Jack left the force four years ago, no one thought to get the cut back, and it had been the last thing on his mind to return it. He hadn't used it since his last undercover job five or six years ago and had been surprised it still fit. If anything, it was loose. Like everything else he owned. Lately, food wasn't exactly a priority for him.

His current actions were nothing to do with the department. This was his own undercover job, and the cut was the perfect cover. There was no reason for Haniford or anyone else to know what he was up to. Not even Ray. If things went sideways, it was completely on him.

"Then you'll know we make our bread on the distribution of pharmaceuticals . . . and a few other things," Jack added.

"Enlighten me."

Jack reseated himself. "A little of this, a little of that. Whatever makes the greenbacks. You know what I mean."

Li offered a weak grin. "Your . . . organization . . . has a strong reputation in the city. How is it you come to require services I may offer?"

That reputation was also fed by the department who leaked stories of false arrests and fake cases to the press. Anyone doing a web search on the 666s or gangs in San Francisco would come up with some of these phony stories. If Li knew anything, it came from whatever the department put out, including the story Jack now told Li.

"The relationship with our previous supplier was cut short when he was killed down in Juarez."

"That is unfortunate. Who ran this other organization, if I may ask?" Li smiled but it didn't reach his eyes.

"We only knew him as El Toro—The Bull—and only dealt with one of his handlers," Jack said, bringing another name out of mothballs.

"I've heard of this Bull. A very dangerous man."

Jack chuckled lightly. Another lie. Was Li stringing him along, or did he believe the media spin? "We never had any trouble, but I can tell you the rumors of him going out in a blaze of glory are highly exaggerated."

"What happened to such a man to cause him a dishonorable death?"

"He was in Juarez overseeing a new supply of pharmaceuticals and new girls to bring across the border. While there, he hooked up with one of his *putas*. Her husband came home unexpectedly . . . ." Jack let Li assume the rest.

"A dangerous game, toying with another man's woman, but was he not protected by his men?" Li gave the briefest acknowledgment to the two men behind him.

Jack nodded. "Of course, but the husband saw El Toro's guards, so he took a secret tunnel into the house and found his wife with El Toro's cock in her mouth. He shot them both execution style—one bullet each, right between the eyes." Jack made a gun with two fingers and thumb, and fired it sideways, gangster style, toward the ground. "Bang. Bang. *Muerto.*"

Li seemed unsurprised. "This can happen. Did his second not step forward to continue your relationship?"

"He tried, but others thought they were the rightful heir to the kingdom. When a civil war kicked off, we backed away. We don't need that kinda heat blowing our way."

"Yes, understandable."

"We've been sampling gear from a few suppliers. That's how we found Armstrong. He sold us some good shit and we told him we wanted in on it. It took some *encouragement*," Jack flashed Li a dark grin he hoped said he'd roughed up Armstrong, "but he finally gave up your name. So here I am."

"I see." Li looked at Armstrong who leaned against the glass display counter containing the knives. Li didn't speak, but his expression said he expected a reply from the guy.

Armstrong nodded quickly. "I don't know about that stuff in Mexico, but yeah, Jack's been buying stuff off me. He asked me who my supplier was, but I wasn't about to tell him. That takes money out of *my* pocket."

"Yet you did tell him."

"Only after he smacked me around. I mean, look at the size of him," Armstrong said, giving Jack the once over. "I didn't want to die."

"You still could," Li suggested.

Armstrong stepped forward, gesturing between Jack and Li. "Yeah, but what would you gain by killing me? Jack's looking for weight. It's more than I can supply, but it would mean a lot of money for you." He paused, then added in a lowered voice, "And I wouldn't say no to a little finder's fee, if you know what I mean." He rubbed his thumb and fingers together on one hand.

Li didn't acknowledge Armstrong's last comment as he turned his attention back to Jack. "What kind of weight are we talking about?"

"How much have you got? I know Armstrong here is peddling light weights of weed, coke, heroin, and a little meth. We'll place a substantial order."

"Mmm," was all Li said.

Jack played the hand he was fairly certain would make Li bite. "Armstrong also said you might have something else in the works. If what he said is true, we want in on it."

The last comment made Li give Armstrong a slow look. His expression changed to one of surprise. "Did he?"

Jack nodded. "We want something people can't get anywhere else. Smokables, edibles, injectables, snortables . . . I don't care if the user has to shove it up their ass. We just want to sell the best high on the market, whatever it is. Armstrong says you're the man to get it from."

Li continued looking at Armstrong. His expression made

Armstrong straighten his spine and step back. "Yeah, you know," he said with a shaky voice. Lower, he added, "I think I mighta cracked it." Then in a whisper, he leaned in and said, "This could be big."

Li eventually looked back at Jack. "I must consider my options, Mr. Jack." Over his shoulder, he said, "*Ná bǐ hézhǐ.*" Kenny stepped behind the counter and retrieved a pen and a small notepad. "*Bǎ zhège gěi tā.*" As Kenny was passing the items to Jack, Li said, "Write down what you want and how to reach you. I will consider these things and let you know if we can do business. I do not know what Logan has told you about anything else. He and I will talk. For now, these other things are all I will consider."

"Fair enough," Jack replied, writing the information on the notepad. He gave Li the number to the burner phone which he had tucked inside his jacket pocket in case anyone decided to check it.

Kenny took back the pen and notepad when Jack was done, and handed the pad to Li, whose good eyebrow lifted. "This is quite a substantial order."

Jack shrugged. "Is it?"

"Tell me, what do I get out of this arrangement, should it come to that?"

"Lots of greenbacks," Jack responded with a chuckle.

"And if I require something more, what would you be prepared to give . . . to show your trust in me?" Was Li trying to prove Jack wrong, that his thugs trusted him without fear? What more could Jack promise Li to seal the deal?

"Protection. Give a deal on the gear we can't refuse and we'll protect you . . . and all of your business dealings."

Li stared at Jack for a long moment before rising. "You may go now. I lose business with a locked door." When Jack stood and offered a hand to shake, Li said, "We have not made a deal yet, Jack. If we come to an arrangement, I will shake with you then."

Jack pulled out his sunglasses and slipped them on. "Okay, chief. Thanks for your time. I expect to hear from you soon or we'll go elsewhere for the gear." Li gave him a smile telling Jack

Thank you for coming, now fuck off. "Logan. A word."

Armstrong looked to Li, as if asking for permission to go with Jack. Li extended a hand toward Jack, but his expression told him he wasn't going anywhere.

Kenny was already holding open the door.

Fresh air slapped Jack in the face, instantly clearing his sinuses of the pong inside the shop. He inhaled sharply as he strode to the Harley.

"Dude, that was intense," Armstrong excitedly said under his breath.

As soon as the shop door closed, Jack turned on Armstrong. Jack poked him in the chest as he spoke. "I thought he knew I was coming. That could have gone assways in more ways than I care to think about."

"But it didn't, man. He talked to you. He doesn't talk to just anyone." Armstrong swatted at Jack's hand.

"Maybe, but it doesn't mean we're going to do business. You need to impress upon him how serious I am about my offer." Jack grabbed the helmet off the gas tank and slid it on. Before dropping down the visor, he poked Armstrong in the shoulder this time and said, "You and I need to talk more about that side project you've been working on for him. That's got my attention more than the other stuff."

Armstrong stepped back. "Yeah, okay man. Just stop doing that. It hurts."

Jack chuckled. "You haven't felt hurt yet. This deal goes sideways, I'll be looking for you. I have a lot of questions still needing answers." Like *where the hell is my wife?*

Jack threw a leg over the saddle and pulled the bike upright, off the kickstand. He slammed his weight down onto the kick starter with one powerful thrust. The bike roared to life.

He looked hard at Armstrong one more time before flipping down the visor and pulling out of the space.

Jack took his time leaving Chinatown via Kearny Street to Broadway. It didn't take long to know he was being followed.

Two people dressed in matching black bike gear and helmets rode together on a small black rice rocket. He caught them in his rearview mirror as they wove through traffic, trying to keep up with him. He doubted it was Kenny and Kai simply because they wouldn't have had time to change into bike gear.

When Jack reached the Embarcadero, he casually signaled left and joined the traffic heading west. The pair followed. They stayed back just far enough they probably hoped he wouldn't notice.

The light at Bay Street had just turned red so Jack gunned the motor and raced across the junction just as oncoming traffic started making its way across the intersection. The rice rocket had no choice but to stop at the light and wait.

Jack chuckled as he immediately veered off the road into the lanes for the Pier 39 parking garage. He wove between the cars waiting for the Muni to pass, then turned to follow the trolleybus as it joined Bay Street. He hugged the right side of the bus as it turned right to join the Embarcadero heading east. In his rearview mirror, he saw the rice rocket speed across the junction on its green light and up Bay Street. They hadn't seen him.

Jack pulled back the throttle and sped toward Broadway.

CHAPTER TWENTY

Jack backed his Harley into his space in the alley beside Tommy Wong's. He flipped down the kickstand and removed his helmet before pulling his leg over the saddle.

He caught movement from the corner of his eye and looked up the stairs leading to the apartment. He wasn't taking clients and had even removed the sign from his door—*Jack Slaughter, Private Investigations and Security*. Had things gone to plan at his house, he wouldn't be here right now, so who was up there sitting in the shadows?

His heart kicked up a beat. Had Li's thugs found out who he really was and where he lived? He didn't think so. Whoever this was, they were much taller than Li's crew.

Jack took off the cut and quickly folded it inside out; whoever this was didn't need to know what he was doing or that he still possessed department property.

As he approached the stairs, the figure at the top stood up. Halo from the automatic light over the apartment door caught the man's profile.

Jon Cutter.

Relief washed through him. "Been waiting long?"

"Not too long. I tried calling a few times, but it kept going to voice."

Inside the apartment, Jack set his helmet and cut on the side table then flipped on the overhead light. Cutter must have seen the cut when Jack pulled into the alley, as he looked between it and Jack with curiosity in his eyes.

"I was undercover and left my phone here."

K.A. Lugo

"Haniford bring you in on a Sixers case?"

Jack shook his head. "Nah."

"You still have the cut." It wasn't a question or accusation, just an observation.

"Yeah."

Cutter followed Jack to the desk, dropping the subject. "What's with all the boxes?"

"I decluttered." It wasn't a lie. "Thinking about repainting." That one was.

"Ever think about moving?"

"Sometimes." Cutter's questions echoed Ray's. It was obvious the two men had talked. "I was going to order something brought up, or would you rather go down?" The smell of food, even Chinese, awakened the beast in Jack's stomach, reminding him he hadn't eaten today.

"Yeah, sure. How do you feel about Italian? My treat."

Moments later, Jack and Cutter entered Capo's Restaurant on Vallejo Street around the corner from the apartment. The exposed red brick walls, gently aged natural timber, vintage décor, and diamond tufted red leather booths screamed San Francisco Italian.

It wasn't just the Detroit and Chicago-style pizza aromas assaulting Jack's senses from the brick ovens in back making him salivate. Capo's also specialized in traditional Italian dishes created with regional ingredients—calamari from Monterey, garlic from Gilroy, and artichokes from Castroville. The scent of garlic, tomatoes, and fresh pasta made Jack's stomach tighten from hunger and his chest ache with memories of his mother's cooking. And Leah's own marinara.

They sat at the end of the bar closest to the door. The bartender slid a couple Italian Peroni beers toward Jack and Cutter and took their order before heading back down the bar. After a ceremonial clink, Jack took a long pull off his bottle before setting it on the counter. The icy cold liquid traced a path down his esophagus and into his empty stomach.

"Long day?" Cutter asked.

Jack nodded. "Long week."

"I didn't think private investigations involved much undercover work."

Jack chuffed to himself. Cutter hadn't waited long to get to the point. "A lot of it is undercover because of the surveillance and stakeouts, but with this case, I was deep under. As you saw, I still have the department cut, so I used it."

Before Cutter could ask, Jack gave his friend the pared down version of what had been going on the last few days and how it tied into the dead man in his house. He left out the part where Haniford tore him a new asshole but did tell him about the interview with Armstrong and discovering what had happened to his family.

"Oh, man!" Cutter sat forward in his chair, focusing on Jack. "How do you feel now that you know what happened?"

Jack thought for a moment. He really didn't know. Of course, he was gut-sick over what had happened to Zoë, but until he found Leah, he wouldn't allow the pit of despair to open up and swallow him whole. Yet.

"I don't know, but I haven't told Ray. I'd appreciate you keeping him in the dark until I'm ready to tell him."

"Goes without saying. It's your story to tell," Cutter said. "What're you gonna do if things go sideways with this Li character?"

Jack had thought about that before making his decision to meet Li on his own, and the only thing he could come up with was, "It's all on me."

Cutter scowled. "Is there anything I can do to help? If you need to populate your 'crew', it'd give me the chance to pull out my old bobber. Been few enough of those days lately."

Cutter's '48 bobber, aka bob-job or cut-down, was an old panhead he'd stripped back to the bare minimum during restoration. Getting rid of excess weight, like fenders, fairings, saddlebags, and other superfluous accessory weight created a much faster bike without having to do expensive motor modifications. The bike had a matte black frame, and the gas tank and a reduced size rear fender were painted dark surf green with seafoam cream pinstripes. The fat tires had wide whitewalls, making them look like car tires. The bobber had a classic look right out of the forties but with the speed of the twenty-first century.

Cutter's only lament was the bike wasn't built for carrying his boards.

Jack lifted his bottle to Cutter with a, "Thanks. If it comes to that, I'll let you know. So far, I've only met with him once. If he needs proof of a larger organization, I'll definitely need asses in saddles."

Just then, the waitress brought over a thick Detroit-style pepperoni pizza—a traditional rectangle thick crust pan pizza loaded with extra pepperoni with well-browned cheesy edges. She set it down between them along with a couple plates topped with cutlery wrapped in cloth napkins.

"Can I get you anything else?" she asked, looking between the men.

Jack tapped his bottle and Cutter said, "Another couple Peronis and we're good. Thanks."

Jack grabbed a corner of the pizza and dropped it onto his plate. He pulled off a piece of the crunchy edge and let the metallic taste of burnt mozzarella wash over his tongue.

A few minutes later, Jack reached for another slice. He glanced at Cutter. "Are you going to tell me why you really wanted to see me?"

Without looking up, Cutter replied, "No special reason. It's just been a minute since we've shared some *kaukau* and talked story."

His friend wasn't wrong. "Sorry. The last few months have been crazy."

Cutter then gave Jack a long side look. "You okay?"

Jack's heart pumped hard twice before he put a smile on his face. "Sure. It's all good."

Between bites, Cutter said, "You were MIA there for a while."

"You've been talking to Ray."

"He called."

Jack swallowed the last bite of pizza and pushed away his plate.

"I needed some time. It's been four years now—" He left the last hanging.

Cutter nodded. "I bet it's not any easier now, knowing what happened to your family. I'm sorry."

"I expect to find out what happened to Leah once I get through this thing with Li."

"Then you can get on with your life."

Jack quickly glanced at his friend. "Then I can get on." By that he meant go back to the Sunset house with his Beretta. "Speaking of getting on, how are you getting on with finding records on Kyle Warren and Daniel Chin?"

Cutter shook his head. "There's absolutely nothing in the system. I had someone run through stored hard copies from that time and there's nothing there. Sorry, brah."

"Maybe they're in hiding like Rybak was, or Li had them disappeared." Jack didn't want to think about all the disappearances Li was responsible for.

At the end of the meal, the waitress cleared the bar in front of them then brought over a couple rich Italian espressos.

CHAPTER TWENTY-ONE

Monday – April 5

Jack stood with a steaming cup of coffee in hand, staring out the window to the bustling intersection below but not really seeing it. His mind spun.

Li Zihao still hadn't called, which made Jack more nervous with each passing day. That nervousness gave birth to all the questions he didn't have answers to.

If Li accepted Jack's drug order, how the hell was he going to pay for it? With the quantities he'd told Li he wanted, Jack knew it could cost him at least a cool quarter million. He didn't have that kind of money. Even with the price of real estate in the city, the current available equity of his house was worth nowhere near that amount. Not that anyone would want to buy a house with that kind of history.

What was he going to do with the drugs once he had them? If he turned them over to the department, Haniford would know Jack was still in the thick of the Rybak investigation. Even though right now, the only tie the department had to the Jade Dragons was Armstrong.

Could he take the drugs over to the house and burn them in the tiny fireplace? Maybe he'd just dump it all in the living room and set fire to the house. Since no one would want to buy it, and he didn't see Ray doing anything with it, burning it down and releasing all the spirits living within the walls was probably the best option.

And if Li rejected his proposal, how would he find Leah?

He couldn't think about any of it. He had to stay positive. It would all work out. It *had* to work out.

If he'd been thinking straight, he would've called Ray to organize a drug sting, despite his former lieutenant making it clear Jack needed to shit or get off the pot—get back on the job and take full advantage of the department resources, or stay away. The fence Jack had been sitting on had been torn down and a wall had been erected in its place.

As much as Jack knew the reality of it for a long time, Ray had been right about Jack never being a cop again. That part of his life was over. It had been since the night he lost his family, but there was some relief in admitting it to himself, even knowing how his end game would play out. Admitting it to himself would make it easier admitting it to others. Why string them along with false hopes?

As much as he hated admitting it, he was in over his head with Li. He'd been so angry last week he ignored all the warnings and jumped into the fire with both feet. This wasn't like him. He was never *this* reckless. He didn't know what was wrong with him. He was behaving like a petulant five-year-old saying, *You can't tell me what to do.*

A text notification drew his attention to his phone. He turned to the desk and saw the screen light up—Ray. Jack clicked on the message: *Where are you?*

He pulled out the chair and dropped into it before setting his mug on the desk. The Beretta pressed against the small of his back. He'd started carrying again since meeting with Li. Since he was on his own, he couldn't be too careful. He could only afford to drop his guard once he found out where Leah was.

He pulled his to-do list in front of him and winced at the first line—background checks. He now needed to run those himself. They were a normal part of private investigating, but Ray could do a much deeper dive in department files.

Jack put his elbows on the desk and leaned his head into the palms of his hands, pushing hard on his forehead to relieve the tension.

Nick, he sighed to himself.

Jack wished his friend was still up at St. Frank's. He needed someone to talk with, about Haniford and to some degree Ray too, and this case and what had happened to his family.

The text notification sounded again. *Don't make me ping your phone again.*

He groaned as he grabbed his phone off the charger. *I disabled GPS,* he lied. *What do you want?*

A moment later, the phone vibrated. He'd turned off the ringer last night. The quiet was nice while it lasted.

"Hey," Jack said on answering.

"You're one hard *ese* to reach these days."

"I'm here now. What's up?"

"I got back some of those background checks you suggested. I wanted to go over them with you."

"I'm off the case, brother."

"What do you mean you're off the case? We're in the middle of it. You can't just quit, *hombre*." The tone of Ray's voice told Jack his friend was definitely annoyed. He was sure Ray hadn't been prepared for the way the conversation was heading.

"Talk to Haniford. He doesn't want me getting involved in department cases anymore. You were right. I'm not going back on the job. Honestly, I don't think I ever was. I've wasted too much of everyone's time letting you all live with false hopes. Especially you. I'm sorry."

"Jack—"

"Haniford was right too about me always calling in favors. I can't keep doing that. It's made me lazy, and it's not fair to you. I'm sorry about that too."

"I'll email over the reports, and you can have a look anyway."

"Don't do it. Despite Rybak killing himself in my house, Haniford made it absolutely clear this is a department issue; I'm not allowed anywhere near it. My hands are tied."

Ray was quiet on the other end of the line. Jack waited for him to say something. Then, "Where are you?"

"Look, Ray. I'll call you this evening when you're home. We both have a lot of work on today."

"We need to talk. I don't want to do it on the phone," Ray insisted.

Jack didn't want to shut Ray out, but if he kept pushing him away, he was bound to get suspicious. "Fine. I'll come to you. Where are you?"

Jack's door swung open. "At your place."

"What the fuck, Navarro?" Jack said in a raised voice.

Ray cut to the point. "I tried reaching you all weekend, but I kept getting voicemail."

"I was busy."

"Too busy to check messages?"

"I checked them. Nothing sounded urgent. Just a bunch of *call me's* which I was going to get to this afternoon." Jack sat back and folded his arms in front of him. "Was that all you needed, to look over the reports?"

Ray remained standing as he glared down at him. "I was going over to Armstrong's again to see if I could find him. I thought you'd want to tag along."

Jack shook his head. "I'm done tagging along, Ray. What did I just tell you about Haniford?"

"Yeah, I get it. I guess it's different when the shoe is on the other foot."

"What's that supposed to mean?" Jack's anger rose. He really didn't want to fight with his best friend again, but things felt like they were edging in that direction.

"Every time *you* need help, it's *Ray, run this name for me*, and *Ray, I need a file*, and *Ray*—"

"Stop."

"Even when I tell you my job is on the line, you still con me into doing favors for you," Ray told him. "But you know what? Even when Haniford ripped my head off and explicitly told me to keep you out of this, I still showed up at your door to take you to the university with me. And over to Armstrong's. Now I need your help and it's all *Haniford this* and *no-can-do that*—"

"Ray, just stop," Jack insisted. His friend wasn't wrong about any of it. They'd been friends for so long, Jack knew how easy it was to get Ray on side. It wasn't always work related, but he had to admit, lately most of it had been.

"You're some kinda *hipócrita*."

Jack didn't care what Haniford did to *him*. Since he was no longer on the force, the worst his former LT could do was ban him from the department, which he'd effectively already done by disallowing the liberty of calling in some favors.

What he *was* concerned with was Ray. Jack didn't want to be the reason his friend didn't get his promotion. Yet as they both got deeper into the Rybak bullshit, the more they needed each other to work the case. Jack needed access to files from the department and Ray needed backup. He'd blown through so many new partners, Haniford finally conceded and now let Ray ride solo, which came at its own cost—not having a partner to back him up or bounce theories against.

Where Jack was concerned, Haniford had been clear . . . very clear. If he didn't back away from the case and stop asking Ray for favors, Ray would never see his promotion, and worse, if Ray didn't stop encouraging Jack, Ray could find himself getting bumped back down to street patrol. Jack didn't want any of it on his conscience. How could he make Ray understand? Jack wasn't being a hypocrite. Far from it. He was protecting his friend.

"I'm sorry, Ray. Haniford—"

Ray was on a roll. All Jack could do was listen.

"Haniford, Haniford . . . blah, blah, blah. Since I couldn't reach you, this morning I went back to Armstrong's on my own. I thought if I caught him early enough, he wouldn't run, and I could interview him. Imagine my surprise when I find you've already been there and had a nice long chat with our boy."

"So?"

"So, *ese*, he didn't want to talk to me because he'd already told you everything. Said he had some kind of deal going with you and couldn't risk getting on your bad side." Ray removed his jacket—a sign Jack took his friend planned on staying a while—threw it onto the sofa then started pacing the small room. "What the fuck is that all about?"

"What did he tell you?" If that little shitbag had said anything about anything, he'd nail his scrawny burnout ass to the wall.

"And sit down before you wear a hole in the floor."

Ray threw himself into the chair in front of the desk. "That's just it. He didn't tell me anything. All he said was, *Talk to Jack*." Leaning forward with his elbows on his knees, he demanded, "I'm here, *homie*, so talk."

"I think Armstrong is being overly dramatic, and so are you. Why couldn't we have talked about this on the phone?"

"Because I want you to look me in the eye when you lie to me."

"Lie to you?" Jack huffed. "About what?"

"Tell me what you've been doing behind my back." Ray suddenly didn't sound angry. He sounded hurt.

Quietly, Jack said, "Haniford pissed me off last week. When I left the department, I got on my bike with the intention of driving down the coast to clear my head. I had a lot to think about since Haniford kicked me out of the department. By the time I reached Skyline Boulevard, I reminded myself I'm a private investigator and can investigate on my own. So, I rode over to Geary to see if Armstrong was home. Long story short, he was there, and we talked." He wasn't ready to tell Ray about what happened to his family. "We eventually came to an understanding, and he agreed to set up a meeting for me with his boss, Li Zihao."

Ray sank back in his chair. "The same Li Zihao who runs the Jade Dragons?" Jack nodded. Under his breath, Ray asked, "What are you doing, Jack? You can't go to this guy on your own."

"I didn't," Jack assured him.

"Wait, what?" Ray's voice hitched up an octave. "You've already gone over? When?"

"Saturday morning."

"And you didn't go alone. You're working with someone else now." It wasn't a question but an accusation.

"Don't get your tighty whities in a knot, Ray. I met Armstrong at the Dragon's Lair shop over at Portsmouth Square. Everything went fine."

"Don't bullshit me, Jack. I know what your *fine* means. You walked out alive."

"I'm sitting here with you. He didn't even threaten to shoot me. So yes, it went fine."

"What did you talk about?" Ray pressed. "I mean, you're an ex-cop and he's a gang leader. What could you possibly have that he wants?"

"I wasn't there as a cop."

"If not a cop, then what? You offering him private investigation services or something? You'll search for his enemies and tell him where they are so he can kill them?"

"You didn't just go there, did you?" Ray had never disparaged Jack's decision to become a private investigator. If he was going to start now, this conversation wasn't going to end well. Ray must have realized what he'd said because he instantly went quiet, but his gaze on Jack never wavered. "Maybe you'd better leave before this goes somewhere there's no coming back from."

"Or," Ray finally said, "we talk this out now, because, *ese*, you're not thinking straight." He tapped the side of his head.

"I'm thinking just fine," Jack assured him.

"I don't think you are. The background checks are just one thing we need to discuss."

"There's more?"

"The department cut."

Jack's stomach flipped over in his gut. "What are you talking about?"

"You know exactly what I'm talking about. You wore it to the head shop, didn't you?"

Jack just looked at Ray for a long minute before asking in a lowered voice, "Does Haniford know?"

"What do you think? I heard your name when he started screaming in his office, so I logged into the system. When I saw what Haniford was screaming about, I came right over to give you a heads up."

"How did Haniford know?"

Ray shook his head. "You do know those cuts have GPS trackers on them, don't you?"

"So? The battery only lasts a couple years at best."

"I'm guessing yours has been sitting in the closet since you left the department. But the motion sensor switched it on, and it pinged at the department. It was tracked across the city and back on Saturday. Now that you've told me where you were, the cut certainly wasn't out for a joy ride on its own. Care to tell me why you were wearing the department cut at the head shop? You certainly didn't need it just to talk with Li." Ray resumed his position of leaning forward with elbows on his knees and waited for Jack's response.

"What do you want me to say? Yeah, I wore the cut to the meeting. I had to make it look like I was a gang member or how else could I justify a large buy? I had to show Li I was serious about making a deal with him. So what?"

"You really aren't thinking, are you?" Ray muttered.

"What?"

Ray growled as he shot out of his chair, stomped across the room then pivoted and glared at Jack. He ran his fingers through his hair before crossing the room again, slapped his palms on the desktop and leaned forward. Ray's posture didn't scare Jack, but it was a surprise. Ray was normally such a laid-back person. Now his Hispanic temper was showing as he raged at Jack, up one side and back down the other, in Spanish. They had been friends long enough that Jack picked up about every fourth or fifth word and got the gist of abuse being slung at him.

Just then, someone pounded on his door. Ray was here, his business sign was down so it couldn't be a prospective client, he didn't owe Tommy rent and he was sure if Li had found out who Jack really was, he would have sent thugs already.

Pounding again.

As Jack rose and went to the door, he slid the Beretta from the small of his back. Whoever it was, they weren't happy.

At the door, he glanced back at Ray who stood with his own weapon drawn.

"Who is it?" he asked through the door, holding the weapon at the ready.

"Your worst nightmare. Open the door or I'll shoot off the lock."

Haniford.

His former LT had never come here. Whenever he needed to meet in person, Jack had always gone to the department. Coming here, and the tone of his voice, told Jack some serious shit was about to hit the proverbial.

Looking at Ray, Jack asked, "What's he doing here?"

"I was just about to tell you Haniford's on the war path."

After clicking on the weapon's safety, Jack tucked the Beretta into the waistband at his back. Ray had already holstered his weapon at his hip by the time Jack swung open the door.

Not waiting for an invitation, Haniford pushed past Jack and stopped in the center of the room when he saw Ray standing in front of the desk.

Jack shut the door and walked past both men to the opposite side of the desk. It felt safer than being on the other side between two men who looked like they both wanted to kill him.

"To what do I owe the pleasure, Lieutenant?" Jack stood with his legs wide and arms folded over his chest. He felt defensive as two of the three men he trusted most in the world glared angrily across the desk at him. The third man he trusted as much was Cutter, and Jack didn't think there was an angry bone in the man's body.

Haniford scowled at Ray for a long moment. "I'm not even going to ask why you're here, Ray. I'll deal with you later." Looking back at Jack, he continued, "I thought after our discussion last week you would have kept your nose out of department business."

"What are you talking about? I have been," Jack told him.

"It's true, LT. I came here asking Jack for some help with an interview and he refused. He said you told him to back off and that's what he's done," Ray said.

Haniford glared between the two men before settling on Jack. "Whatever you're doing, Jack, your shit is still raining down on my parade. Anything I tell either of you falls on deaf ears, or you pointedly ignore me. So, I'm here—"

"LT," Ray cut in. "I think you need to hear what Jack has to say."

The crease between Haniford's eyes deepened. "I have a feeling

I need to sit down for this." He moved to the sofa and sank into the center cushion, then shot up quickly, a hand on his ass cheek. "Jesus!"

"Fuck, Jack, when are you going to get a new sofa?" Ray growled as he reseated himself in front of the desk.

His tone was full of sarcasm when he said, "Somehow a new sofa doesn't seem as important as finding out what happened to my family."

CHAPTER TWENTY-TWO

Ray and Haniford sat in stunned silence before Ray asked, "Are you sure?"

Over the past hour, Jack had said things he hadn't been ready to talk about yet but his hand had been forced. To his surprise, he felt some relief. He didn't know why he thought he could keep Zoë's and Trax's killer to himself until he found Leah, but now it was out, he breathed easier.

"As sure as I can be." Jack sat back in his chair, but his spine remained stiff. Having Haniford in his place made him nervous.

"You're going to take the word of some shitbag junkie?" Ray asked.

"He wasn't always like this," Jack said. "Remember what Ms. Fong told us at the university? Armstrong had been at the top of his class until he met Rybak and Warren."

"And Rybak and Warren maintained their grades until they met Armstrong," Ray said. "The point is, how can you trust anything he says *now* about what happened *then*?"

"Because back then none of them were hopheads. They were just three guys who met over a video game and got pulled into the wrong one, *Head Shop Heist*. They made the wrong decision to start robbing actual head shops." Jack filled in Haniford about what the game was about and the website features. "They monumentally fucked up when they hit the Dragon's Lair. Warren was killed, Rybak went into hiding, and Armstrong was left holding the bag for all three of them. When Li found out what Armstrong's major was, he kept him close for his own benefit."

"That's some weight to carry," Haniford said. The anger on his face eased but Jack knew he wasn't out of the woods.

"And how could Armstrong forget what they'd done to Zoë and Trax?" Jack continued. "No amount of drug abuse can erase a memory like that."

Haniford nodded his agreement. "Are you sure it was your family?"

"When I talked with Armstrong on Saturday, he told me what address Li had sent him and Rybak to. He recited the night in clear detail, as if it had been the night before. It was my house. Zoë and Trax died exactly like he said. Leah is still missing. Armstrong said he didn't know what happened to the woman that night. Just that Li told his guys to," he used finger quotes when he said, "*take care of her*. How could it have been anyone else?"

Ray shook his head. "I don't know, Jack, but something about it doesn't add up right. You said Li told Armstrong and Rybak that this husband owed him money and he wanted these guys to act as debt collectors?"

Jack nodded. "So?"

"And they took the wife because the husband wasn't home?"

Jack nodded again. "Your point?"

"It means if Armstrong remembered everything from that night," Haniford said, "*you* were the husband. Were or are you in the habit of borrowing money from Chinese gangs?"

"I've only ever borrowed money twice in my life and both times from the bank—to buy my first car and for the mortgage on the Sunset house."

"My point. So why would Li have sent guys over to collect a debt on a man who didn't owe him anything?" Haniford asked.

Damn Haniford for being reasonable.

"I don't know, man. Maybe he was testing those guys. Maybe the address was random, and he wanted to see how far he could push Armstrong and Rybak." Jack sat back and pressed his fingers into the space between his eyebrows to relieve some of his tension. "What I do know is if I can get on Li's good side, I'm hoping to find out what they did with Leah. Even if it's just an address or location where they buried her."

Ray asked on a lowered voice, "Does this mean you've conceded Leah's dead?"

Was he?

Given what Armstrong had told him happened, he doubted Li's men would have spared Leah's life. *Take care of* someone usually meant to kill them and dispose of the body. "Unfortunately, the facts say she probably is. I just need to get my head around it. I won't be sure until I find her—dead or alive."

Jack's confession must have startled the men because the room went quiet. Jack finally broke the silence by asking Haniford, "Are you going to tell me why you're here, and how I'm still shitting on your parade?"

Haniford sat forward. "I'm sure Ray didn't waste any time telling you the Gangs Task Force got a ping off the department cut still in your possession."

"It wasn't the first thing out of his mouth when he walked in, but yeah, he mentioned it. Are you here to take it off me?" Jack asked.

"First I want you to tell me what's going on. What precipitated wearing a department issue undercover garment? Especially without telling me—or asking, for that matter." Haniford's voice began rising again.

Jack took a deep breath and brought the lieutenant up to speed, echoing what he'd told Ray about meeting with Li Zihao.

"After what Armstrong told me about what happened that night at my house, the only question left unanswered is what happened to my wife. The only ones who know are Li and the two thugs he sent away with Leah. Armstrong swears he doesn't know, so if I'm going to find my wife, I need to get friendly with Li. Armstrong was my way in. Since he deals small quantities, the only way to Li was to place a larger order than Armstrong could fill." Jack gave Haniford a rundown of the quantities of heroin, cocaine, and methamphetamine he'd ordered from Li.

"Are you shitting me? Do you have any idea how much money that is?" Haniford shouted.

Jack shrugged. "Yeah. Somewhere around a quarter of a million."

"Do you have that kind of money lying around, Jack? And what are you going to do with all that dope once you have it? You do realize, if you're stopped after the deal, carrying that amount of dope, one wrong move with the wrong patrol officer and you could land in prison for the rest of your life."

"I've been asking myself those questions since Saturday, but I'm hoping Li is the one who goes away. And no, I don't have that kind of money, and I don't know what I'll do if he agrees to such a big sale, or what I'll do with it all. It was the only thing I could think of at the time to get my foot in the door with Li. Everything else . . . I'm just winging it." Jack paused at the look on Ray's face. He'd been quiet while Haniford rode Jack with questions, but now his friend looked angry and disappointed at the same time.

"What did wearing the department cut have to do with this buy?" Haniford asked.

Jack slowly moved his gaze back to the lieutenant. "I went in as a buyer for the Triple Sixers. The meeting had to look realistic. I told Li I'd been buying small quantities off Armstrong since we lost our previous source. When he couldn't supply what we needed, I asked for a meeting with his boss to buy quantity. To protect Armstrong, I told Li I roughed him up until he agreed to arrange a meeting." Jack didn't want to add that he'd walked in blind because Armstrong had failed to tell Li about the meeting. That would have made both men in front of him more nervous about what he was doing. "And as I told Ray before you arrived, the meeting went fine. He's taking some time to decide if he wants to do business with the Sixers."

"Jack," Haniford started. "I think you may have some trouble already. Part of why I'm here is to let you know the cut wasn't the only thing that pinged at the department. Someone in-house ran your bike's license plate. You didn't switch out your plate for a cold plate and now Li knows exactly who you are—Jack Slaughter private investigator and former SFPD. You blew your own cover, Jack."

Shit! He hadn't even thought about using a cold plate. Guys on the 666 crew who had their own bikes always removed their plates or swapped them out for cold plates before going out on a job—untraceable plates used in undercover work.

"I was tailed after I left, but I lost them down on the Embarcadero," he said. "I'm sure I was too far ahead of them to get a clear reading."

"Are you sure?" Ray asked. "Because Li doesn't fuck around. If he knows where you live, he'll send out his enforcers to kill you if he doesn't trust you, and he won't wait long to order the hit."

Jack thought. Someone could have taken down the plate number while the bike sat in front of Dragon's Lair. *Shit. Shit!*

"Very sure," Jack lied. "It's been two days and I'm fine." *Think, Jack, think.* What would he tell Li if he was confronted? "Like you said. I'm *former* SFPD and now independent. Li doesn't know the Sixers is a department gang. There's no reason why he shouldn't believe me or my offer. And if he reads the papers, he'll know just how far I've fallen off the grid."

"You better hope so, *ese.*"

Jack looked at Haniford. "Hey, what do you mean someone in-house ran my plate? Does Li have someone working on the inside?"

"Looks that way."

"Have you run the ID on who accessed the system to run my plate?"

"Of course I did. I'm not a rookie," Haniford said.

"But?" Jack asked.

"It came back to David Perry."

Jack sucked in his breath. "Harry's partner? But he died a couple years ago." Inspector Deborah Callahan, nicknamed Harry because of her Debbie Harry smile and not Dirty Harry, had been partners with Perry in more ways than one. He'd been killed in a *doorknock* while questioning neighbors after a spate of break-ins.

"Exactly. Whoever ran your plate under his name either had intimate knowledge of Perry's login or has access to the system," Haniford said. "I have someone running time stamps on anyone who accessed your file in the last few days. We should be able to locate the computer used to log in, and we'll see all the files they accessed."

Ray shifted in his seat. "Do you have any first impressions of who it could be? You're not thinking it's Harry . . . are you?"

"Right," Jack said. "I'm sure Harry would be the last person who would do something like this. She and I are on good terms, so why would she run my bike plate? Besides, how would she be connected to the Jade Dragons?" Jack was more than sure it wasn't her. But if not Harry, then who? He drew a blank.

"I don't want to be the one stating the obvious, but Amy's brother did work for the Jade Dragons before he disappeared," Ray said.

"She's crazy, but I don't think she's that crazy." Jack turned to the lieutenant. "She's been on the watch list since day one, because of her brother's ties to the gang, hasn't she? Has anything popped?"

Haniford shook his head. "Nothing substantial. She looked out for her brother, but nothing that would've got her in trouble at work. We've had no reason to suspect she's involved with the gang at all, especially since her brother disappeared."

"Shit!" Jack growled.

Haniford rubbed the bridge between his eyes. Jack knew he was trying to ward off a headache. He looked up then and squared his gaze with Jack's. "I'm curious. Just what did you offer him in exchange for making a drug deal with him? It can't possibly be as simple as walking in and asking the leader of the biggest gang in the city to sell you some drugs and expect he wants nothing in return. I'm almost afraid to ask."

Anger forced Jack's eyebrows together when he scowled. "Money, protection, another body on the ground selling his gear . . ." The part about selling the drugs wasn't a lie. He had told Li he wanted in on the new party drug, and he'd made it clear he wanted the exclusive on it.

"Protection?" Haniford shouted. "Jesus fucking Christ, Jack, are you fucking kidding me? What the hell is wrong with you?"

"It's not like I was actually going to do it."

"It doesn't matter. If you don't follow through with the promise, Li will eat your liver for breakfast and your heart for dinner," Haniford warned.

Jack turned to Ray. "You not going to say anything?"

Ray sat with his arms crossed over his chest but waved one hand. "No, *ese*, you're digging your own hole well enough on your own. You don't need my help."

Jack looked back at Haniford. "So, what happens now? You going to take the cut off me?"

Haniford's frown curved into a wicked grin. "When I'm through with you, you'll wish I had come here just to take the cut off you."

"Do tell." Jack wasn't the type of guy who scared easily, nor could he be intimidated. But when it came to Haniford, the line between *you just got away with this* and *oh, shit, you're fucked* was very thin. Just then, Jack felt he was sliding into the latter but tried not to show it.

"I'm going to let you keep the cut, for now. Keep wearing it to your meetings with Li. It will allow us to track your movements, and it'll give you some credibility." Haniford leaned back, casually rested an arm along the length of the back cushion and crossed an ankle over the opposite knee. "I'm also giving you the money to make your buy, and I'll even take the drugs off you," Haniford promised.

"What's the catch?" Jack asked, knowing his former boss didn't often give something this big without asking for something just as big in return.

"You're going to be *my* man on the inside."

"Your what?" Both Jack and Ray asked.

"Are you shitting me?" Jack all but screeched.

Haniford's gaze bore down on Jack. He couldn't look away. "Since you can't seem to keep your ass out of department affairs and refuse to badge-up, no, I'm not shitting you."

"And if I refuse?"

"Don Corleone said it best. I'm making you an offer you can't refuse."

"Can't or won't?" Jack asked.

"Take your pick. The answer is the same. If you don't do this, you're going to jail for obstruction," Haniford promised.

Ray gasped. And for a moment, Jack couldn't breathe. When he found his breath, he asked, "Obstruction of what?"

"Anything I can hang on you, Jack. As long as it keeps you out of the department and off my back."

"You told me last week to back off and I have," Jack said.

"Yet here I am, and here you are still shitting on my parade." Haniford took a few noticeably deep breaths before saying, "What you'd know if you were still in the department is that a couple years ago the FBI put together a Joint Task Force to bring down Li Zihao and Jade Dragons."

"*I'm* in the department, LT," Ray said, "and didn't know anything about this. What's going on?"

Haniford looked between the two men as he spoke. "Each of these services has been trying to bring down the Jade Dragons for years. A couple years ago, they put together a task force to expedite the process. This gang is one of the city's biggest suppliers of narcotics and weapons, yet their investigation hasn't been able to get anything to stick."

"They also run brothels," Ray said. "That's three counts there for human trafficking, prostitution, and enslavement."

"That's one of those add-on charges once we've got Li and his gang in on trading narcotics and weapons. That's where they'll get the most prison time." Haniford looked back at Jack. "And if Armstrong is telling the truth and Li and his crew are responsible for killing your family, he'll go down on that too—murder for hire and kidnapping, for sure, and maybe extortion. This wouldn't have been the first time he's been involved in deaths under suspicious circumstances."

"What does all this have to do with me?" Jack asked.

"Because you're a new player. We can use you since you've gone in and are working a deal with Li for a quantity of drugs."

"Yeah, for my own purpose. Why not just put in a CI?"

"They have, but there's nothing we can actually hang Li with. The CI hasn't earned any privilege of being on the scene when deals go down. At this point, it appears he's little more than a sales clerk. We need to get something on Li. So far, after all the time and resources everyone has invested in this, Li is still a shadow. Your deal would be the perfect opportunity to finally get him dead to rights."

"And what do I get out of being your man inside?" Jack asked.

"Like I said, you need money for the buy. I'll give it to you. You can't sit on all that product, so I'll take the drugs off your hands. It'll be the evidence we need for the case. That and your testimony, of course," Haniford added.

"Who's actually running point in the task force?" Jack asked, knowing Haniford wasn't high enough in the ranks.

"The FBI has a commander in place for the joint operation, but you don't need to know anything other than what I tell you." Haniford glanced at Ray. "Rather, whatever Ray tells you."

"Wait a minute. Why are you getting me messed up in all this?" Ray asked.

"Consider it penance. I told you to keep Jack out of it, but you've kept him involved anyway. You two want to play cops and robbers together again with my full blessing? This is how." Haniford looked between Jack and Ray. "And I want full disclosure."

"Meaning?" Jack asked.

"Just what it says on the tin. I want complete transparency through the investigation. You report to Ray, and he reports to me. I want to know what you're doing before you do it. You make the deal with Li. Tell Ray how much he wants, and I'll organize the money. When you make the bust—"

Jack's back stiffened. "Hold on. Me? You want *me* to bust Li?"

Haniford's expression didn't change. "You got a problem with that?"

"Yeah. I do. It's just me in there. Normally, these stings mean there's back up waiting outside in case the deal goes assways." What the hell kind of game was Haniford playing?

"What's the difference from what you were already walking into?"

Ray cleared his throat, drawing Jack's and Haniford's attention. "The difference is, you're also asking him to arrest Li. From the sounds of it, Jack has another plan. The guy is surrounded by security. If anything happens and the deal is compromised, Jack doesn't stand a chance of walking out of that shop." When Haniford didn't reply, Ray added, "Come on, Lieutenant, even you can see this is a bad deal."

Jack gave Ray a weak smile. Even after all of the recent arguments and knowing his promotion could be made or broken with this deal Haniford was throwing at him, Ray still had his six.

The deal was definitely dangerous, but at this point, Jack was willing to do just about anything to find Leah. Letting Haniford and the task force solve two of his problems—money for the buy and taking the drugs off him—was the perfect solution for his two biggest worries. But the trade-off was his being asked—no, told—to risk his life by arresting Li when the deal was done.

Would he even be ready at that point to put Li in cuffs? His purpose for getting cozy with the Chinese gangster was to find out what happened to Leah. The drug deal was just his *in*.

Did Haniford expect him to bring in Li immediately after the deal? It didn't sound like the lieutenant wanted to wait, or perhaps it was the task force who didn't want to delay things any longer than they had to since their CI hadn't brought them anything concrete to proceed with.

Already, Jack's head spun with possible solutions and outcomes. If he was expected to bring in Li, he'd have to go in armed to the teeth, but Li's thugs would never let him keep any of the weapons, which was as good as going in empty-handed.

Would he be able to get Li alone long enough to quietly cuff him and take him out of the shop before anyone noticed he was gone? And even if that scenario worked, how would he get Li back to the department? Certainly not on the back of his bike, and definitely not a Fast-Fast Car.

Jack glanced at Ray. Could he ask his friend to park on the corner and wait until Li was apprehended, then bundle him into the vehicle for Ray to drive him into the station? That would be a tricky maneuver to pull off, especially if Jack was going to have enough time to get back to his bike and take off. He certainly wasn't going to leave it behind.

No, there didn't seem to be an easy solution. Not even one he was marginally comfortable with.

"I'm with Ray," Jack said. "I don't like this."

"I don't either, but I can only offer what the task force commander has approved. My hands are tied," Haniford said.

"Nothing in what you're offering me has anything to do with me finding Leah. That's my main purpose for meeting with this guy," Jack reminded him.

"I'm not saying you can't do that."

Ray sat forward. "How's he going to do that while making a drug buy and arresting Li? Getting cozy with Li and earning his trust over time is the only way the man will talk."

"Do you want to partner up with Jack when he goes back to meet with Li?"

"You know how I am on bikes, or I'd be the first one in line to volunteer."

Jack heard the desperation in his friend's voice. "Thanks, brother. I'll figure something out." He turned back to the lieutenant. "Just so you know, if both opportunities present themselves—finding out about Leah and arresting Li—my priority is going to be my wife. Damn your consequences."

Haniford's only response was a shrug and a gesture telling Jack to do what he felt he had to do. He would, goddamn it!

"Something else. You said Li ran my bike's plates and knows who I am. No one has come looking for me, so what if he uses that information and refuses to make a deal with me?"

Haniford cocked his head and folded his arms across his chest. "You're going to have to play this by ear. We know he ran your bike's plates because it popped in the system around the same time as you taking the cut out for a spin. But Li doesn't know what we know. He may keep your information close to his chest and see where this goes. If he's smart and thinks you're working for the department, he may avoid making a deal, or he may string you along if he thinks it's a sting."

"That would be the smart thing to do," Jack said.

"Unfortunately, we won't know anything about Li's plans for

you until you make contact again," Haniford said.

Jack's body went numb. "So, it's all on me. I'm on my own with everything. The only thing that changes is that Ray becomes my handler."

"And you get the money you need for the deal from the department," Haniford reminded him. "And don't think of Ray as your handler. He's actually just the go-between so the task force and I can keep an eye on you."

"Handler. And if I can't make the deal stick, what then?" Jack asked.

Haniford shrugged. "You could still see time for obstruction and wasting department time. Of course, if you lose our money, that'll definitely be on you, and you'll find yourself vacationing at San Quentin."

"You know this really blows, don't you?" Jack grumbled.

"Why do you say that?"

"Because, if you had let me help Ray work the case, none of this would be going down. Or at least I'd know the department had my back on this. From where I'm standing right now, if I fuck up and the deal goes south, I'm on my own to suffer the blowback. It's no skin off the department's nose, or yours, because I'm not officially on the case."

"You're not wrong," Haniford confirmed. "But wasn't that the case before we stepped in?"

Jack spun his chair toward the window and focused on the Trans Am Pyramid building. His heart flipped. *Well, fuck.*

"Jack." Ray's voice was calmer now. "If you're going to do this, I think we need to go over the reports I pulled. There may be something specific in Li's file that you can use to protect yourself."

Protect himself from what? Getting killed? Wasn't that exactly what he was trying to do nearly two weeks ago in his house?

CHAPTER TWENTY-THREE

Tuesday – April 6

Spread across his desk were the contents of the envelope he'd put together before taking his Beretta to the Sunset house for what he thought was the last time. Jack double-checked the documents to be sure everything was in place if this thing with Li went bad.

As he reached for his cell phone to check the time, the ringer on his burner sounded. His heart thumped hard. It could be only one person. Li Zihao. Had he agreed to the drug buy, or now he knew who Jack was, would he try luring him somewhere to kill him?

Should he let on he knew that Li knew who he was, or play it cool?

He thought about not answering the phone at all, but what message would it send? If he severed a possible relationship with the drug lord, would he ever find out what happened to Leah?

Taking a deep breath, Jack tapped the *answer* button. "Yeah."

"Friday. Ten p.m.," said the voice on the line. It wasn't Li. "You bring fifty towsin dowlar to Dragon Layer."

"That's not enough money for what I ordered."

"You bring this money. Mr. Li explain term of deal."

"But—"

"If you wan this deal, you come."

The line went dead.

Ten p.m. at the shop on Friday night.

Why wait so long, and why so late? Not that he was complaining. Three days would give Haniford the time to organize the money and get it to him, but the late hour concerned him.

A trickle of reason suggested Li wasn't likely going to kill Jack in his place of business, but that didn't mean he now trusted the drug lord. The man was a professional when it came to clean-up. Hadn't they got rid of at least three bodies from Dragon's Lair?

Jack reached for his phone and punched in Ray's number. It rang a few times before picking up. Loud rumbling down the line nearly drowned out his friend's voice.

"Jack," Ray said on greeting. "Everything okay?"

"I got the call. Li Zihao wants to meet Friday night at ten in his shop in Chinatown. He wants fifty large. I don't know what he's selling me for that, but it's definitely not enough money for the product I asked for."

"Did he say what you were getting for so little?"

"One of his lackeys made the call. He only said if I wanted to make a deal, that's what I needed to bring."

"Why so late?"

"No idea."

"I'm sure I don't have to tell you all this scares the *mierda* out of me."

"Me too, but I got the ball rolling so I can find Leah. I need to finish this."

A lump formed in Jack's throat. If a buy like this went as it should, the takedown would be done in three easy steps: Order the dope, meet to test the quality of the product and make the buy, then arrests as soon as the transaction was complete. A support team would back up the buyer at every stage.

As it was, and it had been beating him upside his head, he was absolutely alone. Whatever was going down on Friday night, it was all on him.

"Did the caller give you special instructions on the money?" Ray asked.

"No, but we can assume Li wants the usual unmarked, non-sequential bills in the most common denominations."

"All right. Let me call Haniford now. As soon as I'm outta here, I'm going home to shower. Haniford should have some news for me by then. I'll call you to let you know I have it. You gonna be home tonight?"

He checked the time again. "I'm not going anywhere. I'm getting my affairs in order in case Li decides Friday is my last day on Earth," he flippantly added.

"Don't even go there."

"Yeah, yeah." Jack disengaged the call.

He gazed at the paperwork in front of him. After going over it once more, he neatly packaged everything back into the large manilla envelope and set it on the corner of the desk. First thing in the morning, he'd take it all down to City Vaults and give Ray the key when he saw him next. Everything would be secure until Ray collected it.

Until?

Was he already assuming he wouldn't make it through his meeting with Li?

Tired and frustrated, Jack stood and stretched his back then turned to look out the window. Someone stood under the trees kitty corner from his apartment. The person seemed to be staring at Tommy's restaurant. Or was it toward his apartment?

There was one way to find out, but by the time he reached the sidewalk under the *Language of Birds* art installation in front of Tommy Wong's, the person was gone.

CHAPTER TWENTY-FOUR

Friday – April 9

" W hat's this for?" Ray had asked, catching the City Vaults key Jack tossed at him.

"It's a key. It opens things."

Ray huffed. "No shit, but why are you giving it to me?"

Early Wednesday morning, Jack had taken everything he'd gathered—pink slips, deeds, accounts, keys, and anything else he thought important—and took it over to the Trans Am Building and put it into a safety deposit box at City Vaults.

Last night, Ray had stopped by the apartment with the money Haniford had promised, along with drug test kits Jack would need to ensure he was buying drugs and not crushed aspirin. He wasn't about to hand over the money if the shit wasn't pure.

Jack still wasn't sure why Li had only asked for fifty thousand and it made him anxious.

"Someone gets to deal with my shit if this meeting with Li goes tits up. Tag. You're it." Ray kept looking between Jack and the key in his hand. *"You'll need this too."* Jack had slid the paperwork across the desk Ray would need to access the box.

Jack saw Ray struggling for words, so he'd distracted him by saying he wanted to count the money. He knew the bank had already done it—apparent by the currency straps around the ten bundles of fifty-dollar bills—but counting it gave him something to do with his nervous fingers. And it kept Ray quiet, which in turn kept Jack's own anxiety from worsening.

When it was time for Ray to leave, Jack felt his friend's trepidation as he pushed him through the door. On the landing, Ray spun and threw his arms around Jack and held him tightly for a long minute, only reluctantly letting him go, but when he did, Ray quickly wiped his eyes and rushed down the steel stairs.

Jack tried thinking of something to say to lighten things but came up empty. In the end, he shouted down to the alley, "Thanks for everything, brother."

Ray had stopped in his tracks and glared up at Jack. "Just be safe and come home." Then he was gone.

When Jack was alone again, he retrieved the tiny urn that held Zoë's ashes and set them on his desk. Beside the urn was a short note Jack had already written to Ray explaining that should Jack die, he wanted his remains cremated and taken with Zoë's to Holy Cross Catholic Cemetery in Colma to be buried beside his mother in the family plot he'd purchased after her passing.

Jack tossed all night on the sofa, his imagination spinning over possible outcomes when he met Li. Now that Li knew who he was, his chances of walking out of Dragon's Lair alive were slim.

It wasn't the dying part he had a problem with. He just wanted it to be on his own terms. Screw that he was already meeting with Li, but Haniford's using it to his advantage put Jack in an impossible situation which took away his own freedom of choice— meet with Li and probably come out in a body bag, or fail to meet with Li and spend the next few years in prison for impeding an investigation, and whatever else Haniford could throw at him.

With a low growl, Jack threw himself off the sofa as soon as light started filtering through the grungy curtains. He folded up the blanket and set it on the pillow in a neat pile, then went into the bathroom for a shower. He still had the day to get through and a shower would wake him up.

And lots of coffee.

There were two things Jack wanted to accomplish before his drive to Dragon's Lair tonight. The first was giving his potentially last confession at St. Frank's, and the other was one last ride.

At the door, he threw on his jacket then grabbed his saddlebags—Haniford's money in one pouch and the cut in the other. He left his helmet on the table beside the door before descending the stairs to the alley. He didn't look back. He wasn't expecting to return.

It took a hot minute to reach the church on his bike. He gave his confession to a priest he'd never met before lighting candles for his mother, Leah, Zoë, the Navarros, and, of course, Nick.

He didn't have a destination in mind but found himself crossing the peninsula to the Great Highway where he turned south and kept the Pacific Ocean on his right. Weaving at speed through traffic, he passed through Pacifica, Montara, and Moss Beach before approaching Pillar Point Harbor.

At the sign for Princeton, he turned onto Capistrano Road and followed the signs to the Half Moon Bay Distillery. He didn't stop there, but instead, took the narrow, winding West Point Road out to the Pillar Point headland where the Air Force base was located on a clifftop above Mavericks Beach.

Jack took advantage of the quiet harbor beach and rode his bike along the footpath and parked beside the DANGER sign at the entrance to Mavericks Beach. With the saddlebags over one shoulder, he scrambled up a steep cliffside to the back of the base and followed the chain link fence out to Pillar Point, a narrow triangle-shaped plateau on the headland overlooking the rugged, rocky shoreline. The cliff below gave way to a path of jagged rocks out to Sail Rocks and the Mavericks Surfing Zone. He sat with his legs hanging over the cliff edge and tasted the salty sea spray as it washed over his skin.

Jack remembered the last time he'd come here. It felt like both yesterday and a lifetime ago. He and Leah had come to watch Cutter perform at the famous *Titans of Mavericks* surf competition, open to just twenty-four by-invitation-only competitors; an honor in itself. Only the best surfers in the world had been invited, but with winter waves sometimes reaching fifty and sixty feet, even the best of the best thought twice about accepting the invitation to Mavericks.

Today, the waves were much tamer, but as he sat watching them break on the rocks, the ground still rumbled beneath him. It radiated through his ass and thighs and up his spine. The sharp wind cut through him despite the heavy leather jacket he wore.

He finger-combed his tangled hair against the sharp wind and thought about not returning to the city. What would happen if he just kept going? Screw everything and everyone. Draw a line in the sand and start over. The money in the saddlebag beside him would keep him afloat for a while.

Could he do that?

Would Ray and Maria forgive him?

Would it be fair to Leah?

And would Haniford put out a BOLO to get his money back? Of course he would, but this thought didn't bother him as much as letting down Ray and giving up on learning what had happened to Leah.

Guilt reared its ugly head again. This was the closest he'd been to finding out what had happened to his wife. While he knew some would consider it all as a *wrong place, wrong time* situation, it had been a choice Rybak made to kill Zoë and Trax.

Jack also had choices to make. Keep driving and not look back at the city and everything waiting there for him, or return and hopefully live long enough to find out what had happened to Leah. Even if Li killed him, he would die easy, finally knowing what had happened to his family.

And wasn't this the endgame he'd been planning for the last four years? Why was he now looking down the coast for salvation?

He should have been more anxious, but his ride this afternoon helped clear his head. His sole focus was making this deal and trying to live long enough to learn what had happened to Leah. If he didn't see an opportunity to arrest Li after the money and drugs exchanged hands, he wouldn't chance it—*Live to fight another day* kept repeating in his mind—but he would finally get some closure.

As he had two weeks ago at his house, Jack felt somewhere between resolve and relief. Only this time, he wouldn't be the one holding a gun to his head. It would be Li, though Jack tried convincing himself it would be Haniford's hand holding the weapon, as he was holding Jack's life.

Brushing aside these thoughts, he maneuvered the Harley through Chinatown's narrow one-way streets to Walter U Lum Place. He turned onto the street and stopped.

While usually bustling during the day, it was now dark and deserted. Even the homeless he'd seen here nearly a week ago had moved on.

The only light came from his headlamp, which reflected off the fallen cherry blossoms on the asphalt.

Jack's heart raced. He hadn't felt anxious on the ride over, but he was moving that direction.

He gently pulled back on the throttle and moved toward the front of Dragon's Lair where he backed the bike in until the rear tire met the curb. The high beam swept the plaza, confirming its abandonment.

Jack inhaled sharply as he settled the bike before cutting the motor. Reluctantly, he switched off the light and sat listening to his surroundings. Except for the sounds of the busier streets echoing around the district, Walter U Lum Place was quiet and dark as the proverbial tomb.

Anxiety kicked up another notch. He was alone and the surrounding stillness emphasized the deep breaths he forced himself to take in order to keep his shit together.

Li's minion had said Friday at 10 p.m. He checked the time— 10:07 p.m. Maybe the guy was late, though Jack didn't take Li as a man who tolerated tardiness. Something sharp in the pit of his gut told him Li and his thugs stood within the darkened shop, watching him in the blackness and waiting for the right moment.

To do what?

He didn't know.

What am I doing?

The question should have been what wouldn't he do if it meant finding out what happened to Leah, even if it meant putting his life in danger for Haniford.

Bastard!

Why had Haniford thought it was a good idea to send him into this alone?

So what if Jack had already made a deal on his own with Li and would have ended up in a similar situation. Even just one undercover officer would have doubled his chances of survival. But being forced to do this alone, and by a man he had the utmost respect for, ate at every nerve in his body. The weight of the cut pressed him down in the saddle as much as the weight of the Beretta tucked into his jeans at his lower back.

Knowing he also carried fifty thousand dollars in his saddlebags made him feel more vulnerable here on the dark street.

Even if by some miracle he came out of this alive, if he lost the fifty grand *and* the drugs, Haniford would definitely put him in a cell. Jack wasn't sure if it was the chilly night air making him shiver just then, or the thought of going to jail over this bullshit.

The temperature dropped and, just then, the sky rumbled. Just what he needed. Storms were rare in the city, but when they came, they came big. He couldn't see the sky through the cherry trees, and it wouldn't be long until Portsmouth Plaza and all of Chinatown was wrapped in Karl's icy blanket.

"Mister Li say you come now."

Jack nearly jumped out of his skin at the whispered words behind him. "Jesus, man. Sneaking up like that is gonna get you killed."

The thunder grew louder. It was going to be one hell of a storm. The perfect weather for his last night on Earth.

Jack swung his leg over the saddle and stretched his back, took his time removing his gloves and stuffing them into a pocket, then unzipped the cut and the leather jacket.

The jacket Leah had given him was precious. If he was going down tonight, even if he didn't learn what happened to his wife, at the very least, he wanted the jacket on him, as if she protected him herself.

"You come," the minion said, stepping back and waving his hand toward the shop door. "Don't keep Mister Li waiting."

"Yeah, yeah." Taking a deep breath, he pulled the old saddlebags from across his gas tank and slung them over a shoulder. He wanted a free hand for his Beretta if it came to that, and if bullets suddenly started flying, he hoped the bundles of cash and the heavy leather would protect him, at least until he ran out of bullets.

As he stepped onto the sidewalk, the thunder grew louder and more consistent, more familiar. It quickly surrounded him as lights from the Washington Street end of Walter U Lum Place illuminated their way.

Jack's heart pumped hard.

What the hell's happening?

CHAPTER TWENTY-FIVE

Jack shielded his eyes against the headlights as more than a dozen bikes rumbled toward him. They split up as they approached, the first group backing in beside his bike. The second group backed into the curb on the opposite side of the street, their headlights illuminating Dragon's Lair's shop front as well as the interior.

Li stood near the window, flanked by Kenny and Kai. Behind them were several other members of Li's crew.

Ignoring Li's angry glare, Jack watched riders dismount and remove their helmets. Relief washed over him when he realized each wore the 666 cut.

Traditionally in motorcycle clubs, the president rides at the front of the group. He's followed by club members in ranking order—vice president, sergeant at arms, road captain, and others in descending rank.

The club president removed his helmet and placed it on the gas tank of his bike before approaching Jack.

"You weren't going to start without us, were you, Hardcase?" Haniford asked, using the alias he'd chosen for Jack long ago because he wasn't always easy to work with.

"Wouldn't think of it," he said as more than a dozen people he knew and worked with at the department moved in his direction, every one of them having sloughed off their cop persona and were now looking like any other rough-and-ready biker. Many of them had their own bikes in the real world but had changed out personal plates for cold plates, as he should have done a week ago when he'd met Li.

Harry threw down the kickstand of her black Sportster and

dismounted. With her helmet off, she shook out her short blonde hair and checked her makeup in the mirror before heading his direction. Her late partner, David Perry, had given her the nickname Duchess which she used on meets like this one.

Wash met her as they crossed the road. He drove a vintage slate-blue Panhead and went by Baller because of his time playing football with the 49ers.

Bill Waters went by Wild Bill and drove a vintage Harley police bike, now painted in dark red and white. The bike had been adapted for two riders, as Bill and his wife, Lucinda, enjoyed long weekend rides and she rode pillion. What made Jack's heart thump harder was watching Bill's passenger dismount, knowing it wasn't his wife.

Ray!

Jack had to admit his friend fit right in with the others. His dark hair was tamed down with a wide black and white bandana, he'd fluffed out his already bushy mustache, and the cut fit as if it had been made for him. Looking at his friend's badass swagger as he sauntered over, Jack wondered if he'd be able to get him onto a bike of his own someday.

"Lobo refused to sit this one out," Haniford said, using Ray's new biker moniker. Lobo—the wolf. It suited him.

Cutter strolled away from his old bobber. He went by his real title—Doc. He was responsible for the test kits when the department made drug buys.

The air in Jack's lungs instantly dissipated when he saw a tiny woman trotting toward him in a set of skintight dark-red leathers; the matching corset top pushed up her small breasts. Ruby-colored cherries hung from her ears and caught the light off the headlamps. The look on her face was like a cat who got the pigeon—Amy Chin. He knew she did undercover work, but he'd never seen her on a 666 job before. Perhaps she'd got involved since he'd been off the force. Really, he didn't care, but did care about why she was on *this* job.

"What's *she* doing here?" Jack asked Haniford.

"She insisted on coming. Said she grew up in Chinatown and

speaks Mandarin and Cantonese. We can use her to interpret if it comes down to it."

Jack leaned in and murmured, "One of Li's thugs, the guy on the left," he indicated with a glance toward the shop window, "Kenny knows Amy through her brother. He got her brother Daniel a job working for Li. If Kenny recognizes her, we might as well kiss this deal, and our asses, goodbye."

"Got it. I'll keep her out here with the others and call for her if we run into any language barriers. It'll look suspicious if I send her away now."

Jack grumbled. Ignoring Chin's grin, he glanced at the rest of the group, nodding his appreciation to each for coming out.

"We're ready to rock and roll when you are, Hardcase," Haniford said.

"Then let's dance, Prez."

As Haniford was in charge of the 666s as a department organization, he laid claim to the role as president of the club.

Haniford pointed to Harry, Wash, Ray, Bill, and Cutter to follow. He instructed the rest of the club members to keep an eye on things outside and to listen for signs of trouble from inside the shop.

Just as Kai was about to close and lock the door behind them, Chin slipped through and rushed to Jack's side. He wasn't sure whose scowl was darker, his or Haniford's, but neither said anything.

"You will explain the meaning of this," Li bellowed.

"You didn't expect me to come here alone and do a deal with you in the dark, did you?" Jack nodded toward the men surrounding Li. "And you?"

Li frowned. Had his decisions never been questioned? He jerked his head and one of the men closest to the wall reached over and turned on the shop lights. "They are here for my protection."

"And this is *my* protection."

"An unnecessary one. We are here to make a deal, are we not?"

"I'm not a fool, Li," Jack said, thanking God Haniford had decided to bring in backup. He hadn't wanted to do this deal on his own, but if he wanted to find Leah, going it alone was what he had to do. "We're talking about a lot of cash. Alone, what would stop one of your loose cannons from taking me out? My associates are here to prevent that from happening. We don't want to become one of your . . . disappeared."

Li looked startled. Good.

"Explain yourself," Li insisted.

Jack casually shifted his weight to one side. "You have a long reputation for eliminating those who don't agree with you. It's how you took over Chinatown. Gang war shit. Everyone knows what you did." Jack's heart pounded harder. "And we heard about what you did to those people when this shop was robbed a couple years ago."

Li's eyes narrowed. "I know of no such robbery."

Jack snorted. "Really. Armstrong led me to believe you were some kind of Chinese badass. Are you telling me he lied?"

"A mouth like his could get him, as you say, disappeared."

"Don't get your fur up, Li. He was protecting your reputation. I mean, not everyone could disappear five people in one night . . . six if you include the kid's dog." Jack's heart leapt into his throat. Zoë wasn't just *a kid*. She was *his child*. "You ghosted all those people without a thought. Not only two of the robbers, but your own shop employee, and a woman *and* her baby."

"A baby?" Wash said with a deep gasp. "Man, that's some cold-hearted shit right there."

Jack gave Wash a side glance but kept his focus on Li. "Ain't it just. So forgive me for protecting my ass, and my assets." He leaned onto his other leg. "I'm curious about one thing, Li."

"What is that?"

"Where's the woman? You killed her kid and her dog, but she was never found. What happened to her? You disappeared her *real* good."

Li glanced beside him to Kai, whose scowl darkened. Kai said something in Chinese. Then Li asked, "What is it to you what happened to her? She's nobody."

"Curious, is all."

"Come on, Hardcase," said Haniford. "Let's get this deal done."

Jack hated leaving without finding out what happened to Leah, but Li never denied he knew anything about what happened that night. Instead, Jack nodded and said, "It's all good, Prez. If Mr. Li here is so good with hiding people who piss him off, maybe he can handle some of our problematic associates."

Haniford crossed his arms. He gave a short grunt and jerk of his head toward Li, telling Jack to carry on.

"What do you say, Li? Are you up for some extra work?"

Li gave Jack a long look, as if sizing him up. "First we make this deal. After, if we decide to work together again, we can talk of expanding our relations." He snapped his fingers. "*Sōusuǒ tāmen.*" Kenny and Kai instantly stepped around Li and started patting down Jack and the others.

"They're armed, Mr. Li," Kai said, stepping back, hand going to the 9mm tucked into the waistband of his black pants.

"You will remove your weapons before we continue," Li said.

"And what about your men?" Haniford asked. "You want us defenseless if your little tweaker here," he gestured to Kenny, "decides to go all Billy the Kid on us?"

"I trust my men. I do not trust yours."

"I have the same feeling about your boys," Haniford said.

"If you want to deal with the Jade Dragons, you play by our rules. Remove your weapons and give them to my associates while we talk, or . . . you are free to leave." Li shrugged as if he didn't care about the deal one way or another. "Of course, they will be returned to you when you leave."

Jack and Haniford exchanged glances. The others behind them grumbled their disapproval at being relieved of their protection, but Haniford motioned for the group to surrender their weapons anyway. Each pulled out their handgun and set it on top of a glass cabinet nearest to them. Kai nodded when he was satisfied everyone was disarmed.

When Kenny reached for the saddlebag, Jack jerked it away. "I don't think so, squit."

"You must allow my man to relieve you of all weapons," Li insisted.

"This isn't a weapon. If we come to an agreement on the drugs, you can have what's inside. Until then, it stays with me." Jack glared at Kenny. He watched to see if there was any fear in the guy. More so, he wanted to know if he recognized Chin in her getup. He hadn't even glanced her way since they'd stepped into the shop.

"Very well," Li said, motioning Kenny to back off. "Now explain who these people are. I assumed I was only dealing with you."

"I organize the buys." Jack nodded in Haniford's direction. "Our president approves all new deals. If he thinks anything about the deal is hinky—"

"Hinky," Li cut in. "What does this mean?"

"Hinky . . . makes us feel nervous, doesn't seem right, smells rotten. If Prez thinks anything smells rotten, we're out of here." Li seemed to accept this explanation, so Jack continued. "Doc here is our chemist. He'll test your product to make sure it's what you say it is."

Li scowled as much as his scar would allow him, but he didn't challenge Jack. "And what of the rest of these people? Certainly, you don't require so many people to make this deal."

"We're all here to make sure what you're selling is what our customers are buying. Lobo here focuses on our Brown market . . . the Hispanics." Jack motioned to each as he introduced them to Li. "Baller and Wild Bill sell to the Blacks. Duchess caters to the LGBTQ and similar communities around the Bay Area. Prez and I cater to everyone else." Jack hoped Li wouldn't notice he'd left Chin out of the equation, but after Kenny whispered something in Li's ear, he noticed Li's good eye narrow in her direction.

"And this one? The Asian market?" Li asked.

Jack saw Chin's cheeks pinken and wondered what that was about. There was no room for embarrassment in situations like this. To Li, he said, "We'd never step on your toes. Chinatown is yours. Japantown, Koreatown . . . All the Asian markets are yours."

"Then what is her purpose? Or is she just, how you say? Eye candy." There was as much of a sneer in his voice as on his face. Had Kenny recognized her as Daniel Chin's sister?

"She's our interpreter. Just to keep things honest. You understand."

Li stepped closer to Chin and bent to look her over. "She doesn't look like she speaks anymore Chinese than a *gwáilóu* reading a restaurant menu." Li's men laughed with him.

"*Nǐ xiǎng yào yìxiē ma?*" Chin made erotic gestures across her body, pushing herself up on her toes to get in Li's face. Jack's heart pounded hard. If Li recognized Chin as Daniel's sister, he'd instantly know they were all cops, and all of their covers would be blown. But so far, everything remained cool. When Chin huffed and her tone became angry, Jack swore to himself if she blew this deal for them, blew his chance at finding Leah, the little bitch would never hear the end of it. "*Nǐ mǎi bù qǐ wǒ de tángguǒ, lǎotóu,*" she spit.

As if sensing Jack's annoyance, Haniford put an arm between Chin and Li, forcing her to step back. "Put it away, Cherry," he said, glaring down at her. She pouted but stepped back in line with the others.

When Li chuckled, the scar on his face folded over on his cheek, making him appear even more grotesque. He pointed to Haniford and Cutter. "Your president and chemist may come with you. The others will wait here with my men."

"What about me? I'm the interpreter," Chin whined, looking between Jack and Haniford.

Haniford folded his arms in front of him and glared at Li. "We all have a stake in this, so we all go with you." The group behind them muttered their agreement. "We let you take our weapons so you'll let us bring our people."

For a long moment, Li glared at each person in turn before muttering in Chinese as he turned toward the back door. Kenny and Kai herded Jack and the others through the door behind Li. Several of Li's crew brought up the rear, leaving the rest in the shop to keep an eye on the street out front.

What Jack had thought was an office on his previous visit turned out to be a short hallway with two doors—one labeled 浴室 with *YÙSHÌ* below and a toilet symbol below that, and the other at the end of the hall was labeled 私人的 with *SĪRÉN DE* and *PRIVATE.*

Beyond this door, Jack found himself entering the shop's storage area where overstocked merchandise was kept. A wall of boxes formed a sort of privacy wall, but as Li led the group around them, Jack was surprised to see a much larger warehouse open up.

As they were led between stacks of wooden crates, all marked with Chinese characters, Jack glimpsed the butt-end of what looked like a semiautomatic assault rifle under a crate lid that hadn't been properly closed. He gave Haniford a quick eye signal and knew the LT had also seen the weapon. Given Li's reputation, weapon sales were also part of his business, like the drugs, murder, and disappearing bodies. Judging by the number of crates, this confirmed he was very much involved in the dealing of illegal firearms too.

At the center of the warehouse, a large table had been set up. A scale sat in the middle of it beside a closed black briefcase. Two of Li's thugs stood over the case, arms crossed with menacing looks on their faces and nine mils tucked into the front of their belts.

Jack eyed the case. It certainly wasn't large enough to hold his order. Probably not even the fifty K worth he'd been asked to bring with him.

Before they reached the table, Li sharply nodded to Kenny and Kai who drew their nine mils from their waistbands and aimed them at Jack.

Chin gasped as she clutched Jack's arm.

Jack glanced around them. Several of Li's thugs came out of the woodwork, weapons also raised.

Shaking off Chin's grasp, Jack stepped forward and demanded, "What's this all about, Li? I thought we were here to make a deal."

Li narrowed his scarred gaze at Jack. "It seems things have changed . . . police inspector Jack Slaughter."

CHAPTER TWENTY-SIX

There was potential Li would reveal he knew Jack's real name but he thought it would've been done as soon as he entered the shop.

He drew himself up to full height, hoping his bulk would intimidate Li, but the smaller man didn't back down.

"I saw the tail you put on me last week." Jack huffed. "If those shits for brains had done their job correctly, you would know I haven't been a cop for four years. When I lost my family, any support the department had promised blew out the window. My *brothers in blue*," he spat, "called themselves family, but in the end, they abandoned me when I needed them the most."

"You lie," Li said.

In a way, Jack had felt let down by the department, but it was nowhere near the scale he now told Li. He hoped Haniford and the others understood this was part of the act. "When I was a cop, I made some connections with the Triple Sixes—Prez, Lobo, Doc, and others." He jerked his head at the group behind him. "When I needed help, they were there for me. Now *they're* my family. They have my back in ways the cops never did."

"Isn't this what every cop promises . . . to protect each other?"

"You'd think, right? That everyone wearing the same uniform belongs to the fraternity and you can trust they'll have your six no matter what? It's all bullshit. For most cops, the badge just means superiority and nothing more. Look at the news, man, and you'll see cops abusing that power every day." Jack handed the saddlebag full of cash to Haniford, turned halfway then thumbed over his shoulder, indicating the patch on the back of his cut. "This means something. *They* mean something. Except for marrying my wife and my daughter's birth, the day I was patched in was the proudest day of my life. I've sworn my life and my blood to every one of my fellow Sixers." He turned back to face the drug lord. He lowered his voice and said, "The loyalty you have from your gang comes from fear. You wouldn't die for any of them and they know it. You're all about how much money you have and keeping your thugs so scared of you they'll do anything you ask just to stay alive. And if they fail you . . . disappeared. So what? There's always someone else to take their place, right?" They all knew Li killed anyone who got in his way. Prosecuting him for it was another story.

"Yes," Li hissed. "If they fear me, they won't steal from me."

"But where is the loyalty? And respect." Jack jerked his head to the thugs surrounding them. "You don't have even fearful respect. Just fear. For us, it's not about the money. What we make is shared equally within the family. And we take care of the families left behind when one of our own lays down his or her life for us. Can you say the same?"

His heart pounded so hard he felt the blood pulsing through his body, but he refused to break eye contact with Li, even as Haniford stepped up beside him and said, "Starting to smell hinky if you ask me, brother."

When Li remained quiet for too long, Jack said, "Shit or get off the pot. If we're going to do business, let's stop comparing cock size and get down to it. If not, there's always someone else who'll do business with us."

As one, the group took a step forward to stand with Jack. Chin moved out from behind Jack and clutched his arm again.

A long moment later, Li finally stepped away and ordered his men to stand down. "Such dedication to your family. I admire this. We will negotiate, and if it pleases me, you may be useful to me in the future."

Li moved to the opposite side of the table with Kenny and Kai in their usual flanking positions—Kenny to Li's left and Kai to his right. The others maintained their positions around the Sixers but had holstered their weapons. Li nodded to Kenny to open the

K.A. Lugo

briefcase. He did and spun it toward Jack.

"What's this all about, Li?" Jack demanded, still buzzing from the confrontation. The briefcase contained four tightly wrapped packages of equal size.

"You were correct. Logan has been developing a new product for me."

Li indicated with a thin finger to Kenny who produced a small clear pouch from his pocket. He opened it and scattered the contents onto the gray weighing scale tray.

"Candy?" Jack growled.

"Armstrong calls these *Little Dragons*." Li palmed a small, glistening green tablet to show Jack the dragon imprinted on the surface. "Appropriate, don't you think?"

"Yeah, real cute."

Haniford stepped closer to look at the tablets. "What's this shit, Hardcase?"

"This, Mister President," Li said, "is unlike anything else you will find anywhere in the world."

"What the hell's in it that makes it special? Look how small it is." Haniford's chuckle was echoed by the Sixers.

"Yǒu shí, zuìxiǎo de biānpào huì fāchū zuì xiǎngliàng de bàozhà shēng."

The men turned to Chin for the translation of Li's statement.

"Sometimes the smallest firecracker makes the loudest bang," Chin said.

"Correct." Li sounded surprised at Chin's accurate translation. "Anyone who takes just one of these will feel its effects within a few minutes and will last through the night."

"You're living in a fantasy world, Li," Haniford said. "Nothing lasts that long."

Li held the tablet closer to Haniford. "You try, then you tell me if I lie. This one tablet will give you everything you desire—euphoria without hallucinations, infinite energy, increased alertness, lower inhibitions but without losing free will. And more." Jack nearly laughed, thinking Li sounded like an old-world snake oil salesman, but he held it together. "Just one of

184

these reveals your true self and allows you to fulfill your desires." He nodded toward Chin then looked at Jack. "You want to fuck this one all night? You can do it. Orgasm make you cry."

"*Wǒ huì ràng nǐ zài wǒ de jiǎoxià kūqì, lǎotóu.*" Chin stomped her foot, but Li only chuckled.

"You are too bold for such a small woman, but you come to my bed, and I will make *you* cry until you beg for mercy."

Jack spluttered at the thought. "What makes you think I can't do that already?" Why was he baiting the man?

Li held the tablet toward Jack. "Ride the dragon and see."

"Nah, I don't shit where I eat." Li tossed the tablet back on the scale and shrugged. "Whoever called me said you wanted fifty K but didn't say it was for this. I know it won't pay for the quantities of narcotics I asked for, so are we now talking about fifty for the pills or a down payment on the shit I ordered?"

"You are direct. I like that." Li grinned, folding his hands in front of him.

Jack glanced at Haniford who said, "Let's get this over with. We came to make a deal, so let's do it. It's getting late and my old lady is waiting for me at home."

"I hate chewing on bones, Li, so let's get to the meat. If we're talking about the pills, what are we looking at . . . weight and cost?"

The pills had a much better likelihood of getting Li more prison time over common street drugs, but of course, amounts mattered. Since the Little Dragons were a new drug, it's likely they hadn't been tested beyond a couple of Li's volunteers. Haniford would want to get them into the lab as soon as he could to determine the compound and if they had the potential to kill anyone.

Hadn't Armstrong told him previous incarnations of the drug had made people sick?

"So, you wish to negotiate on this product. Does it mean you will no longer require the other items you requested?" Li asked.

Jack glanced again at Haniford who nodded quickly. "Yeah, we still want the other shit, but if this is as good as you say it is, we definitely want in on this too."

Li looked between Jack and Haniford before saying, "Very well. Let us make a deal. We will go to my office."

"We're good right here," Haniford said. "Unless you have a problem with that. The product is here, scales are here, and Doc with his test kits."

"Very well. I had thought we could negotiate as gentlemen in the comfort of my office over a cup of Longjing tea—our ancestral Dragon tea—to celebrate our collaboration."

"Do we look like we drink tea, *puta*," Ray blurted, his tone full of attitude. Jack lifted an eyebrow in his friend's direction. Ray had been silent until now but his outburst made their group chuckle.

"Lobo." Haniford's low voice warned Ray to keep himself in check.

Li jerked his head at Kenny who pulled out each of the four tightly wrapped packages from the briefcase and put them on the scales one at a time. Jack silently calculated as each package was weighed—two kilos in all . . . two point two pounds.

Cutter then stepped forward and extracted several single use reagent test kits. Each kit tested for different drugs. Everyone watched as he added a tablet from each package and crushed it into the liquid in the small pouches. Each changed colors in turn.

Several minutes later, Cutter said, "I've got X, meth, LSD, and trace methaqualone."

"Quaaludes?" Jack asked, using one of the street names for methaqualone, also known as just *ludes*.

Cutter nodded. "I haven't seen disco biscuits in years. I thought they dropped out when the hippies did." He glanced from Jack to Li. "We need to talk with your chemist and see if he's making his own quaaludes or if he's a buyer."

"Good idea, Doc," Haniford said, "but I'm sure this product has been tested. It's safe, right?" he asked, glaring up at Li.

"Of course," Li replied.

Cutter held up the last kit. "Something else is testing positive but I don't know what it is. Bring in the chemist and he can put our minds at ease."

Jack put up a hand. "We know where to find Li if this shit is hinky. For now, let's concentrate on what's in front of us."

Cutter nodded and stepped back from the table.

They had enough here to take down Li. The lab would eventually confirm the last drug. Even if the two kilos of pills had just been X or meth, the prosecutors would be very happy to take Li to trial.

"There are one thousand pills in each package. This is why you have brought me fifty thousand dollars." Li nodded to the saddlebags still draped over Haniford's shoulder.

"What about the other gear I ordered?"

Li rattled off another amount for the weights of coke, heroin, and meth totaling the fifty thousand. "If you would prefer to use your money on that, I am happy to have my men bring the drugs here and take away the pills. It is your choice."

"What if we want both?" Jack asked.

Li grinned crookedly through his scar. "What is the saying? Show me the money."

Looking at Haniford, he flicked a glance toward the crates of weapons they'd passed. The LT nodded.

Jack took the saddlebags from Haniford and emptied the bundles of money out onto the table. "Fifty grand for the pills now. When you have the gear I ordered, we'll come back with money for that."

"Agreed."

Li motioned to Kenny who quickly transferred the pills into the saddlebags and the cash into the briefcase, then closed both before handing the briefcase to one of the thugs behind him. He exited through a door at the back of the warehouse. At the same time, Jack handed the saddlebags to Haniford who passed them back to Waters.

Money and product had exchanged hands. The deal was made, and now Li was done. He just didn't know it yet. But Jack wanted to be sure Li went down for a very long time.

"Let's talk about those." Jack thumbed over his shoulder to the crates.

Li slowly looked up at Jack. "Please explain."

"You're not just dealing drugs, man," Jack said enthusiastically. He quickly went to the crate with the loose lid and slid it off. He'd been correct the first time. Inside the pine crate were ten AK-47 assault rifles in a five over/five under nesting configuration. One end of the crate was filled with magazines and at the other end were boxes of 39mm rounds.

Jack grinned as he lifted out a rifle from the rack plate inside the crate. He turned the weapon back and forth in his hands, inspecting it. He jerked his head at Ray. "Lobo. Check these out."

Li's men became agitated when Ray rushed to Jack's side, but Li motioned for them to hold back. From the corner of his eye, Jack saw several hands move to the handguns tucked in waistbands and holstered under jackets, but Li's thugs remained in place.

Li said, "These weapons are promised to another buyer. I would be happy to negotiate with you if we happen to come across these items again."

"That's not gonna work for us. We want *these* weapons. We don't want to wait, and we have the cash. You can find more AKs for your other buyer."

"I cannot do that, Jack."

"What's it gonna take to sell us *these* guns?" Haniford asked, moving over beside Jack and lifting an AK from its rack plate to inspect.

"You don't understand," Li said. "These weapons have already been purchased. I cannot sell you something which has already been sold."

Haniford said, "We'll match whatever they paid and add ten percent. Call it a *getting to know you* bonus."

Li was quiet for a long moment before saying, "I will contact my supplier and ask for what you want."

"These are what we want," Jack insisted, taking another weapon out of the crate. "You can either give us a price for these crates, or we'll just take them."

In his peripheral vision, Jack saw Ray and Haniford quietly loading rounds into the magazines and carefully placing them into the AKs. Ray flicked him a glance, telling Jack to swap weapons with him. He loaded a magazine into that weapon as well.

Ray lifted his weapon from the crate and aimed it toward the ceiling and various points around the room. "These are real sweet, *ese*."

Time seemed to move in slow motion as Kenny and Kai flipped the table on its side and pushed Li down behind it. Moments later, the thugs spread out from opposite sides of the table and drew their nine mils as they moved toward Jack and the others.

Jack swung his AK around and aimed it at the approaching men, but the threat of the AK didn't stop their advance.

Kai was the first to fire. The bullet shattered the corner of a nearby crate. The splinters felt like a dozen wasps stinging Jack's cheek and neck. *Fuck!* His heart thudded hard and his breath caught. That was too close for comfort. Jack and Haniford's team dove behind the crates for protection.

Between the crates, Jack saw Kenny split off from Kai, both men now firing in Jack's direction. Everywhere the bullets hit sent sharp slivers of timber arcing over them.

Thugs from around the warehouse came out of hiding, firing too as they rushed forward.

Aiming the AK around the crate, Jack randomly fired off a few rounds as Ray pulled out more boxes of bullets from the crates and helped Haniford and the rest arm themselves.

Jack's AK clicked, telling him he was out of bullets. Ray thrust a freshly loaded weapon into his hands and refilled the empty magazine before carefully rising over the crate to see where Li's men were.

Haniford whispered loudly down the ranks. "Try not to kill anyone. Just hold them back. SWAT'll be here any minute if they heard the gunfire."

Jack fired a few more rounds then quickly looked down the row of crates. Everyone was armed except Amy Chin. She crouched on the floor like a frightened child, with her hands over her ears.

Jesus, Jack swore to himself. He didn't need to babysit her at a time like this. Thank God she remained where she was at Cutter's side.

Cutter.

His peace-loving friend had done a one-eighty and looked every bit the pissed off biker as he let go several rounds with a growl.

Jack turned his head and peered between the crates again. Kenny and Kai had rushed back to Li behind the tipped over table and crouched behind it.

Jack took a deep breath and rose. He spun the AK around and carefully fired a single round into the ceiling just above Li. Debris rained down over the three.

"What's this all about, Li?" Jack shouted above the sound of whistling bullets. "I thought we were just talking."

"This is not talking," Li shouted from behind the table. His men stopped shooting but kept their guns trained in Jack's direction.

"Your man fired first. There was no call for that. We're still negotiating." When Li remained silent, Jack added, "To show good faith, we'll put down the AKs. Tell your boys to back off so we can complete our business with you."

A moment later, Li's men back-stepped toward the shadows.

As promised, Jack laid his weapon on top of the closest crate and slowly stepped out from behind the pine boxes, elbows bent at his waist, hands raised to show he was weaponless. Ray and Haniford remained where they were, weapons at the ready.

"Isn't this much better?" Jack asked. He heard Li grunt from behind the table. "Show yourself and let's talk like men. We want the AKs and I kinda think you want the money."

"You don't understand. If I let you take these weapons, a man more powerful than you or I will become very angry."

"Not my problem," Jack said. "Tell us what you want for these. We're taking them with us, one way or another."

Li was silent for a moment before calling out to his men in Chinese. As Jack waited for the drug lord's decision, Chin rushed up to the edge of the crates and whispered, "Jack, he's giving his men orders to surround us and take us out. Take cover. All hell is about to break loose."

Jack and Haniford exchanged a quick glance as Li's thugs started moving in opposite directions around the warehouse. Jack rushed back behind the crates just as bullets started flying again.

Haniford fired his weapon toward the ceiling; the rapid burst of bullets ricocheting off the timber beams and sending chunks fanning out across the warehouse. Li's men dove for cover.

"Your nine mils aren't a match for the AKs. Back off now and we'll let you walk out of here," Jack shouted.

Li roared from behind the table. "You come into my house and disrespect me like this?"

"Your man fired first, Li. If you want to play hardball, we're ready. Remember what I said. My family is prepared to die for me," Jack said. "Can you say the same?"

Li shouted again in Chinese. Jack turned to Chin, who interpreted. "He asks what they're waiting for. He gave them orders to kill us."

For a moment, the warehouse was filled with silence. Were Li's thugs thinking about what Jack had said about loyalty?

Suddenly, Kai rushed out from behind his cover. Screaming in Chinese, he lifted his weapon and started firing as he ran toward Jack. Bullets flew in erratic trajectories, but Jack and the others were tucked safely behind the crates.

From behind a nearby crate, Harry quickly rose, aimed her AK and let off one single shot. Kai jerked back, his feet momentarily off the ground before his lifeless body landed hard, back first, onto the filthy concrete. Blood quickly flowed from the wound in his head.

"Who's next?" Jack asked.

Jack saw movement from the corner of his eye and turned to see a dark shadow move out from behind a steel rack full of cardboard boxes marked with Chinese characters. The shadow drew up his weapon on an extended arm and aimed it in Jack's direction. Jack quickly reached for the AK on the crate beside him and felt someone punch him in the back, throwing him against Chin. He lost his balance and fell to the floor where Chin screamed as she held him.

Ray fired into the shadows. A yell was followed by a thump. "Got him," Ray growled.

Just then, the door on the Grant Avenue side of the building banged open.

"FBI. Everybody, drop your weapons. Get on the ground, face down!" shouted an agent. Jack heard the group rushing around the warehouse and weapons hitting the hard concrete floor.

Almost immediately after the FBI's entry from the rear of the warehouse, another team entered through the shop door. Officers swept their Heckler and Koch MP5s along the backs of the crates. Jack's team had already tossed down the AKs and had their hands over their heads.

"On the floor . . . on the floor *now!*" several officers shouted as they fanned out around Jack and the others. Everyone else did as they were told, but Chin kept holding him tightly.

He turned his head and watched SWAT officers move in quickly to strap flexicuffs onto Haniford and the team's wrists and perform standard pat downs before hauling them, one by one, to their feet and frog marching them out of the warehouse through the shop door.

An officer towered over Jack with his weapon aimed at him. "I said on the floor. Now."

Jack's head swam as adrenaline coursed through him. What else did this guy want from him? He was already on the floor.

Chin's voice sounded like it was coming from somewhere behind him. "He needs help. He's bleeding."

Another officer appeared from around the crate and pulled Jack off Chin and tossed him to the floor, face down. Instantly, he was gasping for air. He struggled to breathe as the officer knelt onto him and performed his pat down.

Chin rushed toward him but was pulled off by the officer who had been patting him down. Jack saw him lift her off the ground like a child as he hauled her against the crates, forced her arms behind her and cuffed her before carrying her kicking and screaming from the warehouse.

He realized then how much his back hurt where the officer had knelt onto him. His vision swam with the pain.

Jack slowly turned to face the other direction and saw a pool of blood beside him.

"Get that board in here. Now!" shouted the officer standing over him.

Jack closed his eyes against the pain, felt himself pulling away from consciousness.

He was jostled back to awareness as he was lifted, then he was rocked back and forth and jolted like he was on some crazy amusement park ride. Only he wasn't laughing.

Loud voices drew nearer and suddenly he was in the middle of the cacophony. Cold air washed over him. He briefly snapped open his eyes as a mask was positioned over his mouth and nose, forcing clean oxygen into his lungs, but he still couldn't breathe. He tried lifting a hand to remove the mask, but his arm was heavy. His body was heavy. Even his eyelids as they obliterated his vision again.

Whatever he was lying on was jostled again, then it landed roughly on a hard surface. He groaned. White lights screamed behind his eyelids. He tried opening them again but couldn't. Where was he? He felt himself floating.

He was thrown to one side and his skin prickled from repeated poking. He attempted to brush whatever it was away, but his arm and hand refused to move.

His mind was dark. He felt himself pulling away from the heaviness, from the pain. The fight went out of him and his body relaxed.

Somewhere around him came a long, shrill sound.

"We're losing him!" someone shouted.

The last thoughts in Jack's mind were those happy times when he'd come home after work to find his family waiting for him in the kitchen. His heart swelled with love and the expectation of being reunited with them at last.

He heard himself whisper, "Is this what it's like to die?" just as he slipped away.

CHAPTER TWENTY-SEVEN

Sunday – April 11

Jack lifted the remote with a shaky hand to turn off the TV, then set it on his tray table. Sunday morning news had just recapped the takedown at Dragon's Lair.

He glanced beside him. Ray had been the first person Jack saw when he'd opened his eyes earlier in the morning. The nurse had told him Ray hadn't left his side since he'd been rushed into emergency surgery after the bust. It had been dark outside when he'd awakened so he'd thought it was still early Saturday morning, not Sunday.

Ray had updated Jack on everything, from the takedown through his life-saving surgery to remove the nine millimeter round and repair his damaged organs.

Jack winced when Ray told him he'd flatlined in the ambulance. It had taken EMTs more than three long minutes to bring him back. Doctors had told Ray, had the round been just a millimeter closer, it would have nicked the artery to his heart, and Jack would have bled out before the ambulance had arrived on scene.

The news he'd died, even for three minutes, stole what little breath he had.

If he'd been dead, where had his family been? Where was Nick? Where was his mother? If he'd truly been dead, there had only been darkness.

He scowled. Was that what he'd have faced if his Beretta hadn't misfired?

His stomach tightened with the thought he'd actually gone to

Hell—but where was the fire and brimstone?

Maybe he'd been cast into Limbo, but hadn't he suffered in Limbo the last four years?

Jack turned his gaze to the other side of the bed where Haniford occupied another visitors' chair, one ankle resting over the opposite knee. He'd arrived just before the news began and had updated Jack on the FBI debriefing. He knew it was a courtesy on Haniford's part, but Jack appreciated it.

One thing confused him though. What had made Haniford decide to bring in backup after all his posturing and insisting Jack was going in alone?

"Jack, you still with us?" Haniford asked.

Jack snapped out of his reflection. "I'm listening," he said, somewhat breathless.

"As I was saying," Haniford continued, "the operation couldn't have gone any smoother."

Jack choked back a grumble. "Yeah, real *smooooth*." He glared at Haniford for a long minute, sizing up how to get the answers he needed. When Haniford didn't speak, Jack inhaled as much as he could and rasped, "Is there anything you want to tell me?"

A groove formed between Haniford's eyebrows. "What do you mean?"

"How about the bit where you sent me in on my own? You were pretty adamant about that. I spent two days putting my affairs in order . . ."

"That's the truth, Lieutenant," Ray said. "I went to his place the other day and he gave me a key to a safety deposit box and the authorization paperwork to access it. Paraphrasing here, but he said if things went tits up, someone had to deal with his shit. Honestly, by the way Jack was acting, I didn't think I'd ever see him again. It scared the shit out of me."

Jack caught the weak smile on his friend's face before looking back at Haniford, waiting for an answer he could believe.

Finally, Haniford said, "I guess we didn't exactly leave our last conversation on the best terms, did we? I know I forced you to put aside your reasons for seeing Li and go in undercover for us . . .

for the task force." Haniford nodded toward the hospital bed and added, "Maybe now's not the time to discuss this."

He wasn't letting Haniford off lightly for what he'd done or for the things he'd said. "No, we didn't; yes, you did; and this is the perfect time. And don't give me the *it is what it is* bullshit." Jack's lungs burned on his raised voice and he breathed through the cough he felt coming.

"Honestly?"

"Nothing but," Jack insisted.

"I was furious with you, and Ray. I still am. I don't want to get into another heated argument, but with Ray continually allowing you to ride shotgun on investigations—"

Jack cut in. "You're pulling Ray's promotion." His gut twisted at the thought.

"Nothing like that," Haniford replied, "but things are changing in the department, and how you treat the department has to change too."

Before Haniford could finish, Ray said, "Lieutenant, I knew Jack would investigate the Rybak case on his own. That's his job. I thought if I kept him close—"

"Goddammit, Ray. I told you I don't need a babysitter," Jack snapped, but the effort took his breath away, making him cough like an asthmatic. He took several shallow breaths to calm himself.

"Ray letting you tag along, even when I explicitly told him to keep you out of things, pissed me off. You and I, Jack, would have had that conversation regardless of Friday night's operation. Since you were already involved with Li, I took the opportunity to, I don't know, teach you a lesson—"

"Teach me a lesson. What the fuck, *Dick*?" Jack ignored the wide-eyed stares he got when he emphasized Haniford's given name.

Jack's heart pounded hard. He felt like it pumped boiling blood through his aching body and struggled to remain composed to keep from breaking out into another coughing fit.

In a word, Jack was pissed. Both with Ray's insinuation he needed babysitting and now Haniford thinking he'd been teaching him some kind of lesson.

"I wanted you to sweat a little, like I do every time your name comes up in an investigation."

"Don't you think I've been doing a lot of my own sweating?" The sharp pains echoing through his body made him add, "I almost didn't go to the meet-up."

"Jack," Ray gasped, concern edging his voice.

"I'm sorry about that," Haniford said. "Believe me when I say I never intended on sending you in alone. That would have been insane. I just couldn't pass up the opportunity to remind you of your situation."

"You're saying it was all a bit of payback?" Jack asked between clenched teeth. Haniford shrugged in a noncommittal way. "Believe me, message received, loud and clear."

"Don't be like that," Haniford said.

"I get it," he fumed under his breath. He tried getting comfortable again, but the effort of trying to punch the pillows into submission made him wince. "I'm no longer on the force and have no business looking for favors from the department. The tie's been cut. I'll stay well clear." Matter-of-factly, he added, "Thanks for the support on Friday, but you can leave now and let me get on with picking up the pieces of my life." He threw himself back against the pillows in frustration, forcing himself to breathe calmly before he exploded.

Jack looked up when the nurse, Markus, rushed through the door to his side. "Are you all right, Mr. Slaughter? The monitors are going off at the nurses' station like a Saturday night disco ball."

"Sorry, Markus. Just trying to get comfortable. Not easy when you're weak as a puppy." Jack glared at Haniford.

Markus' bright smile accentuated the deep color of his complexion. His almond-shaped brown eyes with their long lashes hinted at a mixed heritage.

"Don't you worry, honey. You're still a big dog." He winked at Jack. The coy look on the nurse's face was obvious as he fluffed the pillows and helped him settle back. "You just need some TLC." Satisfied Jack was comfortable and had fresh water in his jug, he asked while making notes on Jack's chart, "Is there anything else I can get you while I'm here?"

"A whiskey is probably out of the question."

Markus chuckled. "I'm sure it's five o'clock somewhere in the world, sweetie, but sadly not here. If you're looking for something more exciting than water, I can sneak you in a cola or a mineral water."

"Thanks. Maybe later."

Markus looked between Ray and Haniford. "Can I get your friends something?"

Before the men could answer, Jack said, "No, they were just leaving."

"If you change your mind, just push the button." Markus moved the nurse's call handset closer to Jack then disappeared through the door.

Jack stared at the TV's black screen, trying to ignore the elephants in the room.

Finally, he said, "I don't know why you're still here, Dick. You said your piece."

"I'm not finished, Jack," Haniford replied.

Jack ignored him and gave Ray a sideways look. "You fell right into your Lobo persona. Think we'll actually get you on a bike one day?"

"I never said I can't ride, I just don't like to," Ray confessed.

"Until you prove otherwise, I'm gonna say you can't ride."

Haniford chuckled and brought the conversation back on point. "I have to say, Jack, you *do* have a set of brass balls on you." Jack's only reply was a lifted eyebrow in Haniford's direction. "I don't think I would have shown up for that meeting with Li on my own."

"It's not like I had a choice."

"You always had a choice," Haniford said. "You chose to meet Li."

"It was the only way to find out what happened to Leah. Even after what went down last night . . . Friday night . . . the only thing I learned is Li did have something to do with my wife's disappearance, but not where she is."

"Sorry about that, Jack, but this operation took priority."

Haniford's voice faded when Jack's mind went back to the warehouse. He knew he'd been making headway with Li and was just about to find out what happened to Leah when Haniford got the deal back on track.

Jack felt the heaviness return. A weight settled on his chest, and something constricted his throat, forcing him to take long, slow breaths, but for a different reason this time. He dug his fingers into the blanket he'd been fisting. All he'd cared about was finally finding Leah. He'd been *this* close . . .

"Jack?"

Haniford broke into Jack's thoughts again. He shifted his weight on the mattress but the pillows propping him up slipped and his wound screamed, bringing moisture to his eyes. Ray stood and helped Jack get comfortable before reseating himself. Jack nodded his thanks.

"I asked what made you take such dangerous side steps," Haniford said.

"What side steps?"

"We went in to buy coke and meth, then Li changed the deal. What's this *Little Dragons* thing all about?"

Jack reminded Haniford about Armstrong and his crew, one of whom blew his brains out in Jack's house. "Armstrong has been working on a new party drug for Li, and I suggested to Li we could add it to the rest of the deal. He'd brushed me off, but it looks like Armstrong came through at the eleventh hour. I figured, the more we could get on Li, the longer he'd go down for."

"Like with the AKs?"

Jack nodded. "More weight on his sentence."

"You leaned on him pretty hard."

"How else was I supposed to treat him? He's a murdering thug who lacks any moral conscience." Jack couldn't make it any clearer.

"I get it." After a moment, Haniford said, "Tell me what's going on between you and Chin."

Jack shook his head. "Absolutely nothing. I just don't like her. I was surprised to see her involved in the sting after I'd told you about meeting her—"

"Your date?" Haniford asked.

"Not a date," Jack corrected. "It was a business meeting to get her to tell us about her brother Danny. I came to you about her unprofessional behavior, so I was shocked seeing her Friday night."

"I wondered the same thing," Ray said.

Haniford looked between Jack and Ray. "You're not wrong about her being assertive."

"Assertive? Is that what you're calling her?" The woman was downright forceful. She'd already proved to him she could go the distance—hounding him for years to take her out, in spite of his repeated refusals.

"I was being nice," Haniford replied. "The point is, she wasn't on the task force. When she showed up, ready to go, it was too late to send her home. Before I could ask her what she thought she was doing, she said we'd need an interpreter since she knows Mandarin and Cantonese. I thought by keeping her outside while we met with Li there wouldn't be any trouble. I hadn't expected her to barge through the shop door. At that point—"

Jack nodded again. "At that point, you were all in, and she knew it. Just as she knew, if she made it clear to Li she was with me, he wouldn't have been suspicious unless I shrugged her off. He may already have been leery since Danny worked for Li until he disappeared, but he didn't give any indication he recognized her."

Ray shifted in his chair. "I'm not making excuses for her, but maybe she took the opportunity to find out what Li did with her brother. No one knows what happened to him either."

"Somehow I doubt it." Jack couldn't keep from scowling. He didn't care what Chin's motivations were. Just talking about her and her behavior pissed him off.

"By the look on your face, there's something else with Chin eating at you," Haniford said.

Jack ran shaky fingers through his hair, remembering how she'd clung to him after he'd been shot, her screaming in his ears.

"She's becoming a loose cannon, and I'm worried she'll do something stupid someday and put those around her at risk."

To Haniford, Ray said, "I've noticed Chin's behavior has changed too. Her concentration is off. During the stakeout at Christmas at the Majestic Lounge, she spent more time watching Jack than looking for our suspect. If we're being honest here, I don't trust her anymore to have my back."

Haniford put up his hand. "I get it, but as Jack is no longer with the department, there shouldn't be any reason for her to be anywhere near him, and I can't tell her what to do on her off-time unless it reflects on the department. At this point, she has a clean record. You know how this goes. Until she does something actionable while on the job, I can't touch her. Let's hope the Majestic Lounge and Friday night are two anomalies and she chooses to stay in her own lane going forward."

"That's fine to say, but I'm telling you, something's not right with that woman."

"I hear you, Jack. It didn't slip my notice how she hung back on Friday when things started going down rather than move into action like the trained officer she is. She refused an AK and froze when bullets started flying. She put herself and others in danger when she went to your side. She could have very well been the one shot. I'll require she sees the department shrink to make sure she's fit for duty."

"A shrink's a good idea," Ray agreed.

Jack nodded with another scowl.

"What's the scowl for?" Haniford asked.

Jack wasn't in the mood to beat around the bush so he gave it to Haniford straight. "I met Li with the express focus on finding Leah. You scuppered that by bringing me into the task force sting. Now Li's behind bars and I still don't know what he did with my wife."

"I'm sorry we had to bring you in this way, but we couldn't lose the opportunity to take down the Jade Dragons. We couldn't have done it without your help."

Jack glared at Haniford. "Make it up to me. Let me question Li."

Ray sat forward and looked at Haniford. Jack glanced between the two men. "What?"

"You gonna tell him or am I?" Ray asked.

Haniford grimaced and crossed his arms over his chest.

"What?" Jack repeated, louder this time, his glare deepening.

"Li's gone, Jack," Ray finally said. "This was a federal operation, and they took control of the prisoners."

Jack stared at his friend. "You're telling me I can't interview Li?" He turned a dark look on Haniford.

"Sorry, Jack," Haniford said. "We didn't know when you'd wake, or if you would. The feds couldn't wait to find out, so they took Li back to their headquarters for interrogation and processing."

"Shit!" Jack cursed. "Then we lean on Kenny. He has to know what happened to his friend. Finding out what happened that one night could answer questions for a lot of people."

Ray shook his head. "He was taken away with Li. It's all in the feds' hands now."

"Goddammit!" Jack shouted, flinching at the pain of air being forced from his lungs. He winced and dropped back to the pillows. "Did they take everyone?" Both men nodded. "What about Armstrong . . . him too?" Jack's gaze fell on Haniford. "What?"

"Remember when I said we had a CI working with the task force?" Haniford asked.

Jack slowly said, "Yeah."

"Armstrong was our CI."

"Are you shitting me? You brought in a junkie to inform on the gang?" Jack couldn't believe what he was hearing.

"Agent Carter told me after an initial interview with Li, that he knew Armstrong had been turned, but kept him alive to feed the task force false intel. That's why it took so long to take down the Jade Dragons." Haniford added, "Without you, we'd still be waiting."

Haniford's confession didn't make Jack feel any better, so he ignored it. "Did Armstrong know he was being played from both sides?"

Haniford shook his head in a noncommittal way. "We haven't been able to find him. Have you spoken with him?"

"No. Come to think of it, I haven't seen him since my intro with Li."

"We have a BOLO out on him, but so far nothing," Ray added.

Jack thought back to his chat with Armstrong in his kitchen. "He's been under Li's and the Jade Dragons' thumbs for years. He's probably taken the opportunity and fled the city."

"You're probably right. I swung by the *abuela's* house and the Trans Am is gone. She hasn't seen him in several days." Ray added, "I don't think there's any love lost there."

To Haniford, Jack asked, "Have the drugs come back from the lab yet?"

Haniford shook his head. "It's still early, but initial tests say it looks like the pills were a sham."

"What do you mean? Li said Armstrong came up with a new formula for the ultimate party drug. That's what he sold us. He blathered on about the potency of his new *Little Dragons*. I assumed he tried them himself."

Ray said, "Doubtful. He probably believed what Armstrong told him to make a sale."

Haniford shook his head. "Armstrong is a pretty ballsy guy. He might have got away with it."

"Tell me," Jack pushed.

Haniford sat forward with his elbows on his knees and looked up at Jack with a look he took as admiration for Armstrong. "According to the lab, Armstrong crushed up *sildenafil citrate*—"

"Wait," Jack cut in. "*Viagra?*"

"That's the trade name, but yeah. He crushed up the blue pills and added a colorant to change the powder to green, then mixed in some *methaqualone*—"

"Quaaludes? I thought ludes faded away with the seventies," Jack said.

"They're still around. Just not as in demand as X and the like," Haniford said.

Jack looked between the two men again. "What about Cutter's tests on the night? They came back for a number of drugs."

Ray chuckled. "Right, but the tablets had only been washed in those drugs. Like a candy coating. There was just enough to test positive, but the trace amounts wouldn't have given a very substantial high. Anyone taking those pills would have only had an all-night boner with an added feeling of euphoria."

Jack would have chuckled if his body didn't hurt so much. *That clever fuck!* If Armstrong hadn't been a CI for the FBI, there probably wasn't enough narcotics in the tablets to get him any jail time. Since he was running, he probably didn't know he was off the hook. Even if it would have earned him jail time, given his CI status, he would have got a walk.

CHAPTER TWENTY-EIGHT

Monday - Two weeks later – April 26

Jack stood in the dining area of his house and slowly looked around with disbelief. From the windows in the living room, past the dining area, and through the vacant kitchen to the back door, everything was gone. Curtains and blinds, carpets and linoleum, cabinets and appliances, and the bloodstained dining table. Even Rybak's bloody halo on the dining room wall had been removed.

He went upstairs and found all the rooms had been gutted too, right down to the fixtures for bathroom appliances.

Gone.

All of it.

What the hell had happened since he'd last been here with his Beretta?

When he hit the foot of the stairs, he found Ray standing in the open doorway, the stained glass of which had been repaired and refitted.

"I wanted to get here before you," Ray said without apology.

"What's this all about?" Jack forced himself to remain calm, in spite of his racing heart.

"Are you angry?"

"Confused. Care to explain?"

"Come on." Jack followed Ray into the living room to stand before the window. "I called in some favors and had the place gutted."

"I can see that. Why?"

"This house is like a boat anchor around your neck, *amigo*." Jack grunted then opened his mouth to speak, but Ray continued, "Let me finish. By clearing out the place, it should give you some breathing space. I know you planned to have the house gutted, but something always comes up. Now you have a clean palette to work from. Restore, sell, or leave it as is and board up the windows. Whatever you decide, there's nothing left to stand in your way from moving forward with your life."

Move forward with his life? Jack still didn't know what Li had done with Leah. Until he knew, how could he move forward with anything?

He gazed through the rooms, once filled with furnishings and family. The house now seemed to yawn with space.

He tried imagining new floors and repainted walls, furniture and new appliances, but all he saw was Leah, Zoë, and Trax, their laughter and love. Anything he did in the house would never replace those memories.

"You don't have to decide now," Ray added, "but the place is ready when you are."

Jack slowly turned toward his friend. "Thanks, Ray," he sincerely said. "And no, I'm not angry. I appreciate everything you've done. Let me know how much I owe—"

Ray put up his hand, telling Jack his friend wasn't taking his money.

Thumbing over his shoulder, Ray said, "I've got some garden tools out in the truck. It's such a nice day, I thought we could tame the weeds in the backyard. If you're up to it."

Jack took a last look around, still not believing what he was seeing, then nodded. "After nearly two weeks in the hospital, I'm ready for a good workout."

A couple hours into the job, Jack straightened his spine and leaned on the hoe he'd been using to clear the last patch of weeds near the ramshackle shed. Using the back of his hand, he wiped away the sweat from his eyes and inhaled deeply. It was a nice feeling, being able to breathe normally again. Agreeing to cardio therapy while in the hospital, to rebuild his strength and lung capacity, made weeding much easier.

He glanced across the yard and grimaced. Leah's beloved garden had been taken over by Mother Nature. Where once Leah had planted herbs and vegetables between colorful flowers, weeds had taken over and made the house look as abandoned as Jack had left it four years earlier.

Jack was grateful for everything Ray had done for him, despite all their arguing. Gutting the house was a big thing, but Ray also knew the yard needed to be put in order too. And today had been a great day for the task.

He gazed over at Ray, who was raking the last of the small piles into the larger one. There were no words to express how much Jack appreciated having such a good friend. *Hermanos de otra madre*—brothers from another mother, Ray always said. He wasn't wrong.

Jack looked around at their handiwork. The only color in the yard came from a big echium in one corner with its large springtime dark-purple cones reaching for the sun. A California lilac covered in large green leaves and fist-size lavender blossoms had pushed itself up and over the shed in the opposite corner. Jack hated the idea of cutting it back, but the shed was falling apart, and he couldn't remove it without pruning the lilac.

"Ready for a break?" Ray asked, pulling Jack out of his thoughts.

"More than ready."

Ray propped the rake against the porch rails. "I have a cooler in the truck with some beers on ice. Be right back."

In the few minutes Ray was gone, Jack placed the hoe beside Ray's rake and sat on one of the porch steps in the shade, dragging his fingers through his sweaty hair. If he'd known he'd be working in the yard, he would have brought a cap.

Ray appeared then with a small cooler and set it beside Jack then sat on the next step down. Jack opened the cooler and pulled out two beers from the icy water before handing one to Ray.

"Thanks. I needed this." Jack popped open the can and took a long slug.

Ray did the same, then said, "I think we made great progress. Not much left to do but take away the debris."

Jack pointed his can toward the shed. "I want to take it down while we're at it, before it falls down on its own." Ray nodded his agreement.

The two men sat in companionable silence, but it wasn't long before Jack caught a look on his friend's face he recognized well.

"Something's on your mind," he said.

Without looking over, Ray replied, "I don't know what you mean."

"I know the look. For fuck's sake, whatever you have to say, just say it."

Ray threw back the last of the beer and cracked open another one, but held onto it. "This is unofficial. Completely off the books."

"And?"

"We questioned Li."

Those three simple words hit Jack in the chest like he'd been shot again and choked off his air. Finally, he said, "We who?"

"Special Agent Carter let Haniford and me sit in with her at FBI headquarters."

"Tell me you asked him about Leah." Even to himself, it sounded like he was begging. He was.

"He only agreed with what went down that night because it was off the record, but he couldn't tell me anything about Leah."

Jack sat forward on the step and stared at his friend. "What does that mean? I feel there's a *but* coming."

"Remember when I said those men would have been looking for you that night? If Li sent Rybak and Armstrong to your house, they would have been looking for the money from *you*."

Jack nodded. "I never borrowed money from him. So what . . . did he send them to a random address, and it just happened to be my house?"

"He gave them the right address."

Jack screwed up his face. "What the fuck are you talking about? Those assholes killed my daughter and kidnapped my wife!" he all but shouted.

Ray turned to face Jack, his gaze intent as he spoke. "Jack. It was the right family. Just not *your* family. It wasn't Zoë or Leah. There was another family in this house before you bought it."

"What?" Jack growled.

"We went through property records. It appears the house had been on the market for an unusually long time. Haniford and I agree, they probably couldn't sell the place because no one wanted to buy a house where murders had taken place. Then you came along, and they never disclosed the full facts to you and Leah."

Jack took the deepest breaths his damaged body would allow, trying to process what his friend had just said. He continued staring at Ray as the implications sunk in, looking for some sign this was a joke, but there wasn't a hint of humor on his friend's face.

"Who was it?" Jack finally asked.

"Hannah Caplan and her daughter, Jenny. John Caplan had been out that night—" He let the last go unsaid then quietly added, "This was a full two years before you bought the house."

Not my family.

This information rained down on Jack like fire. How could he have been so wrong? He recalled his talk with Armstrong. Everything the junkie had told him shouted it had been his family, right down to the dog, even though he couldn't justify his own role in it all. He'd never borrowed money from anyone but the bank, and he certainly would have been home that time of night unless he was on a case.

He scrubbed a hand across his face, trying to make sense of it all, but there was no sense to make. It wasn't his family. It had all gone down long before he and Leah had bought the house. It had never been disclosed about the murders; he would have remembered. And during renovations, there hadn't been any evidence of blood. He recalled though how he'd mentioned to Leah how the subfloors had been in such good condition. Had they been new? He made a mental note to check out the floors when he went back inside.

"You okay, Jack?"

Was he? In this moment, Jack didn't know anything.

He slammed his beer down, shot off the step and stomped across the yard to the shed. Anger boiled through him and poured from his skin. The shed needed to come down and his anger would make light work of it. He heard Ray rush up behind him as he threw the first kick. The door swung on its rusty hinges and fell to the side.

"Jack. Take it easy. I know this must be hard, but I couldn't keep it from you."

Jack glanced at Ray. "I'm fine," he spat. "I just want to get the yard done." He grabbed the shed door and tore it from its remaining hinge and threw it across the yard.

"Let's cut back this triffid. It'll be easier getting at the shed," Ray suggested.

Jack stepped to the side and fisted one of the branches, twisted and pulled it free of the bush. He repeated the action until the plant hung in tatters and broken branches were scattered on the ground.

"Come on, Jack. Do you want to end up back in the hospital?"

"Help or get out of my way," Jack grumbled.

Ray moved in front of Jack and stood in the doorway. "Take a beat."

He went inside and started handing Jack things stored on the old shelves—paint cans, old containers of fertilizer, rusty tools, stacks of plastic pots . . . Jack threw them into a fresh pile beside the lilac branches.

When Ray emerged, Jack pushed past him and started dismantling the old structure. It didn't take much effort. Shelves easily popped off their brackets, the decaying roof was pulled down with little effort, and with a few well-aimed shoves, the walls tumbled to the ground.

Jack stood back, panting hard and gasping for air. His chest hurt with the effort. He dropped his hands onto his knees and took slow, deep breaths to calm himself.

The shed could have been ten times larger, and he still would have been just as pissed off as he still was now. Nothing would change the reality of what Ray told him. It wasn't his family. Li knew nothing about Leah. And likely, Rybak's *I'm sorry* note was probably because he'd killed little Jenny Caplan and her pet, and he could no longer live with himself. He went back to the scene of the crime—the now abandoned house—to make what he probably saw as reparations.

"You okay, *ese*?" Ray asked after giving Jack time to cool his jets.

He shook the sweat out of his hair before straightening. "How am I supposed to feel after that? It wasn't my family. I can't do anything about it."

"I'm sorry. Is there anything I can do?" Ray asked.

"Can you turn back time so I can take my head out of my ass and realize weeks ago Armstrong wasn't talking about my family?"

"Wish I could. For both of us." Ray huffed lightly. "I don't know why I didn't figure it out sooner. It seemed too good to be true."

"Too easy, right?" Jack grumbled low in his chest. It hadn't been his family, and now he was catapulted backward and forced to go back to his own investigation to find those responsible for destroying his family.

"Now what?"

"It'll take a minute to process, but you know what Haniford says. *It is*—"

"*What it is*," Ray finished.

Jack turned his gaze west. "It'll be dark in a couple hours. Let's get this shit into your truck so we can drop it at recycling on the way home."

An hour later, weeds, bits of shed, and the remains of the lilac were in the back of Ray's truck, tarp and rope securing everything down safely.

Jack grabbed a shovel on the way through the yard and used the tip to start lifting the shed's old brick flooring. He placed the bricks in an old bucket which Ray took out to the truck, then returned with the empty container.

When the last of the bricks had been removed, Jack used the

hoe to cut back weeds creeping up around breaks in the shed walls.

Jack pushed the hoe through the compact soil, but it suddenly stopped. He tried pushing it through again, but it refused to move past the obstacle.

He bent over and dug his fingers through the soil to remove the offending item, but it wouldn't come free, so he got down on his knees and buried his fingers in the soil.

"What's up?" Ray asked.

"Fucking rocks, I reckon."

Just then, his phone started ringing in his back pocket, but he ignored it.

"You wanna get that?"

"If it's important, they'll call back. I want to get this rock out of the ground. It's the last thing we need to do before we can get the hell out of here. After this, there's no reason to ever come back here again." Reality kicked Jack in the chest.

He pushed the soil away and a large, round stone appeared. He pushed more soil away to expose the stone.

A few minutes later, the phone rang again.

"Motherfucker!" Jack cursed.

Ray was at Jack's side instantly. "What's wrong?"

Jack moved huge scoops of soil away from the stone. He scraped more furiously, like a dog digging sand at the beach. Soil flew out behind him until the stone was fully revealed.

The phone kept ringing, but he barely noticed it.

"Holy Mother of God," Ray said under his breath, crossing himself.

Jack fell back on his haunches, speechless.

Before him in the hole he'd just created was a perfectly formed human skull.

ABOUT K.A. LUGO

K.A. Lugo is a native of Northern California who grew up on the Central Coast, with San Francisco just a stone's throw away.

Like most writers, Kem has been writing from a young age, sampling many genres before falling into thrillers, mystery, and suspense.

Kem loves hearing from readers and promises to reply to each message. Please visit Kem's socials to stay up-to-date on this exciting new series.

FIND K.A. ONLINE

Website
www.jackslaughterthrillers.com

Facebook
www.facebook.com/KALugoAuthor

Twitter
ttwitter.com/ka_lugo

Blog
jackslaughter.blogspot.com

Goodreads
www.goodreads.com/KALugo

BookBub
www.bookbub.com/profile/1147179734

Tirgearr Publishing
www.tirgearrpublishing.com/authors/Lugo_KA

K.A. Lugo also writes romance as Kemberlee Shortland
www.kemberlee.com

OTHER BOOKS BY K.A. LUGO

<u>JACK SLAUGHTER THRILLERS</u>

SLAUGHTERED, #1
Released: November 2018
ISBN: 9780463775653

Jack hates missing person's cases. He only agrees to search for missing wife, Bonnie Boyd, because the details of her disappearance closely match his own wife's, Leah. Soon, Jack discovers the city has a serial killer officials have dubbed The Butcher. Could Bonnie Boyd be a victim? More important, was Leah one of his victims? With every clue Jack weaves together, the more his own life unravels.

WITNESS TO SLAUGHTER, #2
Released: December 2020
ISBN: 9781005029258

How can Jack refuse a case when he's offered double his fee to follow a cheating husband? Jack is led across the city to the Majestic Lounge, the city's hottest gay nightclub. Owner Chad Lucas hires Jack for added security for the club's drag queen event. Police say deaths of Lucas' friends are suicides, but he convinces Jack something else is going on. Does the city have another serial killer on its hands?

Milton Keynes UK
Ingram Content Group UK Ltd.
UKHW020423281223
435051UK00013B/263